APPALACHIAN AWAKENING

What Reviewers Say About Nance Sparks's Work

Secret Sanctuary

"I love the combination of action and romance. …The crime plot is fast-paced and the story is action-packed and exciting to the end, with some unexpected twists."—*LezReview Books*

"I buzzed through all the action sequences. They felt real and very dangerous, with just enough vulnerability from the main characters to heighten suspense. I was never unsure of who was where and what was going on. The romance made me happy, because both characters have a deep need for love but their lives are highly secretive, giving it a nice tension."—*Lesbian Review*

Cowgirl

"I fell in love with *Cowgirl* by Nance Sparks. This is the author's debut novel, and I'm very impressed with her writing. In fact, I see myself adding a new name to my list of favorite authors. It is the setting that really made the story special to me. The author set this novel on a farm near a tiny town in Michigan, and something about her descriptions of this place really touched me. I kept thinking, 'This sounds and feels like home.'…I recommend this book to everyone. I will also be looking for more from this author." —*Rainbow Reflections*

Starting Over

"This novel works because it's built on a relationship that's grounded, authentic and genuine. Sparks crafts the romance in such a way that it feels believably sincere and honest. She capitalizes on the emotional depth of the characters and their relationship. There's a chemistry between these two ladies that's compelling. Readers see their potential, and they root for them. *Starting Over* reminds readers that love endures and heals, even when one thinks it's lost forever."—*Women Using Words*

By the Author

Cowgirl

An Alaskan Wedding

Secret Sanctuary

Starting Over

Appalachian Awakening

APPALACHIAN AWAKENING

by

Nance Sparks

2024

APPALACHIAN AWAKENING

ISBN 13: 978-1-63679-527-0

THIS TRADE PAPERBACK ORIGINAL IS PUBLISHED BY
BOLD STROKES BOOKS, INC.
P.O. BOX 249
VALLEY FALLS, NY 12185

FIRST EDITION: JANUARY 2024

CREDITS
EDITOR: BARBARA ANN WRIGHT
PRODUCTION DESIGN: SUSAN RAMUNDO
COVER DESIGN BY TAMMY SEIDICK

PROLOGUE

Everyone has a breaking point.
Everyone.

For some reason, I thought I'd be exempt, but there are no exceptions.

My entire life, I've been pushed and groomed to be the best of the best.

Not only do I have a seat at the table, I sit at the head of the table.

I made the cover of *Fortune* magazine the year of my fortieth birthday.

And then, it all fell apart.

It happened on a Friday.

CHAPTER ONE

The late February day started off normal enough. I woke up just before the alarm sounded at four-thirty in the morning. Soon after, I was fast walking on the treadmill for forty-five minutes, getting my steps in while sipping a strawberry and kale smoothie and watching the morning news and market reports, an efficient routine ingrained into me by my mother because it was how successful people started their day.

When I was a little girl, she followed up such a statement with, "and you want to be successful, don't you, Amber?"

Of course I wanted to be successful. It seemed to be the only quality that my mother valued. Like a bobblehead, I responded by nodding wildly in agreement. According to my mother, in order to be successful, I'd have to be relentless, well-informed, driven, and fit. My mother's critical voice was constantly in my head as a shrill reminder of how hard I'd have to work if I ever wanted to meet her expectations. It was a lofty goal that, at forty-five, I was not entirely sure I'd ever achieve.

Two hours later, I was downtown in my office, typing so fast that the clickety-clack of the keyboard held a rhythmic beat. The morning flew by. It was a momentous day. I'd focused solely on the merger for the better part of six months, and it was set to be finalized before the end of business. The company we were merging with would fill out our portfolio and give us the valuation to be in *The Fortune 500*. It was a big deal. A very big deal.

"Knock, knock." Sue, my executive assistant, was more important to me than my right hand. She always said "knock, knock" instead of actually knocking. It was her thing. One of her many things.

I kept typing the closing on my email to ensure I wouldn't lose my train of thought.

"Hey, Amber." When she said my name, it sounded like *Ammbur*. I gave up correcting her years ago. "I'm sorry to bug you again, but Grayson is looking for an update on the final packet. I told him that the update hadn't changed much in the five minutes since his last call, yet he insisted I check again. I swear, this merger has everyone jumpier than a long-tailed cat in a room full of rockin' chairs."

Sue had an unending supply of sayings and self-proclaimed words of wisdom. Most of her phrases were quite endearing when wrapped up in her sweet Georgia drawl. This far north in Hartford, Connecticut, her words could leave a person wondering if they'd been kissed on the cheek or slapped across the face. I adored that about her and envied her skill.

She wasn't wrong about the merger. Everyone was on edge and rightly so. While the merger was the right thing to do for the company, the moment those papers were signed and it became final, almost every level of senior management—beyond the board of directors—overlapped, and someone at each tier would have to go. Those selected to carry the newly merged company forward would be announced by Grayson, the chairman of the board, after lunch. I was certain that my three hundred and sixty degree assessment and the work I'd done to not only present but also secure the merger would prove my worth to the newly formed organization.

I attached my signature and clicked the send button. "I just finished, and the email has been sent to the team." I leaned back in my chair with a smile that I was certain resembled that of the Cheshire Cat, yet another one of Sue's sayings. I rolled my eyes and shook my head. She was wearing off on me more than I cared to admit.

"So if we keep our jobs, are we going to cut out early and grab us a celebratory cocktail or five? My family is expecting another late night, and my credit card is still on file with the Grubhub. Cass and the girls won't mind one more night of junk food." She wiggled her eyebrows.

Sue's granddaughter, Cassidy, had been swept off her feet at a young age and then dumped after she'd become pregnant for the second time. She and her two daughters, ages five and seven, lived with Sue while Cassidy focused on finishing college. She was a determined young woman on year four of a five-year plan. In turn, it added a lot to Sue's plate. Sometimes, she stayed late at the office without being asked. I always welcomed the help. I also suspected she enjoyed the quiet that work offered, though I never called her out on it.

I helped in my own little way by bumping up her salary to show my appreciation for her above and beyond efforts. "I'm all in on the cocktails. What is this, 'if we keep our jobs'? Of course we'll keep our jobs. We're the dynamic duo. They'd be fools to let us go." I wasn't sure which of us I was trying to convince. Without a doubt, I knew we'd done a stellar job, but my email account and phone had become eerily quiet. A tight, nervous feeling took hold in the pit of my stomach. I maintained my confident front because that was what successful people did.

"Your lips to God's ears." Sue pointed a finger in the air. "I'm too old to go job hunting again. Two more years and I'll reach full retirement age. Please, dear angels, grant me just two more years so I can retire to a life of leisure."

I stared into her sweet brown eyes. "Ha, you're not retiring. We're a team. You can't retire until I do."

"Then, you best be planning to do so in about two years." Sue laughed. "Honey, I'm gettin' too old for these long days and all this stress. I need some time poolside with a cabana boy in short shorts."

I couldn't imagine sharing an office suite with anyone other than Sue. We'd worked together for so long that we could practically read each other's thoughts. We'd been paired up since the day I'd hired on. With every promotion I'd ever earned, I'd begged her to join me and negotiated for both of us. She was so much more than my right hand. She was my conscience, my backbone, and one of the reasons I occupied the corner suite. She was invaluable. Over the years, she'd kept me grounded. I wasn't close with too many people outside of work. Hell, I wasn't close to too many people period. Ugly truth honest, Sue was my dearest friend, whether she knew it or not. My career had always been my primary focus, and Sue had been a major constant in my adult life.

I sat there and wondered who might have reported me missing should I have disappeared. The results were depressing. Without a doubt, Sue would be the first, especially if I happened to disappear on a weekday, since she greeted me at the elevator each day with a cup of my favorite coffee. Two others who might eventually notice would be my parents, although it would take them some time. They were both fairly self-absorbed. I suspected that they'd had me… who knew why, maybe it was trendy at the time. Once I was born, they'd quickly realized that they wanted nothing to do with children.

It wasn't until I lived on my own and worked in a professional setting that I was even invited to join them at the country club for the occasional lunch. I'd never fit into their world.

My girlfriend, Tiffany, would most likely celebrate my disappearance and ask for verification. She wasn't currently speaking to me because I'd missed our six-month anniversary dinner. In my defense, celebrations on the half year weren't a real thing. Anniversaries were an annual event, not a monthly or biannual celebration. Besides, the merger had been my priority, and she should've understood that.

A knock on my office door pulled me from my thoughts. "Hey, Grayson, come on in. Everything should already be in your inbox."

"It is. Can we talk for a minute?" He turned to Sue. "In private."

She nodded, excused herself and pulled the door closed behind her.

"Uh-oh, it's something serious." I stood and stepped around my desk. "Your forehead is crinkled, and that vein is popping out. It's your tell. Was there something unexpected in the packet?"

I'd been a direct report to him and the board for the past seven years. He typically flopped in the chair in front of my desk, but today, he stood just inside the doorway and picked at the sleeve of his suit jacket. Something was up, and it wasn't anything good. I remained standing but leaned slightly against my desk for some support.

"The packet was exactly what I've come to expect from you. Spot-on and quite thorough."

"So why do you look like you threw the baby out with the bathwater?" I rolled my eyes. Sue and her sayings.

"Amber, there's no easy way to say this. The decisions have been made for the leadership team and…well…you won't be the CEO moving forward."

My chest tightened, and my heart sank to the pit of my stomach. I'd brought this merger to the board. I'd been the one to pursue it. There were many times that I'd kept it from falling apart. I kept my expression neutral and remained cold as steel, another trait I'd learned from my mother. "I see. When was the decision made? What was the determining factor?"

"The new board feels that you were promoted beyond your skill set."

"Seriously?" I breathed through an inappropriate flurry of curse words. "I've led this company for the past seven years. I've exceeded all goals presented to me. I carried this merger to the finish line. How could that be considered promoted beyond my skill set?"

"Amber, we've talked about this. You've always been too deep in the weeds. You have an entire acquisitions department that should have handled the bulk of the work. Instead, you were the one putting together the merger and creating the final packet. As of today, this company is too big for your control issues. The incoming board wants a change. They're looking for an established leader who's more…traditional. They want experience. Carl Turner will be taking over."

It took a couple of tries before I was able to quench the desert dryness in my throat. I'd been so certain that the board would choose me, choose my style. Of course I was involved. I wasn't a dump-and-run leader. I liked to know what was going on. I liked to be part of the solution. Our numbers were good under my leadership, and turnover was all but nonexistent.

"Carl Turner?" He was traditional all right. A traditional, egotistical, misogynistic asshole. Carl had no love for women in the workplace, let alone in upper-level management. "The board wants a good ol' boy. Is that it? A stodgy—"

Grayson cocked his head and gave me a look that suggested I not finish my sentence. I bit my tongue and focused on my breathing. I had to stay cool. If I had any chance of talking Grayson out of this, I had to keep my composure. Then again, based on his steely expression, I couldn't see a path forward that would maintain my seat at the head of the table. Anger and rage roiled inside. *Breathe.*

"I assume you'll honor the terms regarding my severance package?" I asked.

He nodded and cleared his throat. "Yes, we'll honor your contract. That's the point of doing this before the merger is final. A last order of business in the old books."

My mother had coached me on my contract negotiations. Back then, I'd thought it was silly to ask for stuff in the event that they let me go. It would seem she wasn't so wrong after all. A fresh wave of nausea hit. How was I going to tell her that I'd been passed over? Her disappointment would be more than I could bear. I looked down and noticed Sue's purse resting on my conference table. I'd been so self-absorbed that I'd completely forgotten about her. My heart sank.

"What about Sue?"

"Carl's already fully staffed."

"Are you seriously telling me that you're cutting her? She's been with this company since the beginning."

"She can collect unemployment until she finds something new," Grayson said.

"She's sixty-five. Haven't you heard of agism? No one is going to hire her. She's too close to retirement. Pay her out, including benefits, until she reaches full retirement age. It's just two years. I—" I shook my head. "We put this merger together. You owe her that much."

"No one is going to sign off on that." Grayson crossed his arms as if to end the discussion.

"Is my departure favorable or unfavorable?" I asked because it made a big difference as to what was included in my severance package.

"Favorable." He sighed. "Because of the work you put into the success of the merger."

"Then there's negotiation room for perks beyond my outlined salary and benefits. If I waive some of the other clauses, could I fight for salary and benefits for Sue?"

"Those are two significantly different price tags." He stared into my eyes.

"Mergers tick up the valuation of the stock for both companies involved. I watch the markets. There's room to take care of her." I channeled my mother's bulldog negotiation tactics. If I couldn't save our jobs, the least I could do was keep her from having to search for another one.

"There are senior VPs who aren't getting that kind of buyout. It's not going to happen." He tapped the back of a chair with a finger to drive home his point.

"Grayson, the senior VPs will have no problem with future employment. Sue will, and you know it."

"Six months of salary, no benefits. That's my best and final."

Over the past seven years, I've noticed things. Things that others might have wished I hadn't. Like the fact that Grayson kept his mistress in a high-rise apartment on the other side of town. An apartment that the corporation paid for. Maybe I was too deep in the weeds of the day-to-day operations. It wasn't juicy enough to save my job or Sue's, for that matter. Plenty of people knew about it. But being in the weeds, watching the financials, and questioning things just might have been the leverage I needed to help Sue today.

"I know about the Crescent apartment. I'm not budging. Two years' salary and two years of benefits. Honor that and I'll go quietly. Take care of Sue, and you have my word that everything I know will leave quietly with me."

The color drained from Grayson's face, and the muscles in his jaw tensed. I wondered how many times he'd hear about the Crescent apartment from various executives today. He had plenty of money to pay for the apartment himself, but his wife might be the one to take notice, then.

"Jesus, Amber. Fine. Eighteen months of salary and benefits for the full two years. I'll get it done." He huffed as if the money would come out of his own pocket. "Nothing more."

It was more than I expected. I kept my fist pump of success to myself and maintained my composure. "One more thing, I'd like to exercise my option on all vested stock before I sign off on my severance package."

"That's already been done." He glared at me.

His words sunk in, and my heart broke. All of the long hours and all of the sacrifices that I'd made hadn't meant a thing. My efforts weren't valued or appreciated. My worth was summed up as a final payout checkbox before the merger was complete. I'd been raised to believe that once I became a CEO, I'd hold all the power. I'd be in charge. I'd be valued. In that moment, I realized it was all a pile of crap. Like any other position in the company, I was expendable. My efforts, my success, didn't make much of a difference at all.

"Aren't you a piece of work. No wonder you were calling every five minutes for a status. Cash me out today, including the pay for my twenty-one day decision period. I'll wait here for our payouts and proof of continued coverage for Sue. Then, we'll vacate."

"We'll need all company property, including electronic devices. Stan will stay with you two while you pack up." He unfolded his arms and turned toward the door.

"I love how you trusted me to knit a forty-three billion dollar merger, but you're concerned I'll bolt with a crappy, out-of-date, old laptop. I do have ethics. I could have tanked it all." Anger kept me focused and kept my emotions in check.

"I know you do, or you wouldn't have departed on favorable terms," he said with his back to me.

I bit my tongue. I wanted to tell him off. I wanted to scream and throw something at his smug ass, but Sue's deal would be tanked. I cared too much about her to risk it, so I kept my cool. Grayson walked out and left my office door open.

Sue peeked around the corner. "Well, don't you look madder than a wet hen that's been yanked off her nest and dunked in cold water." She stepped into the room. "I'm guessing we're done?"

Unable to speak, I nodded.

"You still up for that drink?" She wiggled those penciled-on eyebrows. "Win or lose, we've done some good."

God, I adored her. I drew in a deep breath. I had to hold it together. No way I'd show emotion in front of Grayson or Stan or even Sue, for that matter. I'd remained composed until I was alone at home. Another thing I'd learned from my mother. She was always so rock solid, until she didn't think anyone was watching.

"Rain check on the cocktails? I'm afraid I won't be the best company today. Stan is going to watch us pack up." I pushed away from the edge of my desk, hoping my legs would support me. "Sue, I'm sorry I didn't do better by you."

"Sugar, you're a class act in my book. It'll be okay." She pulled me into an unexpected embrace. Wow, was she ever a great hugger. How could I not have known that after all these years? I held on longer than I should have because it felt so good to be wrapped up in her arms. I could have sunk in and remained there, cuddled up all day.

"Don't open your envelope in front of him. Wait until later," I whispered in her ear.

"You been playin' Santa Claus, have ya?" she asked. "These walls aren't that thick. I heard everything. I always have…heard everything. I know that you've always had my back. I appreciate you."

I squeezed her in my arms and held on a bit tighter. Would we stay in touch once we'd lost this connection? Only time would tell. How could I handle possibly losing my one and only friend?

"Stan is staring at us. I best go pack up my desk," Sue said and stepped back.

I nodded, once again unable to speak. I watched her walk out. When she was out of sight, I walked around my desk and sat in my big, comfy, CEO chair one last time. I wondered what it would be like to wake up on Monday and not show up for work. My entire career, I'd focused on climbing the corporate ladder. I'd finally reached the top rung seven years ago. Only recently had I started to consider what my next achievement might be. A bigger company or chair of the board? I hadn't landed on an answer. Instead, my focus had been solely on the merger.

I'd always spent more time at work than I ever had at home. A profound loss washed over me. A deep sadness that I couldn't recall experiencing before. Even my worst breakup paled in comparison. How could I have missed the signs that my position had been in jeopardy? Or was the merger simply the perfect excuse to replace me? All I knew was that I felt angry and numb and empty. I felt like a complete failure.

Once again, my thoughts drifted to my parents' reaction. There would be no condolences. No encouragement that I'd bounce back. They wouldn't feign sympathy. That wasn't their style. Instead, they'd point out my shortcomings and wouldn't bother to hide their disappointment. Their version of a motivational nudge to do better, be better. It'd been that way all my life. No reason to expect anything different now.

Grayson returned. He handed Sue an envelope. She looked at me with a questioning expression. I nodded, and she opened it but kept her reaction in check. She looked at me and smiled. I opened my envelope, too. I'd done the math and knew approximately what to expect. The number on my check was within range. I signed on the dotted line, tucked the envelope into my box of personal belongings and followed Sue out of our office suite, emotions in check, at least for now. My head was pounding, and I needed some time at home, alone, to let everything sink in.

CHAPTER TWO

During my drive home, I was so distracted and lost in thought that I had no idea how I got there or which route I took. It was as if I'd flipped a switch, and autopilot had kicked in. Hopefully, I'd stopped when I was supposed to. I didn't recall any blaring horns, so I must have done all right. I pulled into my parking garage and out of habit, cut the wheel to whip my car into my assigned spot, only to abruptly slam on the brakes.

Both of my assigned spaces were occupied. One by a car I didn't recognize and the other by a small U-Haul truck. I continued until I reached the guest parking area and found a spot there.

Just when I thought my day couldn't get any worse, Tiffany stepped out of my private elevator holding a large cardboard box. She was smiling that sexy, flirtatious smile that had captured my attention six months earlier, except this time, she was focused on the brunette who stepped out of the elevator behind her, also carrying a box.

"Well, well, what have we here?" I asked while walking up between the car and the U-Haul. Okay, maybe it was more of a power strut. I did know how to make a commanding entrance. I'd already had an epically shitty morning, and there was a stranger stepping out of my elevator, apparently helping my girlfriend move out.

Tiffany stopped in her tracks, and her eyes grew wide. "What are you doing home?"

I wasn't about to explain, not when she was flirting with another woman. I perched a hand on my hip and offered her my best expectant stare. "Better question is, what are you doing? Were you hoping to be long gone before I came home from work?"

"I, um, left you a note."

Tiffany's helper or friend or whatever tripped on the ramp that led into the truck. The box shot out of her flailing arms and skidded to a stop at my feet. I smiled just a little bit. Petty, but at that moment, petty felt pretty damned good.

Tiffany set her box down and ran to the woman's aid. "Jesus, why do you have to act all tough and intimidating?" She glared at me as if her friend's clumsiness was somehow my fault. "Bridget, are you okay?"

Silence was a powerful tool when used well. My mother was a grand master. She could have made the most arrogant person crumble and stutter with the appropriate expression and well-timed silence. As a child, I was a quick study and prevailed in many playground disputes. Over the years, I'd perfected the craft. The trick was to hold one's ground. *Don't flinch. Don't move. Don't blink. Maintain the eye daggers, the strong jaw, and the posture.* Held long enough, words poured out of the recipient as if I could offer absolution for all their sins.

Tiffany helped her friend up and turned with a huff to face me. She mimicked my pose and tried to stare me down. She was totally out of her league. Her gaze dropped. Her hand fell from her hip. "I'm moving in with Bridget."

"I see." I held my icy stare to hide my surprise, but on the inside, there was still enough of that young, insecure girl from my childhood to wonder, *what does Bridget have that I don't?* I kept the question to myself, remained poised, and waited for more.

Tiffany opened her mouth, closed it, opened it again, and closed it, apparently at a loss for words.

"And how long has this been going on?" I motioned to the two of them.

"We met a few weeks ago. She was our server at the anniversary dinner you couldn't bother to show up for. She ate with me after her shift ended, then we hung out. We've sort of hit it off." Tiffany reached for Bridget's hand. "We're in love. She loves me and isn't afraid to say so."

"Oh, you're in love? After just two weeks?"

The crux of every relationship I'd ever had: everything was hot sex and good times until the "I love yous" started flowing. I wasn't opposed to saying it, but I'd vowed not do so unless I sincerely felt it.

In the house I grew up in, I wasn't entirely sure my parents liked me, let alone loved me or each other, for that matter. My father had described their marriage as a mutually beneficial arrangement. I'd watched my parents fawn over each other in front of people they wanted to impress. Then, once the visitors had gone, each would sneak off to be with whatever side lover was waiting in the wings.

I refused to live like that. I wouldn't simply say the words, not without the feeling, period. If it was love, it had to be real love, and I'd be all in. Apparently, what I'd had with Tiffany hadn't become real because even at that moment, knowing that she was leaving, I couldn't bring myself to say those three words with the hope that she'd stay.

"How much more stuff do you have?" My question was a bit harsh and matter-of-fact. No emotion. No apology. No begging to try again.

Sadness flashed across her face. Was she expecting me to fight for her? I couldn't. I wouldn't. There wasn't any point in doing so. She'd already made her decision. "These are the last two boxes. I left the keys on the counter." She picked up the box at my feet. "I'm sorry it ended like this, Amber. I thought we'd be…" She shrugged. "I thought I meant more to you."

"I'm sorry, too." It was an honest response and the best I could do at the moment.

I fought the urge to wave as I watched them pull away. I was sure I should have felt sadness, loss, hurt, and a thousand other emotions; instead, all I felt was seriously pissed off. She wasn't going to find anyone better than me. I had my own fucking elevator, for Christ's sake. I owned a penthouse in downtown Hartford. A proverbial rooftop paradise. All of the other condos had a tiny four-by-eight balcony. My balcony was a four-thousand square foot, wooden, rooftop haven, complete with an outdoor kitchen that included a wood-burning oven and grill, not that I'd ever used either, a fully stocked bar, which I used often, and a private Jacuzzi where swimsuits were frowned upon.

My home was two thousand square feet larger than my private outdoor oasis. Everything was the best of the best. It was spacious and airy, with incredible city views from most every room. How could Tiffany want to leave that? Was life with me really that bad?

I released my breath with a huff and went to retrieve my car and my box of belongings. Less than five hours had passed since I'd left for work, and I'd not only lost my job but also my girlfriend. I'd never felt like more of a failure. Seriously, what else could go wrong? Perhaps an asteroid was on a collision course with Connecticut?

The house felt far too empty. I'd lived alone for much of the time that I'd owned this place, but all of a sudden, it felt far too big and far too quiet, cavernous and claustrophobic at the same time. It was too cold outside to open the windows and listen to the sweet sounds of the city. I slid my box onto the kitchen counter and glanced at the note. I caught a few sentences about how Tiff had felt like a neglected afterthought.

My ego had already been beaten badly enough, so I didn't bother to read the rest. Instead, I folded the note in half and tossed it in the garbage. In the blink of an eye, I'd been replaced at the office and at home. I stood there, staring out the window, and wondered where I could go from here? I felt like a fish out of water, flopping around on the shore, drowning in too much oxygen. Shit, I needed a drink.

Within an hour, I had changed into some fuzzy lounging clothes and had Chinese takeout delivered. An obscene amount of takeout, including two orders of deep fried, sugar covered, doughnut holes. I dug into those first. They were fresh and piping hot. I mindlessly devoured them while searching for something on TV that could distract me from my life. I decided on *Wild* with Reese Witherspoon. I settled beneath a blanket on the couch with a box of kung pao chicken and a scotch on the rocks, then pressed play.

While watching that movie, never, ever, in all my life, had I felt such a connection and such a profound yearning to do something so completely out of the ordinary. The main character set out on her journey feeling lost, floundering in her own personal abyss, and ended her travels feeling whole and went on to live a happy and fulfilling life.

I needed that feeling in my life. Regardless of my accomplishments, I hadn't felt any of those emotions. Whole and happiness were foreign concepts. Even after I'd been promoted to CEO seven years ago, it hadn't filled the void, just my bank account. I couldn't put a finger on what might have been missing. Maybe, just maybe, it was time to try something totally different.

The movie impacted me with such power that I watched it all over again. I was captivated with the prospect of walking away from everything and toward something entirely new. When the credits rolled for the second time, I went online and purchased the audiobook. It felt so much more powerful. The ten hours of narration filled in all of the gaps. I listened until I could barely keep my eyes open and resumed play again the next two mornings the moment I woke up. I was obsessed. I was transfixed. I finished listening to the last chapter of the book on Monday morning and called Sue, who'd recommended the book earlier in the year after it was chosen for her book club.

She picked up on the second ring. "Good morning. I've been expecting your call. How's my unemployed boss lady holding up? You missin' the delivery of your morning latte?"

"Hey, good morning. Listen, do you remember reading the book *Wild* by Cheryl Strayed?" I hadn't been this excited in a long time. I felt like jumping in place, as if I was six years old and in line to see Santa Claus.

"Yeah. Why?"

"I'm going to do it. I've decided to hike the Pacific Crest Trail." Saying it out loud made it real. I was really going to do this.

"I'm sorry." Sue coughed into the phone "You decided to do what now? Is Tiffany on board with this?"

"She was moving out when I got home on Friday. She's in love with Bridget." I waved my hand as if Sue could see me. That was old news. I was on to new, bigger, and better things. I was going to hike the Pacific Crest Trail.

"So you watched a movie, and now you're going to take off and hike for months on end? Are you out of your ever-lovin' mind? Should I come over? Are you having a moment?"

"Sue, I've got to do something. I need to get out of here." I paced in the kitchen.

"Then go on an all-inclusive trip to some tropical paradise. If you need a buddy, I'll come with ya. Honey, beaches are for get-out-of-here moments, hiking a death-defying trail screams of an identity crisis. Are you havin' an identity crisis?" Her southern drawl made it all sound so much more desperate than it was. "There's a drought out west. That *Wild* author nearly died of dehydration. Oh, and you do remember the rattlesnakes, don't ya? Lots and lots of snakes out west."

She had a point about the water…and the snakes. Water had been a big issue in the book, and the drought out west was much worse now than it had been in 1995. I lifted the lid on my laptop and did a quick search of hiking trails like the Pacific Crest Trail. To my surprise, there were several, and one was sort of close by.

"What about the Appalachian Trail?" I traced the multi-state path on my laptop. This could work. This trail had three-sided wooden shelters that were spaced relatively close together and most had a reliable water source.

I could hear Sue sigh through the phone. "Sure, the southern start of the trail is a stone's throw from my hometown in Georgia, but a luxurious beach vacation sounds more like something you'd enjoy. You could have a personal chef, cocktail delivery, and all that pampering. So much better than hikin' alone in the woods."

I did enjoy having a personal chef, and cocktail delivery would be an added bonus, but the two things weren't the same. One was just that, a vacation. Time away while being spoiled and pampered to no end, but the other was about finding my identity. Finding what might make me feel happy and fulfilled. "I hear what you're saying, Sue, but I feel deeply compelled to do this. My answers are out there." My words were not conveying how desperately I needed to do this. It was as if my future existence depended on this trek. I wanted Sue's support, and I really hoped she'd be my base camp person.

"Honey, you know I love you. I hope you also know that the shelters out there on the trail aren't cozy log cabins with all of the amenities you're accustomed to. There are no showers. There are no toilets. There's only you, your tent, and bugs…lots of bugs, and cold camp food and walkin' for days and weeks and months on end."

"Jesus, you make me sound like a spoiled powder puff. I need to do this more than I've ever needed to do anything. I need to figure out what I want for the rest of my life."

"I hear you, and I'll say this, what you'll want for the rest of your life is ever-changing. Believe me. I've got close to twenty years on you. What you think you want today may not be what you want tomorrow, and that includes hiking for two thousand miles."

"Sue, I've felt this deep unsettled feeling for as long as I can remember, and no matter how much success I've achieved, it hasn't gone away. Instead, it gets louder, as if I'm not listening. I'm listening now, and I need to walk in the woods." I didn't know how else to explain how unsettled I felt despite the money, despite the penthouse, despite all of it. I hadn't been happy.

"And I'll ask you again. Are you having a moment? Do you need me to come over? Have you slept at all since Friday? Honey, how much have you been drinking? What's your momma say about all this? I don't need her knocking down my door. She scares me a little bit, and not much scares me."

Sue knew how to take the wind out of my sails. My parents. Hell, I hadn't even told them that I'd lost my job or that I'd lost my girlfriend. She was right, best to hit them with the trifecta all at once. "Not yet, you were my first call. I was hoping you'd be my box mailer, like in the book. I've been researching what all I'll need for the past two days. I don't have much time to prepare. I'm headed to REI next."

Once again, Sue sighed heavily. "Is there anything I can say to stop you from dropping an obscene amount of money on an adventure that may or may not last a week?"

Sue had always been my conscience, but I didn't want a conscience today. I wanted a cheering section. She didn't think I'd make it, just like people didn't think that Cheryl would make it. Okay, so all I had to do was prove her wrong.

"No, there's nothing you can say to change my mind. I'll call my folks and tell them next, and then, I'm going to REI. When I have the boxes packed up, I'll show you what I'd like you to do. I'll pay you for your time and effort, of course." I had to force myself to stop talking. It was time to be silent and let Sue decide if she was going to help me or if she was going to bow out and enjoy retirement.

"At least you didn't ask me to join you. Yes, if you do this, I'll mail the boxes, but only once I get confirmation that you'll be hiking to the next drop. You'll be taking your cell phone, right?"

I smiled a smile bigger than I can ever remember smiling, or at least that's what it felt like. "Yes, I'll take my cell. I thank you. I adore you. Thank you again. By the way, how are you doing with being unemployed?"

She laughed. "Are you kidding me right now? Well, technically, I'm on a two-year paid vacation, then I'll officially retire. I was just sitting here wondering what I might do. That was mighty wonderful of you to fight for me the way you did. I'd still like to buy you a drink and properly thank you. I appreciate you more than I could ever say."

I smiled as if she could see me through the phone. "You're my dear friend. Of course I'd fight for you."

Sue laughed. "And because of that, I'll mail your boxes." She was in my corner. I could hear it in her words and her tone of voice.

"You're the best."

We said our good-byes and hung up. I didn't call my folks right away. I did a bit of a deep dive on the Appalachian Trail first. I wanted the answers to the questions I was certain they would ask, or at least, I'd always hoped they'd be interested enough to ask. The more I researched, the more excited I became about the AT, as it was commonly referred to, over the Pacific Crest Trail, or PCT. There were frequent shelters on the AT, frequent reliable water sources, especially if I had a proper water filter, and frequent enough towns for hotel rooms, showers, and a meal. I could have everything. The hike, the meals, and with any luck, the answers I'd been looking for.

Finally, I dialed my parents and held my breath. Lady Luck was shining down on me. They didn't answer, so I left a message, stating that I'd not been the CEO chosen to move the merged company forward and that Tiffany had moved out and finally, that I was taking a long vacation and would call when I could. All of it true, for the most part.

CHAPTER THREE

S ue stood next to me, and we stared at the mountain of gear piled high on the bed in one of the guest rooms, so high that it dared to clean the dust from the ceiling fan blades. It overflowed on all sides and onto the floor until it created a moat around the king-sized bed. My flight for Georgia departed in just ten days, on the twelfth of March. That left me little time to figure out how to use all this stuff, let alone how to pack it as efficiently as possible.

REI was every bit the hiking oasis it claimed to be. Sue hadn't been wrong about the spend, either. I'd dropped an obscene amount of money—okay, way more than obscene—on gear, food, clothing, and more gear, more clothing, and more food. In fact, I'd filled, no, stuffed my car on my first trip, and then, after more research, I went back, again, and again once more. Mind you, I wasn't taking my car on this journey. I was limited to what I could carry on my back, and yet, with each visit to REI, it me took several trips up in the elevator with overflowing armloads to get my haul into the house.

There was the obvious stuff: the tent, the sleeping pad, the sleeping bag, and the backpack. Each of which required a stuff sack or rain cover. I'd created a spreadsheet with each item I'd need, each placed on a line with a column for the importance to the success of my journey and then another column for weight. The four noted above tallied at priority one for importance. I totaled the weight in ounces and then converted to pounds and remaining ounces in bold below the list. Because having a list with data was something that kept me feeling centered and in control, and at that moment, after losing my life's work, my girlfriend, and just ten days from embarking on a journey into the depths of the woods, I really needed to feel centered and in control.

The tent, a Big Agnes Copper Spur two-person, three-season affair—because I wasn't hiking in the dead of winter and didn't need the extra weight of the four-season setup—was two pounds, eight ounces. Just a couple ounces more than the one-person tent. I liked the idea of a bit more space and not feeling like I was in a coffin. The sleeping pad and down-filled sleeping bag added another three pounds, twelve ounces. Yes, I'd gone as ultralight as possible, while not setting out on my hike with a plastic furniture tarp and a box of matches. The backpack, on its own, empty, weighed in at two pounds, fifteen ounces. So with the absolute bare essentials, I was already looking at toting a little over nine pounds across more than two thousand miles.

Nine pounds seemed totally doable as a starting point. I'd lifted significantly heavier weights when I worked out. A quick google told me that the standard pack weight of a thru-hiker was between fifteen and twenty-five pounds; that didn't leave much room for what I expected to add.

According to Kit, my REI sales associate, a lot—or in Kit's words, "a shit ton"—of advancements had been made in gear since 1995 when Cheryl Strayed had hiked the PCT. My pack had something called a "dynamic free-float system" that allowed the hip belt, shoulder harness, and lower back panel to adapt and conform to my body's unique shape. This free-float system also allowed my pack to flex with my natural movement. It was life-changing, breakthrough technology that would take my hike from daunting to delightful. At least, that was what Kit told me. I took her word for it since it fit well empty, and because, in all honesty, I hadn't yet tried it on stuffed full of gear. I sincerely hoped the hype was real.

Packing the pack was today's project. Actually, packing the boxes and then packing the pack was on the docket. I'd invited Sue to join me. Well, to be more accurate, Sue had begged to come over and help. She needed a break from Cassidy and the girls since she'd lost her quiet time at the office, and I needed her to be here, to be my person. A win-win in my book.

It was two in the afternoon. We'd already finished lunch, and with our second cocktail in hand, we planned to inventory my haul, pack boxes, tally the weight, and pack my pack. I figured it would take an hour, tops.

"Say, Amber, back in high school, I had this favorite pair of jeans. It was the late seventies. Jordache, remember them?" Sue's accent amplified when she was about to make a profound point with a story from her youth, and at that moment, her southern drawl was dialed up to eleven, so, I had a feeling she was trying for a monumental statement.

I shook my head. I'd been a drooling baby in the late seventies. Whatever fashion I was wearing back then involved Pampers or Huggies.

"Well, trust me, Jordache were all the craze. Anyway, back then, I wore a size four. Can you believe that? Me? I can't hardly believe it myself. Now look at me. I've had children, and I can't be accused of havin' skipped too many meals." Sue wiggled her hips for effect. "I now wear a size twenty-two, and there are days that I've pushed the seams. I say all of this because lookin' at that pile mounded up on the bed and lookin' at that itty-bitty backpack, well, packing you up for this trip is like me stuffin' my fat ass back into those, itty-bitty jeans. It's gonna be ugly, and it just ain't gonna happen." She tipped her glass and drew in half her Bacardi and Coke.

She wasn't wrong. I surveyed the pile and hoped it would dwindle quickly once we got started. While I'd planned out most everything, I might have gone a little overboard with the shopping. Hell, I might have gone a lot overboard. "Not all of it will go in the pack. Some, okay, maybe two-thirds, we'll pack into the boxes you'll mail to me. Fresh socks, food, clean clothes, and all that. I'll have them numbered so the clothes in each box match the weather as I progress. I'll also put a rough estimate of dates and locations."

The prospect of crisp clean clothes every week or two appealed to me with a deep, desperate need. I'd watched the *Wild* movie twice and listened to the book at least as many times and had found a book on the Appalachian Trail called *A Walk in The Woods* by Bill Bryson and had listened to that audiobook as well. They'd all put filthy clothes back on after finally getting a shower because that was all they had to wear. I'd quickly decided that I wanted fresh clothes every seven to ten days. It would be my self-indulgent reward while out on the trail.

That wasn't too much to ask, was it? If I didn't need the extra outfits, I could ship them back home or put them in a trail box of free items for hikers, if that was a thing on the AT like it was in the book about the PCT.

"Honey, there's a lot of stuff in that pile. You're gonna need a shit ton of boxes." Her eyes bugged out, and her mouth was open wide.

Yup, I was most definitely going to need a shit ton of boxes. There was a bundle of thirty somewhere at the bottom of that heap; I'd purchased them on my first trip to REI. I estimated approximately one every week or so, as a reward for making it another seven days on the trail. I'd need to resupply food more often, but there were plenty of places to stop on my northbound trip from Georgia to Maine, or as the trail sites called it, a NOBO trek. The boxes would add some food variety too. I planned to leave them unsealed in case I needed Sue to add something special before mailing it.

I dug them out, causing quite the avalanche. Sue and I folded flaps, taped the bottoms, and lined the wall with them after I'd weighed one empty and entered that into my spreadsheet as a baseline. Next, we made an assembly line: sorting stuff for boxes and stuff for the pack. Each was weighed and catalogued. It was a solid plan, and I felt confident. Okay, I put on a confident front until I saw how it all sorted out.

Each box earned two pairs of panties, a pair of shorts for hotter months, lightweight hiking pants fitted around the ankle to keep ticks at bay, fresh socks, a clean shirt, and a bra. Once each of the boxes was set, I stacked the balance of the clothing on the floor by my pack.

Next, we sorted and boxed up the food: nutrition bars, freeze-dried and dehydrated meals, teas, energy drink packets, and instant coffee pouches so I had something to drink besides water for the next six months. We also sorted candy, turkey jerky, granola, raisins, and other dried goods that would last well beyond the mailing date. Again, I divided up my haul between each box and set the balance to the side for my pack.

My system was working well, and my purchases were dividing without too much surplus. One point for the excessive planner, or as Grayson put it, the woman who was too deep in the weeds.

Fucking asshole.

"Well, isn't this a cute little potholder." Sue held up an item that did indeed look like a potholder but was, in fact, an anti-microbial, anti-bacterial, hygiene cloth. "Why do you need so many spares? Wouldn't one suffice for your entire trip?"

"It's, um…well, a feminine hygiene item." I repeated the words Kit had used to sell me. There was a cloth for every other box and one for my pack. I figured that after a couple of weeks of use, I'd be ready for a new one. I could leave the clean, freshly laundered ones in the free box. Buying so many extras wasn't the most environmentally friendly thing to do, but I was who I was, and I had my standards.

Sue wasn't on board. "A what now?"

"It replaces toilet paper for when I just need to pee. It snaps in half, and the other side is waterproof so it will protect anything that comes in contact with it. See here." I snapped it on the diagonal. "Like this. It's so the pee doesn't get on my pack. I can rinse it out when I come across a water source and wash it with my laundry."

"Amber, that's just fuckin' nasty." Sue gave me a crumpled nose look. I'd seen it often enough over the years. She made the best faces that always made me laugh, unless I caused the angry face. Then, there was no laughing.

"I read that I should pack out used toilet paper, which seems nastier, so it's that cloth for pee or a bigger baggie of used toilet paper to haul to the next town," I said, as if my words made any of it less nasty.

"I'm sorry, say again, you're going to do what now?" That was Sue's favorite saying when she questioned something I'd shared.

"As you mentioned on the phone the other day, there aren't bathrooms, so I have to do my business in an eight-inch cathole that I dig and mark with a stick, but it's recommended that toilet paper not be left behind. Ever. Ya know, in case an animal digs it up." The information was from my research. I'd needed to know what I was getting into so I wasn't a complete newbie on the trail. It was an aspect of my trek that I was least looking forward to, but I chalked it up to personal growth.

"Let me get this straight. Amber Shaw, who graced the cover of *Fortune* magazine and had an annual salary greater than the GDP of several small nations is going to dig an eight-inch hole to pee and poop in? Oh, sugar, I'm gonna need a moment and another very, very, strong cocktail." Sue burst out laughing.

Soon, both of us were laughing. One of those good deep belly laughs that made us gasp because we couldn't catch our breath. I couldn't recall the last time I'd laughed like that. Maybe never. It felt energizing and wonderful. Once I'd regained some control, I made each of us another drink, and we got back to work sorting and packing up the last few items into the boxes, like tick and mosquito repellant and a few replacement plastic shovels for along the way because "plastic shovels can and will break," according to Kit. I really hoped she earned commission for all her efforts with me. Finally, we added replacement water filters for my handy-dandy water filtration system and small packs of wet wipes for when I needed clean hands or other parts.

To the hiking industry's credit, there had definitely been some amazing advancements in gear beyond the backpack since Cheryl's 1995 hike. For example, my headlamp no longer needed replacement batteries. It accepted a quick charge from the same device that would charge my phone between stops, when electricity wasn't available. The closer we came to finishing the project at hand, the more excited I became to set off on my journey. Within a few hours, we had the mountain of stuff sorted and had a much smaller mountain next to my backpack. The stuff that needed to be stuffed into my pack looked to be double the size that might actually fit inside. But I'd already decided to tackle that another day.

"Oh, these are cute." Sue held up a pair of lightweight Keen sandals.

"They can go with the pack."

Sue tossed them onto the ever-growing pile. "Seriously? I thought they'd be a summer treat. If you have hiking boots, why do you need a cute pair of sandals?"

"Because once I stop hiking for the day, I likely won't want boots on my feet until the next morning. Or maybe my boots fall off a cliff, and I need to hike twenty more miles to the next town. Remember what happened to Cheryl in the book? Thank goodness she had camp sandals. I have duct tape, too, just like she had in her pack. Hikers have to be able to improvise."

"I love how you watched a movie twice and have since become a long-distance hiking expert." Sue set my trekking poles near my pack.

More and more lately, I spoke of Cheryl Strayed as if she was my nearest and dearest friend. My hike would be more closely related to what Bill Bryson had experienced with his college buddy, Steven, but still, whenever I considered what it might be like out there, I thought about Cheryl and what she'd experienced and endured, perhaps because I was looking for the closure she'd found at the end of her hike, whereas Bill Bryson had simply stopped hiking and gone back to his normal life with his amazing wife and had written a bestselling novel that had also become a movie.

Sue sat in the rocking lounge chair next to the guest bed. "I can't believe you're actually doing this on your own, all alone, voluntarily. Promise me you'll quit if it gets too hard."

"You know me. There's no such thing as too hard." I laughed that executive laugh that my mother had so eloquently trained me to do. "I eat challenges for breakfast and kick ass by lunch. It might sound a little crazy, but I'm excited to get started. I'm looking forward to conquering the entire thing." I flopped on the bed and propped myself up with several pillows, a luxury I soon wouldn't have. In all honesty, my enthusiasm was a bit overstated due to the unknown.

Sue spun the chair and fixed her eyes on mine. "Sweetie, I wasn't all that as a mother. Quite honestly, I've fucked up plenty. I'm trying to make up for that now. I consider you to be an adopted daughter that I might have done all right by. I'm here for Cass and the girls because my sweet baby girl is in rehab for the fifth time of Cass's young life. Let's not dance the dance. I've known you for far too long, and I've had a few too many cocktails to play that game."

I couldn't turn away from her gaze. Unlike what I'd been able to do with my own mother, I'd never been able to pull one over on Sue. I'd never been able to feign self-confidence and self-resilience. She'd never fallen for my, "I'm fine, I'll power through" bullshit, and I loved her dearly for that. I depended on her for that.

It was time to be completely honest. "I need to do this. I need answers. There's an emptiness inside me that no amount of success has filled. I thought making manager would fill the void and make me happy, but it didn't. Neither did managing director or VP or CFO. So I bought the primo penthouse…and still, nothing. I've filled the hot tub with plenty of beautiful women and enjoyed my fair share of great sex. Still, the emptiness inside remained. I made CEO and more of the same. A lifetime of achievements and still, there's this void deep in my soul, and I don't know what will fill it."

"And you expect to find that out on the trail?"

"Cheryl did. I hope I can, too."

"Cheryl battled her demons and found peace inside that let her welcome love into her life. Do you have demons to battle?"

"I don't know if demons is the right word, but there's something inside that has me unsettled."

"I think you just need to find your one true love. Maybe you find love on your walk, maybe not, but it seems to me that love is what's missin' in your life."

I let Sue's words soak in. I marinated in them. Love would have been nice, but I wasn't entirely sure it existed. My parents weren't in love. Not with each other or any of the countless flings, as far as I knew. "If only it were that easy."

"Have you ever felt love, Amber? Real, kick you in the ass, knock the wind right outta ya lungs kinda love?"

It wasn't hard to imagine what she was talking about. I'd dreamed of finding that kind of love forever, and no matter how hard I looked, the women who'd graced the hot tub weren't anyone who might tick that box. I was forty-five, and I still hadn't felt that kind of love. "No. Never. Does it even exist?" I answered honestly. "I'll focus on that after the hike. I need to do this first before I can consider what might be next."

"You go on ahead and walk your walk. If you ask me, you already have the perfect life. The money, the home, and I know you can find another perfect job. Your resume will ensure that happens. But all that ain't shit without someone who loves you and who you love without condition."

I wasn't sold on her comments. I was certain that my answers were somewhere out there on the trail. Some profound epiphany that would help me feel centered and ready for what might come next. Just like what Cheryl had experienced. I needed to feel that resolution, that clarity, that vision for the future. The answer was somewhere in the hike. Of that, I was certain.

Sue leaned back in the lounge chair. "Just don't forget to leave me a key to the elevator. I'll hold down the fort, mail your boxes, and water your plants while you're away."

"I don't have any plants."

"Cass and the girls don't need to know that. Hell, I might just have to stay overnight a few days a week to make sure the place looks lived in. Oh, and don't lock up that hot tub." She winked at me and smiled.

Ah, it was then that I understood. "My home is your home. Your key to the elevator is on the kitchen counter. Stay as often as you want."

The subject of my love life was dropped. We had dinner, and then Sue made her way home. Rather than pack the rest of my gear, I threw my four essential items, some clothes, my headlamp, the camp stove, and some snacks into my pack and made my way out to my rooftop oasis. It took longer than I'd like to admit to set up the tent and inflate my sleeping pad. There was also quite a learning curve on using the camp stove, but I was determined to make a hot cup of tea on my stove before I went to bed. Eventually, I managed to boil water and was surprised by how giddy the accomplishment made me. I sat cross-legged on the wood planks, munched on some granola, and sipped my tea while listening to the sounds of the city. It was peaceful.

Before long, I crawled into my tent and zipped myself into my sleeping bag. I felt safe, secure, and toasty warm. More than that, dared I say, it seemed that anticipation had filled a portion of that void in my soul. I let that thought lull me to sleep.

CHAPTER FOUR

Time flew by, and before I knew it, it was travel day. I'd spent the last two days arranging and rearranging my pack so it could be my one carry-on item. Everything about my life for the next six months or so was in this nylon bag, and quite honestly, I was terrified to let it out of my sight. While researching, I'd read story after story about those who'd checked their pack into the belly of the plane only to find out that it had never made it or had gone to an entirely different state. All that time planning and selecting the perfect gear only to have the ultimate hike delayed or derailed by the simple act of checking a bag.

There were a few blogs from experienced hikers with suggestions on how to properly pack for a flight. I followed the recommendations to a tee. The information was a godsend. My food items, along with my toothpaste, and a baggie with my shampoo bar and deodorant, were all buttoned up in my clear blue bear vault, which I'd kept at the top of my pack for easy inspection. There were just two items that I'd had to leave at home: the fuel canister for my camp stove and a multi-tool. I'd purchased them without even thinking about the inability to carry a sharp knife or flammable pressured gas onto an airplane. A quick search on the internet also told me that there were plenty of places to stop for replacements once I arrived in Atlanta.

Following the guidance certainly paid off. I made it through the security check in record time, which left me with two hours before my flight departed. Type A personality for the win. I'd rather have had the extra time on this side of the TSA than to have not prepared and risk missing my flight. On my walk toward my gate, I passed a lounge and decided that a Bloody Mary might be the perfect reward.

The lounge had seating that protruded onto the concourse. It was divided from the fast-paced foot traffic by a waist-tall railing and was the perfect place to people watch. I made a game out of it and tried to imagine where everyone was going and why. A couple in their sixties walked by wearing Hawaiian shirts and sporting floppy hats. That one was almost too easy. No doubt they were headed to some sandy beach vacation. Right behind them, a teenager shuffled by, laser focused on his phone and was either very young, like early teens, or very clean-shaven. He flopped at the gate area across the way and pulled a Ziplock baggie of snacks out of his small backpack. He was probably on spring break and off to visit a parent or grandparents.

I pulled an olive off the spear and popped it in my mouth. A woman stopped on the other side of the railing so close that I could have reached out and touched her. Her eyes were puffy and red. Her nose was red, too, as if she'd been crying. She had three children, and all looked to be younger than five. The oldest seemed like the spawn of Satan. Damned Sue and her sayings. He swiped the boarding passes out of Mom's hand and played keep-away by running around the stroller just out of reach. He slowed only long enough to pinch the plump pink skin of one of the toddlers in the stroller. The victim started screaming, and soon, the other one joined in.

Mom looked ready to snap. She finally caught the instigator and tucked him under her arm like a football. His arms and legs flailed wildly. How she managed to hang on to the slithering monster, I'd never know. Likely, this wasn't her first time wrangling that kid.

"Fuck my life," she mumbled and tucked a rogue strand of hair behind her ear with her free hand before snatching the boarding passes back.

The poor woman was a hot mess. If it weren't for the three kids, I'd have offered to buy her a drink. Best guess, either there'd been a death in the family or an ugly divorce. My money was on the divorce. Such a contentious event that it sent Mom and the kids back to her hometown to stay with her parents while she got on her feet. I silently wished her luck while also secretly hoping she, or more accurately, the flailing spawn, wasn't on my flight.

I finished my drink and still had a fair amount of time before departure. Hoisting my pack wasn't yet second nature, but it was becoming a little easier each time. The airport had been a good test since all I'd done so far was to walk a few hours on the treadmill while wearing it stuffed to the hilt. Rather than ordering another round, I dropped my empty glass off at the bar and decided to wait at the gate. People watching could occur from there, too, although a couple hundred people staring at their phones held little entertainment value. Certainly nothing like watching the events of the child and his mom.

From what I could gather, the flight was going to be a shoulder to shoulder sardine can. The gate attendant said as much after a few frantic people, inquiring about space for their standby tickets, walked away. Apparently, there had been scheduling issues on earlier flights that were causing quite the headache. I'd never been more grateful for the perks of diamond status and the roomy seating of first class.

"Would passengers Andrew Paulson and Leslie Brown please report to the ticketing counter at gate C14?" the gate attendant announced over the loudspeaker.

The approaching man was wearing so much aftershave, it assaulted my senses well before he passed by. The ticketing agent blinked a couple of times and crinkled her nose. I was glad I wasn't the only one offended by the overpowering fragrance.

"I'm Andrew Paulson." He slapped his hand on the counter.

Head to toe, his appearance screamed pushy car salesman. Regardless of his profession, it was obvious by his cheap suit and plastic smile that he'd keep pushing until a no became a yes. His teeth were so overly bleached, they were iridescent white. Completely over-the-top, much like his presence; so much so that it hurt to look.

"I'm sorry, sir, but it seems there was a glitch in the computer system, and you and another passenger were assigned the same seat.

Coach is full, and we're wondering if one of you is willing to take a different flight. We have a hotel voucher if that helps your decision."

"I have a very important business meeting in Atlanta. I can't take a different flight." He stabbed the counter with his index finger to make his point.

"Very well, since you were the first to respond to the page, I'll honor your boarding pass and get the other passenger on the next flight."

"Well done, I appreciate your integrity, and I'll be sure to give you a good review." He offered a thumbs-up and a wink. Definitely over-the-top.

Panting breathlessly, a woman ran up behind the aromatic salesman. She was the first person I'd seen all day with a large backpack like mine, and believe me, I'd been scanning for anyone who might also be hiking. She appeared to be close to my age and had a dark, golden surfer tan that made her pale blue eyes even more striking. Her shoulder-length, dirty blond hair was mostly hidden beneath a rainbow tie-dye bandana. She sported a stocky build with thighs nearly as big as my waist. It wasn't quite a bodybuilder's physique, but in those formfitting leggings, she looked like she'd hiked her fair share of miles.

"I'm Leslie Brown." She shoved some papers across the counter. "I heard my name over the speakers just as I got through security. Please don't tell me it's bad news. I've already had all I can handle of bad news."

"I'm sorry, Ms. Brown, but you and this gentleman were both assigned the same seat. Coach is full on this flight. He was here first and has declined a different flight, therefore, he gets the specified seat." The gate attendant pushed the papers back and offered a newly printed paper to Mr. Paulson.

"But I have a ticket and a boarding pass for that seat." She held up the papers again.

"Me, too." Mr. Paulson held up his new boarding pass. "I have a business meeting that I can't miss…and I was here first. Too bad, so sad." He clicked his tongue while pointing at her and cocking his thumb as if he was a porn star from the eighties.

Ms. Brown touched the gate attendant's arm. "Look, I'm begging you. I've had a week from hell. I would have been here before him, but the cab broke down on the way to the airport, and it took forever to get another one to pick me up on the expressway. This is the last flight to Atlanta today." Tears welled in her eyes. "Please, I'll sit on the floor. I don't care. I just need to get to Atlanta. I'm expected in Amicalola Falls this evening." The tears started rolling down her cheeks. She wiped at them with her sleeve. "Help me out here. I've already moved out of my apartment, and everything I own is in this pack. All of it in preparation for this trip…and…I have a valid ticket." She waved two sheets of paper.

I perked up at the words Amicalola Falls. I was headed to the same state park after arriving in Atlanta. Not only was she a hiker, but it was also likely that she was going to hike the AT. An unusual sense of giddiness took hold of me. I might get the chance to glean information from someone with experience.

The gate attendant offered a weak smile. "I'm sorry you've had a rough day, but all I'm permitted to offer is a hotel voucher and book you on the next flight out. There is one open seat in first class, but you'd need to pay for the upgrade."

Ms. Brown started pulling crumpled up bills from her pocket. "How much? Maybe I have enough on me."

"I'm sorry, I can't accept cash at the counter, and boarding is about to start. We can't hold the plane for the time it would take you to go back to ticketing and upgrade. Do you have a credit card?"

"I don't do credit cards. I have a debit card, but my account's a little lean until I get the deposit back from my apartment."

I couldn't sit by and let this happen. If I'd learned anything in all my research, it was that hikers helped each other out. It was a trail thing. "Excuse me, I am a diamond status member. I have several first-class upgrades on my account. Perhaps that would work? I have my account number right here." I opened the airline app on my phone and passed it to the agent.

"Really? You'd do that for me? Oh, thank you. You rock. Thank you, thank you, thank you." Leslie placed a hand over her heart. "I'm happy to pay you the value of the upgrade."

"Don't worry about it. You don't owe me a thing. It's my pleasure." I smiled at her.

The gate attendant did her magic and handed Leslie a first-class boarding pass. Bonus, it appeared that she would be seated next to me.

"Hi, I'm Leslie."

"I'm Amber." Her hand was thick and strong, yet her grip was warm and gentle.

"It's nice to meet you, Amber." She looked at my pack in the seat next to me. "Is the Osprey yours?" A warm smile spread across her face.

"As a matter-of-fact, it is." I returned the smile.

"Nice gear. Hiking the AT?"

I nodded.

"Section or thru?" she asked.

"Thru-hiking," Accepting any other option was not an option.

"Yeah? Me, too." Her smile broadened more, as if that was even possible. Her full lips and dimpled cheeks could have lit up the room. There was something about Leslie that caught my eye and made a few butterflies stir deep in my belly. The fluttery feeling surprised me because I'd never really been attracted to the sporty type. I'd always dated women who were more feminine, like me.

I looked at my own outfit and realized we were similarly dressed in clothing designed for a hike in the woods. Who knew what type she was when not wearing trail clothes? I chalked the stomach flip-flops up to being excited about meeting a fellow hiker and let it go.

Before she could remove her pack and sit, the first-class section was called for boarding. She grabbed my pack as if it wasn't another twenty-eight pounds, then followed me to our place in line: the very front of the row. I always choose the front aisle seat on the starboard side of the plane if it was available. I liked to see what was going on around the cockpit. Mr. Aftershave glanced at us with a confused expression. I mimicked that arrogant porn star gesture he'd done at the counter. Leslie gave him a nod and waved her first-class boarding pass at him.

I knew I'd made the right choice. I much preferred to sit next to her anyway.

She followed me onto the plane and lifted my pack, suspending it at shoulder height while she opened the compartment with the other hand. Impressive. She placed both mine and hers in the overhead bin with one hand. Wow, she was strong. I had a hunch that there was no way I could stand there like that and support thirty pounds at full reach.

I stepped off to the side so she could get to the window seat. As she stepped past, I caught a whiff of an earthy, floral fragrance I couldn't place. It could have been shampoo or lotion or simply an essential oil. Whatever it was, it complemented her chemistry and smelled quite nice. Far better than Mr. Aftershave. I sat next to her and watched the plane fill up. Before long, the flight attendant started the spiel about the safety features and what to do in the event of an emergency. At last, the jet pushed away from the terminal. Georgia was getting closer by the second.

"Have you—"

We both started talking at the same time and stopped.

"You first," Leslie said.

"I was going to ask you if you've hiked any other long-distance trails, or is the AT your first?"

"Oh, I've got a few miles under my belt. I'm on a mission to hike all of the National Scenic Trails by the time I'm forty."

"When is that?" I asked.

"This next December." She removed her lightweight down jacket and draped it over her lap.

"How many National Scenic Trails are there?" I made a mental note to research it more once I was settled for the night.

"Eleven, for a total of almost twenty-five thousand miles. It's a pretty big deal to hike them all. For the most part, I've hiked the spring, summer, and fall of every year for the past twenty-one years."

My first response was to offer one of Sue's favorites: *No, fuckin' way. You're shittin' me.* But I held that inside. "You've been hiking for twenty-one years? Eleven long-distance trails? I had no idea there were so many footpaths."

"There are way more. The eleven are just the scenic trails. There are also historic trails and a few other categories that I can't think of at the moment."

I was sure my expression was every bit the disbelief and admiration I felt inside. "Still, twenty-five thousand miles over twenty-one years? How? Why? What about work and a life?"

"How? One foot in front of the other…until it feels like your legs will fall off." She smiled. "It started out with smaller, local trails and then state trails, and then I was hooked. I haven't reached the full twenty-five thousand quite yet. That's where the AT comes in. I saved the best, at least in my opinion, for last, and then I'll be one of only a couple dozen people to have ever accomplished all eleven." Leslie lit up when she talked about reaching her goal. I couldn't blame her. It was quite a feat. Her eyes sparkled with excitement, and I could hear the elation in her voice, as if her soul was overflowing with enthusiasm. "Why? I'll answer with, why not? Everyone needs a goal. I have nothing tying me down. Why not accomplish this one thing for myself?"

"What do you win when you've finished? Is there a monetary payoff for dedicating so much of your life?"

"If only." She laughed. "No, nothing like that. The reward is knowing I did it."

I wanted to feel that deep sense of accomplishment and enthusiasm. Hopefully, I could feel that with one trail and wouldn't need the other ten to give me that sense of euphoria. "Wow, twenty-five thousand miles. What was the longest? Do you hike alone, or do you hike with a group? Have you always felt safe out there? Do you ever get lonely? What are you going to do after you've accomplished your goal?" I asked questions in a rapid-fire sequence. I had so many more questions, but I forced myself to rein it in. No doubt, I hoped she was hiking the AT alone and that she'd wanted a buddy.

On second thought, she was such an experienced hiker, it was unlikely that I'd keep up with her. Still, I held out hope.

She laughed again. "Wow, that was a lot at once. Okay, the longest I've tackled is the North Country National Scenic Trail at forty-eight hundred miles. It was my third of the eleven, and it took three years to accomplish that one. There was a small group that I hiked with on the first leg, and half of that group returned to join me for the second. I'd expected to do that trail in just two years but had to cut the second half short due to a knee injury. I finished the last stretch alone and have pretty much hiked alone ever since. There's less pressure and less dependance on others to get moving when you hike alone."

So much for my newfound hiking buddy. The flight attendant came by requesting drink orders. I decided to stick with vodka since I'd already had the Bloody Mary and this time mixed it with cranberry juice.

Leslie ordered the same and swirled her glass when she got it. "Have I ever gotten lonely? Yeah, there are times when it gets lonely out there, but I've been known to make friends easily, too. Anymore, most hikers have heard of me and know who I am. I almost always feel safe. I've encountered a few situations that made me nervous. Far more because of creepy people than because of animals." She took a sip of her drink "Hey, vodka and cranberry is refreshing. Good call." She set her glass into the cup holder on the arm rest. "I really have no idea what might be next. My focus has been on completing the scenic eleven for so long, I haven't considered what to do once I've actually done it."

I decided to back up a bit instead of asking more about hiking. She'd said something when trying to get on the plane that had caught my attention. "I heard you say that you've moved out of your apartment. For this hike? I knew I'd be gone for the better part of six to seven months, but I can't imagine giving up my home. Is everything you own in that pack? Seriously? No car, no other clothes, no furniture?"

"Just what's in the pack. Back in the day, I couch surfed instead of even bothering with an apartment, but once my hiking pals hung up their packs for college, marriage, kids, and careers, they became less enthused with me crashing for a few weeks or months. I can't afford to keep an apartment during hiking season. I can either pay rent or pay for what I need out on the trail. I also can't afford to store stuff just to have it. Same goes for a car. I've found that furnished studio apartments are much cheaper than living in a hotel for a few months. I pick up whatever I need at thrift stores and then donate it all back when it's time to hit the trail. It works out pretty well."

"What do you do for work that allows you to be away so many months of the year?"

She shrugged. "This and that. I only look for work when I need a little something extra."

Her way of life was foreign and totally baffled me. I couldn't imagine living with such financial uncertainty. "How can you live like that? What about your future? What will you do after you've finished hiking? What about retirement savings, home security, equity, or some kind of asset portfolio or even a basic emergency fund?"

My tone must have been somewhat harsh because Leslie recoiled. "Condescend much?" She glared at me. "Just like a first-class, diamond status member to think I'm destitute if I don't sell my time and soul for a retirement plan, home equity, and all that. You don't know anything about me. I manage fine. I'm following my dreams, not everyone else's expectations."

"I didn't mean it like that." That wasn't entirely true. I'd meant it exactly like that. What I hadn't meant was to sound patronizing. All my life, I'd adhered to everyone else's expectations. So much so that I didn't know if I'd ever had my own dreams. I wasn't sure whether to be appalled by her views or envious of them. "And how have you been lucky enough to avoid life's expectations?" This was the most unusual aircraft conversation I'd ever had.

"It's easy to avoid expectations when you don't have any," she said quietly. She turned and looked out the window.

Curious response. "Don't have any? How could you grow up without expectations? All parents have expectations for their children, often totally unreasonable ones, believe me." I couldn't imagine a life where expectations weren't raining down on me like a summer monsoon. "What's going to happen when you're done with the eleven trails? You don't have a job or a home. You'll be forty and starting as if you've just finished high school." It dawned on me at that moment that she was very much like the *Wild* author, hopefully without the bout with heroin.

She twisted in her seat so fast that it startled me. "Drop it, Suze Orman. I didn't ask you to worry about me. I'm good. The white picket life isn't for everyone."

"I didn't mean to imply—"

She tossed a dismissive wave in my direction. "What about you? Any other long-distance trails under your belt?"

I'd never, in all my life, met anyone like her. My curiosity was piqued. I had so many more questions, but the look on her face made it clear that she was done talking. Perhaps another time. "I'm afraid my answers are much less interesting than yours. This will be my first, and I, too, am hiking alone."

Her hand froze with her drink about an inch away from her lips. She lowered her glass. "First hike or first thru-hike?"

"Is there a reason for the distinction?" I hoped she wasn't about to tell me that I'd set myself up for failure. "If I'm honest, it's a first for both."

"I guess I should have known when I saw the brand-new pack. Top-of-the-line, latest and greatest, I'm surprised the tag isn't still on it." She raised her glass as if to offer a toast and finished off her drink. "Okay, out with it. Which author inspired your decision to uproot your perfect, financially secure, white picket, Connecticut life and rough it on a twenty-two hundred mile trail? Cheryl Strayed or Bill Bryson? Movie or book? What pushed you over the edge? A good ol' fashioned midlife crisis brought on by an unexpected divorce?" She leaned a little closer, and when she started talking again, her voice was just above a whisper. "Tell me, Amber, were you dumped for a young office assistant with perky tits and a tight ass, or maybe you lost that fancy job that made you a first-class, diamond status member to begin with? What happened to make you want to escape to the dark and dangerous woods for six long months?"

"Excuse me?" I wasn't ready to admit that she'd damn near pinpointed every bit of my truth in a flurry of sentences. "You weren't so critical of my diamond status when it allowed you to get on the flight, so you might want to tone the attitude down a notch."

She stared at me. "You look like the type swooned by *Wild*. Not that I blame you. Women, it seems, are more able to connect to Cheryl's story on an emotional level, whereas men get a kick out of the dude humor in Bryson's book. Truth be told, I enjoyed both novels myself. Most who hike solely because of one of those books drop out before they cross the first state line. Might that be you, Amber? Will you tap out before we get to North Carolina?"

Utterly annoyed, I held her gaze. Annoyed because I felt called out. Annoyed because Sue, who'd known me for years, had pretty much said the same thing, albeit with gentler words. Great, now I had to prove both of them wrong. "Stick around and see what I'm capable of. If you took a moment to get to know me instead of judging me for my successes, you'd learn quickly that I'm not prone to tapping out. I don't settle for second best, and I'm no quitter."

"Ah, so, you're the only one who gets to judge other people?"

I felt taken aback, as if she'd slapped me across the face, but I recovered quickly. I probably had that coming. "Touché." It was my turn to lean close and whisper. "Oh, and for the record, believe me when I say that my tits are plenty perky, and I've been told I have a very nice ass."

Leslie's eyes dropped to my chest. "Good to know. I'll keep that in mind." She regarded me for a moment, then leaned back and smiled. "Come on, ease up on the glare. Just because our lives are totally opposite doesn't mean we can't be trail pals. It'll be fun to have you out there. Who knows, you might just surprise me."

I sat quietly for some time, lost in my thoughts. Had I bitten off more than I could chew? Would this adventure prove to be too much? We returned to the safety of small talk until touchdown in Atlanta.

When the plane parked at the gate, I stood and opened the overhead bin. She was right about the contrast of our lives. It was quite apparent when looking at our packs side by side. Mine was bright, crisp, and pristine, while hers was faded, worn, and dingy. Was one better than the other? Likely not, but who could say? One thing I knew for sure was which pack I'd chosen to carry. I hoisted mine onto my back and then pulled Leslie's down. I tried to hold it out like she had, but my arm was having nothing to do with that. She was most definitely stronger than me.

"Thanks again for getting me on the plane. I really do appreciate it. I hope I didn't royally piss you off. I can get carried away when I get on a roll. The *Wild* hikers are kind of a joke on the trail."

"I never admitted to being a *Wild* hiker. You made that assumption all on your own."

"You didn't deny it, either." She winked at me. "Don't worry, I owe you, so your secret is safe with me. I won't out you on the trail."

How someone could be so intriguing and so infuriating at the exact same time was beyond me. I waited for the cabin door to open, all the while hoping I was up for the demands of the trail. I wanted to finish it just to see Leslie choke on her snarky opinion.

"Hey, Amber, how are you getting to Amicalola? Want to share an Uber? My treat," she asked when we made it into the terminal.

Was this her way of extending an olive branch? When I'd set up my travel plans, I'd debated on ordering a car and driver, opting instead to try out the rideshare apps, since I'd need to depend on those to get from the trail into town every week or so. In that moment, I was very happy I hadn't scheduled the car. I never would have heard the end of it.

I spun around, walking backward so I could face her. "I'm in. If you're buying, how about I leave the tip?"

She agreed and shoulder bumped me when I was once again at her side. A flicker of renewed hope took hold. Maybe I'd have a hiking pal after all.

Chapter Five

We exited the car in front of the Lodge of Amicalola Falls State Park. Through the glass entryway, I could see a group of fifteen or so milling around the lobby. With the sound of the automatic doors, they all turned and in unison, hollered, "The legend, Munch! Nom, nom, nom."

Leslie stopped and took a bow, and the group erupted in catcalls and applause. She slid her pack off and set it in a nearby chair. I was in her world now, and these were her people.

"Munch?" I asked.

"My trail name." The smile on her face beat anything I'd seen from her all day.

"I gathered as much, but what's the meaning?"

"I'll leave it to your imagination. If you make it to North Carolina, I'll tell—" She was pulled away by the group mid-sentence.

Guys and gals alike clapped her on the back and pulled her into bear hugs. I stayed back and watched the group make a fuss over their hero. I'd never felt more out of place or further from my element. "The last of the scenic eleven. What's it feel like to be here?" someone asked above the rest.

Leslie beamed. "Surreal, that's for sure."

"Oh, hey, we've got campsites one through six. There's plenty of space if you want to pitch your tent with us. Boondocks brought a fifth of Jack to pass around the fire later tonight."

A tall lanky man wearing a flannel shirt, shorts, and camp sandals with knee-high white socks let out a whoop and scooped up

Leslie's pack. Was that Boondocks? Unexpected pangs of jealously slathered with a hefty coat of envy-green frosting gripped my spirit. I didn't know what I expected to happen when we reached the resort. I guess, I'd hoped that Leslie would grab my hand and introduce me to her friends as her new hiking pal.

While working my way up the ranks in my career, I'd always been the leader, sort of isolated and off on my own, but despite that, I'd never wanted to belong to a group as much as I did in that moment. Part of me wanted to compete with the campsite offer and counter with a lush bed in a multi-room suite, complete with indoor plumbing, room service, and tons of pillows. But Leslie had already made it perfectly clear that luxuries weren't important to her. She'd say we weren't here for pampering. She'd say that tonight was merely a time for camaraderie before the treat of the trail tomorrow.

I had a desire to see if campsite seven was available, where I could pitch my tent and join in on the fun. The group swarming Leslie made their way outside into the waning evening light. I caught her eye through the glass. She gave me a wave good-bye instead of the beckoning wave I'd hoped to see and said something, but I had no idea what. I'd never been one to read lips.

After check-in, I scanned into my hotel room and dropped my pack on the luggage rack. I didn't know why my heart was so heavy. I hadn't set out on this journey to be tucked beneath someone's wing. This was something I needed to do for me. This was my journey of self-discovery, and I couldn't discover anything if I was following someone else. I needed to snap out of this funk.

I pulled my phone out of my pocket and called Sue. She answered on the second ring. "How's my favorite boss lady?"

"You're going to have to think of something else to call me. I'm no longer anyone's boss lady." It was good to hear her voice. The tightness in my chest let up a bit, and I could breathe again.

"How's about I call you my favorite hiker?"

"I don't feel much like a hiker yet, either. If I make it a week, you can call me your favorite. I wanted to let you know I've arrived in Amicalola Falls safe and sound." I flopped on the bed. It was surprisingly comfortable.

"The seven-hundred-foot waterfall is pretty spectacular. You be sure to check it out on your way to Springer Mountain tomorrow, okay?"

"I will. I pretty much have to. It's part of the Approach Trail." I'd memorized the map for the side trail I'd need to follow from the hotel to Springer Mountain, the actual beginning of the Appalachian Trail.

"You okay, sugar? You sound like someone dun' gone and stole your tea set."

I hadn't heard that one before. I wondered if Sue's accent would be this pronounced the entire time I was in Georgia. The funny part of it was, everyone I'd encountered in Georgia so far sounded exactly the same way. "It's been a long travel day, and I need to grab some dinner."

"That's not it, and we both know it. You don't get hangry, and hunger has never made you sad. You gonna tell me who's been tuggin' on your smile? I thought you'd be more upbeat to make it to the park."

She had a sixth sense, and I knew she wouldn't let up until I spilled. "Sue, am I condescending and judgmental?"

The line went quiet and stayed that way long enough that I thought we'd been disconnected. Nope. The call timer was still ticking away.

"Are you there?"

"I am." She sighed across the miles.

"Did you hear my question, or did the line cut out?" Here was to hoping the line had cut out.

"Oh, I heard you. I'm wondering why you're askin', is all."

"I met another hiker on the plane. Apparently, I made that impression within the first hour of the flight."

"I see. Well, then." She remained silent for another long moment. "Sugar, for as long as I've known you, you've held a particular opinion about how people should act and how things should be. It's what got you up to the top rung of the ladder." Her pronunciation of the word particular always sounded like "paa-tick-ule-e-la," with a lot of emphasis on the word tick. I'd tried a few times to help her pronounce it properly, but she'd assured me she was saying it right, and I was the one who was wrong.

I shook my head, realizing that I just made her point more valid. "Ah, okay, so I'm particular, condescending, and judgmental. Any other adjectives I should be aware of? Let's not forget that I wasn't able to retain my position at the top."

"Isn't that what your hike is all about? Figuring out who you are and what you want? If you don't like an adjective, swap it for something you like better. Darlin', I have no doubt that you can do anything you put your mind to."

"How is it that when this hiker called me out, I felt slapped across the face, but when you say much the same thing, I feel wrapped in a hug?"

"Because that hiker doesn't yet know your heart. I do. While you may expect certain things in a certain way, your heart is every bit as big as the state of Georgia. I love you like you're my blood. I'll always be the first in line to wrap you up in a hug."

"I love you, too. Thank you."

"Well, all righty, then. Go on now, grab yourself some dinner. If these kids don't settle down, I may have to go to your place and check on the plants. I wonder where my bathing suit is?"

That made me laugh. She always had a way of making me feel better. "No suits needed when checking on the plants. None of the buildings in the area are taller than the Jacuzzi, unless the paparazzi shows up in a helicopter. Bath robes are hanging on pegs next to the sliding door. You know where the bar is. Make yourself at home."

"Oh, honey, I will, believe you me. Thanks for calling and letting me know you're safe."

I could see that toothy smile in my mind. "No problem. I'll call again in a few days. Have a good night."

"Will do. You, too. Bye now."

I put my phone on the charger and set off in search of a hot meal and a stiff drink. It would be a week or more before I'd enjoy either of those luxuries again.

❖

Everything was still and quiet at six-thirty in the morning. I'd already had my morning coffee and an obnoxiously long, hot, sudsy shower. I registered as an Appalachian Trail thru-hiker, number eight hundred forty-three, and obtained the necessary permits that I'd need for the Smoky Mountain National Park in North Carolina. It was hard to believe that there were so many people out on the trail already. It was barely mid-March. I continued down my checklist by charging my lightweight e-reader that boasted a ten-day battery life, my phone, headlamp, and my charging brick. Once that was done, I repacked my pack, placing everything in the most efficient order given frequency of use and need, including the new fuel canister and multi-tool.

Breakfast wouldn't be served until eight in the dining area, and I wasn't so sure I could sit in my room that long waiting to get my day started, so I ate an orange, a banana, and a granola bar from the complimentary basket. I tucked the apple and other two granola bars into the last available crevices of my bear vault. After that, I triple checked the room for anything I might have left behind, especially attentive to my one charging cord for all my devices and set off to tackle the almost nine mile Appalachian Approach Trail.

Bathed in the golden light of daybreak, Amicalola Falls State Park was breathtakingly beautiful, even this early in the year. The trees were waking up from a long winter slumber, some canopied in an abundance of fragrant white flowers. It'd been an unusually warm spring, and the dogwood trees were already in full bloom. While it was a visual spectacle, it was more so an olfactory sensation. I drew in deep breaths and savored the sweet scent reminiscent of a honeysuckle vine. It was now my new favorite fragrance, and I couldn't get enough. Birds fluttered about while singing the songs of the season. The area was more picturesque than I could have ever imagined. Certainly different than Hartford, Connecticut in what we called the bleh winter months.

I followed the path downhill to the beginning of the Approach Trail and stood for a moment in awe of the iconic stone archway. I'd seen the archway and sign off to the left countless times on the internet, but to see it in person stirred an emotional response that I wasn't expecting. I teared up as I read the white lettering on the topmost board, Appalachian Trail Approach. The next board down read, *Springer Mtn. GA, 8.5 miles*, and below that was, *Mt. Katahdin, Maine, 2,108.5 miles*. The rest of the sign read, *Benton MacKaye trail, 8.7 miles, Amicalola Falls, Dawsonville, GA*. I'd made it. I was really here.

I pulled out my phone and took a photo of the arch and the sign and a selfie of me next to part of the sign and another of me with part of the arch. It was momentous. It was time for some self-discovery.

Because the Approach Trail was a side trail, blue blazes marked the path. It followed along the Little Amicalola Creek to the triangular-shaped Reflection Pool and continued to the notorious Amicalola Falls. The trail was fairly flat and easygoing all the way to the pool. The incline picked up dramatically from there. I expected as much considering the falls began over seven hundred feet above.

The views from the lower observation deck had me pulling my phone out again for pictures. It was breathtaking. The sound of the rushing water was unlike anything I'd ever heard. The water crashed straight down onto a rock shale, then cascaded over more dark gray scaly rock only to crash vertically again with more cascading. Beneath my feet on the observation platform, the base of the falls burbled along with the natural flow of the river. Each sound was distinct, and the scent of the woods, the flora, and the crisp, clean, flowing water was unlike anything I'd experience in my isolated Hartford life. I could have spent the entire day savoring the sounds of the waterfall and everything about the splendor surrounding it, but my future awaited.

I was embarrassed that my legs were screaming by the time I'd climbed the six hundred and four steps to the top of the falls while wearing my pack at its absolute heaviest, and that was with short breaks on each resting platform. The view was even more spectacular from this vantage point. I was mesmerized. It surprised me that I hadn't seen another soul since checking out of the hotel. I was sure that other hikers would be out and about, eager to get going like I had been. I held on to the rail, closed my eyes, and just listened to everything around me.

I still had the better part of eight miles to go before I reached the actual beginning of the Appalachian Trail and three miles after that before I reached the shelter where I'd planned to set up camp my first night. I had a feeling that Leslie was right about walking each day until it felt like my legs would up and fall off. The funny part was that while I fully expected the day to be daunting and exhausting, I was excited to get going. No time like the present.

I adjusted my straps and put my foot on the next stage of the Approach Trail. This was it. There was no turning back now.

I followed the blue blazes over a footbridge and pushed through a steep climb to the top of Frosty Mountain, panting breathlessly the entire way despite my frequent stops. In an area that leveled out a bit, I found a nice spot to stop for a snack and was surprised to find that it had been several hours since I'd left the falls. I opted for lunch instead, which was a hefty snack, along with my hotel apple. It was crisp and sweet and couldn't have been more perfect.

The view of valleys were magnificent. There was such depth and dimension to the landscape. I saw the remnants of a long-gone fire tower. It was surreal to see landmarks I'd read about a week or so ago. I finished my lunch, swapped my empty water bottle for a full one, and broke in my cathole shovel and the "pee holder," as I'd renamed my hygiene cloths, for my first time ever urinating in the woods. Squatting with my pants around my thighs and my ass hanging out for all the world to see, I had a funny thought: *If the board of directors could see me now.*

According to my trail map app, I was about halfway to Springer Mountain, the actual start of my journey. Climbing uphill and then descending for a bit only to climb a bunch more. I stopped whenever I reached an opening and took in the incredible views beneath the clear blue sky, then I'd get going again. One last uphill push, rising six hundred feet up the south side of Springer Mountain, would deliver me to the trailhead. Feeling excited, accomplished, and breathless, I dropped to my knees when I made it to the top.

Once I recovered, I was rewarded with some of the best views of the day, along with the legendary bronze plaque sporting the Appalachian Trail logo that indicated the real kickoff point of the AT.

Next to the plaque was the trademark white blaze painted on a rock. Following the blazes meant that I was actually on the Appalachian Trail. I'd made it. Was this the beginning of the rest of my life? What lessons awaited me in the woods? I was committed to learn them, good and bad. There was no turning back now.

In a waterproof baggie, I found the infamous AT registry: a spiral notebook for hikers to sign and share their thoughts before embarking on their journey. My first entry. I fished my pen out of a side pocket of my pack and flipped the book open. I scanned the lines for Leslie's name, fully expecting her to be ahead of me. There hadn't been any entries since yesterday. Mine would be the first of the day. I wrote the date and then sat and stared at the page. My mind was completely blank. I waited, tapping my pen on the paper, hoping for a profound limerick or tidbit, but in the end, I went with: *I hope I find what I'm looking for, else, I hope I find what I need.—Amber Shaw.*

I took pictures and had a snack. In all, I'd climbed two thousand feet in almost nine miles. My legs burned with exhaustion and protested any further movement. However, I couldn't sleep here. I had to push on.

I had almost three more miles before I reached the Stover Creek Shelter and could set up camp for the night. There were two shelters that were closer, but Leslie had mentioned that she intended to camp at Stover Creek, mostly because the Springer Mountain Shelter would be totally overcrowded. I'd hung on her every word and trusted her knowledge.

It might also have been true that I'd hoped to see her again.

The thought of actually using my shiny new gear put a little bounce in my step. Before long, I saw the blue blazes indicating a side trail, and the three-sided wooded shelter came into view. According to my research, this one could sleep sixteen people. There was also an area leveled for tents, a water source, and an outhouse. Far better amenities than anything I'd read about on the Pacific Crest Trail. I understood why Leslie had said she'd saved the best for last.

I checked out the wooden structure. Despite it being empty, I wasn't excited to set up my sleeping pad inside. I wanted to spend my first night in my own tent. I spotted the registry book and jotted down the same message I'd used up at Springer Mountain and added, *Made it to Stover Creek, one of many shelters in my future.*

I scouted out the tent pad and picked what I thought to be the perfect spot. The ground cloth went down first, then it was time to erect my tent, inflate my sleeping pad, and spread out my sleeping bag. I stood back and marveled at my nylon home away from home. After I'd refilled my water bottles, I pulled out my camp stove, including the new fuel canister, my thirty-ounce titanium pot, handy titanium spork, and set about cooking my first trail dinner. Freeze-dried chicken pesto pasta for the win.

Never before had I ever cooked anything that smelled so good. Dared I say, it tasted better than it smelled. It felt incredible to eat a hot meal after a long day of hiking.

After dinner, I rummaged around the woods and collected quite the armload of sticks and kindling. The waxed paper wrappers from my granola bars and some dried pine needles made for great starter beneath the small twigs. I would never have admitted it to anyone, but I was pretty proud of my first fire that involved more than turning on the gas valve and pushing an igniter button. I clicked my fancy butane zippo that I'd picked up when I bought the new fuel canister and marveled at my accomplishment. Once again, research for the win.

My pack was secured in my tent, and my bear vault containing smelly things that attracted wild animals with teeth and claws was stashed a safe distance away. I called my first day on the trail a fantastic success. Hopefully, I wouldn't be too sore to walk tomorrow. I had ibuprofen in my pack, just in case.

CHAPTER SIX

I sat there sipping on a hot cup of tea, enjoying the pop and crackle of the small campfire, when I heard female voices coming up the path toward the shelter. I didn't recognize either of the women approaching. Maybe Leslie had decided to hang out at the campground for an extra day or had stopped at a different shelter all together. Unexpected disappointment washed over me like a weighted blanket. I reminded myself that this was my trip, my journey, and so far, I'd done a pretty stellar job.

The hikers shed their packs at the picnic table and stepped close to the fire. "Hi there, I'm Cricket," the shorter, stouter one said. She removed her knit hat and freed long brown hair from a twisted bun hidden beneath it.

"I'm Bobber," the taller woman said. Her hair was light brown, boasting the softest-looking curls I'd ever seen. They both spoke to me as if I was any other AT hiker. For reasons I couldn't explain, this made me very happy.

"Hi Cricket and Bobber. I'm Amber."

"Is that your trail name? Like the petrified sap?" Bobber asked.

"No sappy story, I'm afraid. I don't have a trail name yet." The solitude of the day had been nice, but it was also nice to have a couple of women to visit with.

"Amber Shaw. I saw your entry back at Springer. I liked the honesty of it. You'll get a trail name at some point. It's happened to all of us. Be smart, pick your own, and let no one be the wiser." Cricket said. "Otherwise, you'll eat a live cricket on a dare and never live it down."

I chuckled at her admission.

"No, don't pick your own. There's no fun in that. I got mine skinny-dipping in a pond when we hiked the north half of the AT a few years ago. A group walked up to filter water and refill their bottles. Let me tell you, there's no keeping these girls submerged." She wiggled her eyebrows and framed her large breasts with her hands. "At least, not without a fair amount of effort, hence the name Bobber."

I laughed. "That's not an issue I expect to encounter." No matter how much I pushed my chest forward, I couldn't come close to making my breasts look anywhere near as large as hers. How she carried them and a pack I'd never know.

"The fire feels nice." Cricket held her hands closer to the flames. "Mid-forties and clear skies tonight should make for some great sleeping. Although, I don't think anything could keep me from crashing the moment my head hits the pillow. The first day back on the trail totally kicked my ass."

"I bet I could keep you awake," Bobber said close to Cricket's ear but loud enough for me to hear. "How about I go make us a fancy bedroom while you scrounge up something to eat? I like Amber's plan of the tent off to the side. I expect the shelter will fill up quickly tonight."

"Deal."

Cricket was spot-on about the exhaustion of the first day. I didn't know if even the allure of an orgasm would have kept me from crashing later. I found it comforting to have a female couple as the first to arrive at the shelter. Even if Leslie didn't show up, at least I wouldn't be the only lesbian at Stover Creek.

A twig snapped in the direction of the side trail leading into camp. I watched and waited for movement. When the person came around the final bend, my heart did a little happy dance. Leslie. I didn't know why I was so excited to see her.

Whatever the reason, I couldn't contain my smile. "Hey there, stranger, you made it. I was beginning to wonder if perhaps you'd been overserved at the campfire last night."

"Well, well, what do you know?" She had that same beaming smile that she'd had when we'd walked into the lodge and seen all of the people waiting for her, only this time, the smile was for me. "First Class survived her first day on the AT."

"I did more than survive. I beat you here, didn't I?" I hoped that if I ignored the snarky nickname, Bobber and Cricket wouldn't pick up on it. "Where's your entourage?"

"You mean the group from the lobby? They're probably still at the campground nursing hangovers."

"Ha! You do have a trail name." Bobber clapped me on the shoulder.

So much for glossing over it. "That's not my trail name." I wasn't entirely sure how I felt about being called First Class.

"Sure, it is. Trail names are given, and it seems only fair that I'm the one to give you yours. Besides, who wouldn't want to be considered top-shelf? Your gear." Leslie swiped my titanium cup, looked it over, and gave me a nod of approval before returning it. "The way you look and dress. The way you carry yourself. Come on, all in, you're First Class." She removed her pack, walked past, and set it on the wooden platform of the shelter behind me.

"Hell, I'd be okay with being called First Class. It's better than my name," Cricket said, holding her camp stove.

"Bobber, Cricket, this is Les...I mean, Munch."

"It's nice to meet you both."

I could feel Leslie's presence directly behind me. Rather than turn, I watched Bobber and Cricket to see if they recognized the name. They lit up. Munch, it would seem, was larger than life.

"No shit, you're Munch? The Munch? That's it, First Class, you're back to being petrified tree sap. You didn't tell us that you're tight with Munch." Bobber clapped me on the shoulder again. No doubt I'd have a bruise tomorrow.

Did I want to share that we weren't tight? Should I confess that I barely knew her? That was not to say I wouldn't like to know her better. Rather than correct them, I let the issue drop.

"We were glued to your interview on the Hiker Radio podcast last night," Cricket said. "We also enjoyed that big article about you in the last edition of *Hiker's Life*. The last of the scenic eleven. You're a frickin' legend."

"I haven't finished all eleven yet."

"Podcast? So that's why you needed to be in Amicalola last night?" I asked.

"Yeah, that's why I needed to be on that plane." She sat next to me on the long log. "The podcaster had been promoting the show for weeks. Sorry they pulled me out of the lobby like that. She was set up at the campground and wanted to do the interview outside, with all of the natural sounds of the woods."

"I'm sorry I missed it. I would have liked to have heard you."

She had the goofiest smile on her face. I probably had a similar look. I was so happy that she'd sat next to me.

"Oh, you can still listen. That's the best thing about podcasts, you're not forced to listen at a certain time," Bobber said.

Over the next couple of hours, hikers continued to filter in. Twenty was my last count. The hiss of camp stoves emanated from every direction, along with the scent of stew, noodle dishes, and the occasional whiff of sweetened oatmeal. The inside of the shelter was a sight to behold. The floor was wall-to-wall with backpacks and sleeping bags. A second story of slumber had been created by stringing hammocks and packs from the rafters.

Looking in at the maze, I was very glad that I'd set up my tent rather than risk being pinned beneath and between bodies. It would have been just my luck that once everyone had settled in, someone would inevitably disturb one and all with a desperate need to use the privy. No, thank you.

"Will all the shelters be this crowded?" Cricket asked no one in particular. The four of us had staked claim to the log I'd been sitting on when Cricket and Bobber had arrived. We'd kept to our own little group, and being an introvert, I was very happy with that.

"Naw, the trail from here to North Carolina is sorta like trying to go to the gym in January. It'll be packed, but much like committing to the gym, hiking isn't for everyone. Trust me, it'll thin out dramatically as we make our way north," Leslie said without looking up from her cup of cheesy noodles. "Lots of people start out with the intention of thru-hiking, but few actually make it to Maine."

"When we hiked the upper half of the trail a few years ago, none of the shelters were this crowded," Bobber said.

"When and where did you start that hike?" I asked.

"We started in late May, at the midpoint in Pennsylvania, and hiked north to Maine. Most of the time, we had shelters to ourselves, but every once in a while, we'd come across other hikers. Never anything like this."

"Thank God. It worked out beautifully, given that it was our honeymoon." Bobber wiggled her eyebrows.

"Wait, you went hiking for your honeymoon?"

"Yeppers. I recommend it highly, too. There's no better way to really get to know someone than to spend three months together, day and night, on the trail," Cricket said.

"I was raised with a pack on my back. My family's hiked the Big Horn Mountains, sections of the PCT, and Ice Age Trail, but the AT is the wet dream of long-distance trails."

I envied Bobber's ability to speak so freely. She was so animated and unedited.

"She's not wrong about the AT being the wet dream. Many of the scenic eleven are rarely thru-hiked because they're fragmented and unfinished, with big gaps that require miles on the shoulder of the road to get to the next section. There are few, if any, shelters, unreliable water sources, and lack the organization and volunteers that make the AT amazing. It's why I saved it for last. Go out on a high note and all that."

Listening to the three of them, I was very grateful that Sue had talked me out of the PCT and that I'd stumbled onto the AT on the internet. I'd take that bit of good fortune.

Watching everyone around the shelter was far more interesting than it had been watching people at the airport. For starters, no one was focused on an electronic device. Instead, some quietly focused on tasks like cooking or refilling water bottles, while others enjoyed friendly conversations that almost inevitably migrated to a discussion about backpacking gear. At that moment, there was a lively chat going on behind me, in front of the shelter, about the pros and cons of camping with a hammock versus lugging and pitching a tent. I was soundly on the tent side of the equation. There was something about having my own private space that appealed to me.

The sun was low in the sky when a group of four women staggered into camp. Twigs and leaves and clumps of mud created a head to toe camouflage over brightly colored clothing. Two had dried blood soaking through patches of torn fabric on shins, elbows, and knees. Another woman's entire left leg was covered in a thick, crusty layer of mud. I couldn't imagine how that might have happened. The only place I'd seen thick mud like that was back at Nimblewill Gap, where a couple of Jeeps had been bogging in the muck, which meant she'd likely been walking for six miles with a crusty leg. Yuk.

Bobber and Cricket were on my left, scraping the last of the stew from their cups. One of them gasped. The closest one nudged me with an elbow. "Are you two seeing this?"

I nodded. Leslie was on my right. She halted the movement of her spoonful of her chicken cheesy noodles and looked up. "My God, they look like ten miles of bad road." The words were out of my mouth before I thought about what I'd said. I hoped my comment was quiet enough that the women hadn't heard it. I shook my head. Sue and her sayings.

Bobber chuckled. "You're not kidding. I wonder what happened?"

"*Wild* hikers, mark my word," Leslie said, just loud enough for us to hear. "Twenty bucks says one of them will mention the movie and say something about how it wasn't what they expected."

"What's a *Wild* hiker?" Cricket asked.

"Wait, are you talking about the book about the woman who hiked the Pacific Crest Trail? Remember, Cricket? We read it eons ago," Bobber said quietly.

"Vaguely. Was that the lady who lost most of her toenails?"

"Yep, her boots were too small," Leslie said.

"Hey, wait a minute. You called me a *Wild* hiker on the plane yesterday." I was shocked to see the association. "You expected me to roll in looking like that?"

Leslie shrugged. "Yet, you beat me here smelling like you just stepped out of the shower. Aren't you full of surprises?"

I playfully slapped her arm. "Sorry to have disappointed you."

"Excuse me." The leader of the group stopped on the far side of the picnic table. "Is there room at this shelter for a few more? The others were too full."

"This shelter's full, too, but there's plenty of space to pitch tents," one of the men behind me said.

"Thanks. Don't suppose anyone wants to volunteer to help?" When no one responded, the women limped and shuffled to the tent area. Until then, our tents had been the only three. Bobber and Cricket had a roomy two-person tent, larger than mine, pitched between my tent and the shelter. Leslie had pitched hers on the other side of mine. We'd created our own little neighborhood.

The newest additions shed their packs and turned them upside down, emptying all contents in a clatter of tin and plastic. All conversation in the camp ceased. Everyone turned and watched. The stuff sacks containing tents and sleeping bags were the last items to tumble out. The lack of planning and organization astounded me. Those items should have been closer to the top where they'd be most accessible. Everything, including food and clothing, was now sitting in the dirt. Another of Sue's sayings, something about coming upon a train wreck with stuff strewn everywhere, popped into my mind. The scene unfolding before us offered a similar hold on my psyche. While appalling, I simply couldn't look away.

"I can't believe I let you talk me into this, Jackie," one woman said, then snapped out her ground cloth, creating a vast plume of dust. I was glad my tent was zipped up tight. "I'm too fucking old to hike uphill all day long. My heart can't take it."

"I swear, there was nothing about it being such a steep hike. Maybe the PCT is an easier trail?" a woman I assumed to be Jackie said.

"Apparently, no one ever taught you how to read a map. I keep telling you that the swirling lines are changes in elevation. We must be, like, two miles closer to the heavens. The air up here is so thin, I can't hardly breathe," the third woman said. She skipped the ground cloth and was spreading out her tent without the layer of protection.

"My body hurts all over. I wonder if my knee needs stitches."

Someone behind me chuckled. I didn't dare turn to see who for fear of missing something good.

"I tried to warn you about the drop-off, Clara, but *no*, you had to take a selfie on the edge of the rock," Jackie said with a snide tone.

"Shut up, just shut up!" One of the bloodied women shook her tent pole at Jackie.

"Let's hike like Reese Witherspoon. If she can do it, we can do it. It'll be fun. We can bond and drink wine." The woman with the mud leg screamed and threw her sleeping bag at Jackie. A direct hit to the face. "You're a fucking idiot. I wonder if it's too late to return all this camping shit."

"Definitely too late if she sticks that goop leg inside the sleeping bag," Bobber whispered.

"I don't know about any of you, but tomorrow, I'm hiking back to the hotel and drinking my body weight in alcohol. They can pour me into my room" Clara had no sooner finished her sentence than her tent collapsed. She kicked at some of the contents from her pack and let out a primitive, guttural sound before resuming efforts on the tent.

I wondered if they'd been this animated during the entire hike or if the pressure had been building all day, and this was the colorful explosion. Regardless, it was captivating.

"Me, too. I wish there was a car service that would pick us up. I'd like to be back at the hotel right now. Jackie, you can take your *Wild* movie and your wild hiking ideas and shove it all right up your wild ass!"

"Quit yelling at me. No one had a gun to your head. It wasn't what I expected, either. We'll head back tomorrow," Jackie said. "Now, shut up and go to bed."

And that was the end of their conversation. When the tents were kind of erected, they collected most of what was scattered on the ground and crawled inside with their packs. A minute later, the evening resumed as if nothing had happened. It would appear that Leslie was spot-on with her assessment, and I was grateful for my over-the-top research because without it, I could have ended up with a similar experience on my first day.

Bonus, I'd managed to impress Leslie.

The moment darkness settled in, exhaustion caught up with me, and my eyelids grew heavy. I'd had enough social time. I bid a good night to Bobber, Cricket, and the few others who were lingering around the campfire. Leslie was off somewhere in the woods washing her cup and spoon. I figured I'd catch her before I turned in. I made my way to my tent to retrieve my headlamp. I didn't need to be the newbie who became lost trying to find my way back from the outhouse. I unzipped my sidewall tent flap and crawled inside for my pack, careful to leave my feet outside.

I heard footsteps approaching and saw a faint light on the side of my tent "Did you enjoy your first day on the trail?"

The sound of her voice stirred a little something inside me. "I did. It was good. We'll see if I can walk tomorrow, but today went well. How about you? Do you still think you saved the best trail for last?"

"I do." She crouched and crawled inside my tent next to me. Her headlamp was tilted up and lit the inside like a lantern. "Wow, this is nice. Spacious. It's like an ultralight hotel room. So this is how a diamond status member hikes, eh? The inflatable sleeping pad is so plush and comfy."

We were side by side, diagonal on top of my sleeping bag like two bugs snug in a rug. She smelled of campfire smoke. Who knew the scent could be such a powerful aphrodisiac? The weight of her body on my sleeping pad caused me to rise up slightly each time she shifted and moved. The motion did little to tame the arousal that stirred within.

"Really? Again with that? What will it take for me to lose that nomenclature?" We were almost nose to nose.

"Well, for starters, you need to ditch words like nomenclature."
Leslie grinned and arched an eyebrow in the faint light.

"It means—"

"I know what it means. It's still a dumb word."

"Noted."

"Yeah, that one's gotta go, too. Only yuppies, well, in your case, muppies, say things like noted and nomenclature. Did you take a special course on words that no one else uses?"

"I'm afraid to ask. Muppie?"

Leslie nodded. "When yuppies stop being young, they become mature urban professionals. Fair bet that you've tipped over into that grouping."

"Aren't you just full of compliments."

My second time this close to Leslie, and again, such a dichotomy of emotion stirred inside. How she could be so irresistibly alluring while also incredibly insulting in an ornery, five-year-old kind of way, I'd never know. Dichotomy, another great word and certainly on Leslie's list of words to avoid. Were muppies even a real thing? I'd look it up when she vacated my ultralight home away from home. Still, I wasn't ready for her to leave.

Bobber's head popped through the opening. "Hey, you two, you're doing it wrong. Clothes off, light out, tent closed."

Cricket's head popped in next to her. My tent was getting quite crowded. "What shelter are we all meeting at tomorrow?"

"I was thinking about Gooch Mountain. Roughly thirteen miles. Does that work?" Leslie asked.

"Sounds great. We'll see you two there," Bobber said. "Remember, clothes off, door closed. You can leave the light on if ya want, it'll be fun to watch." Bobber and Cricket chuckled and disappeared.

Leslie focused on me. "How about you? Think you can manage thirteen miles tomorrow?"

"I'll manage better if I get some sleep."

"Does that mean you're kicking me to the curb? Ah, but your bed is so cozy." Leslie gave me a pout before winking and backing out. Her presence was immediately missed.

I successfully found my way back from the privy and crawled into my sleeping bag. As much as I still felt like an outsider, I'd met some nice people my first day on the trail. In the woods, degrees and backgrounds weren't discussed. Careers were forgotten. It would seem that we were all connected because we were hikers. It really was a trail thing. I closed my eyes and allowed the murmurs of hushed conversations to lull me to sleep.

CHAPTER SEVEN

Research had led me to believe that due to the physical demands of hiking, I'd sleep like a baby while out on the trail. Nothing could've been further from the truth; at least that wasn't the case on my first night in the woods. It wasn't to say that my sleeping pad wasn't comfortable, it was, but camping in the woods was a far cry from camping on my safe and secure outdoor rooftop deck. There was a noticeable lack of city sounds. Horns and sirens emanating from the bustling streets below were ominously absent. The woods were way too quiet and at the same time, filled with heart-stopping noises.

I tried to listen to the snoring hikers and pretend it was a white noise app. Instead, their rattled breaths were drowned out, with acute clarity, each time a twig snapped somewhere nearby. Later, an owl landed directly above my tent and hooted for the longest time. When it left, I finally started to relax and drift off, only to be jolted into a sitting position by the sounds of what had to be a hundred wolves killing something that squealed loudly until it squealed no more. Growling tussles off in the distance made it clear that wolves don't like to share any more than small children did. Later, the pack howled about their victory for what seemed like hours. I remained in my tent, frozen in place, clutching my sleeping bag until dawn broke, and I could see well enough to pack up and get out of there.

The early morning air was crisp. I added an extra layer beneath my down hiking jacket and snuck out to collect my bear vault. I couldn't believe how loud each carefully placed step landed. Apparently, there was no tiptoeing in the forest. How hunters were ever successful was beyond me because despite my best efforts, each step sounded like a moose busting through the brush. No one stirred, so I guessed I wasn't as loud as I thought. I used the privy, washed up, and topped off my water bottles. After all of that, I dug a hole so I could brush my teeth and spit out the minty flavored foam somewhere besides the forest floor. Leave no trace: that was the trail creed.

Rather than fire up my camp stove and create even more noise, I decided to make my morning tea later when I stopped for breakfast. Instead, I disassembled my nylon home as quietly as I could. Everything inside my tent had already been stowed, and I was collapsing the poles when I heard a zipper behind me. Leslie. More than once, I'd hoped she'd wake up while I was still in camp.

"Aren't you the early bird?" Leslie stuck her legs outside of her door and slid a boot on each sock-clad foot. She stood and stretched with great deliberation, much like a cat after a sunny siesta. "Good morning."

"Good morning to you, too. I hope I didn't wake you." I whispered. "I couldn't sleep last night, stupid wolves."

"You mean the stupid coyotes."

"What?"

"If we're being accurate, those weren't wolves. That yippee, high-pitched howl is distinctively coyote." She slid her arms into her down jacket.

Good to know I wasn't the only one who was particular about facts. "So what I'm hearing you say is that you didn't sleep any better than I did."

"Yeah, not so much. Between the owl and the coyotes, it was a restless night for sure," she said, then disappeared into the woods behind the shelter.

I returned my attention to packing up my tent and ground cloth. To say my legs were stiff and achy was the understatement of the century. My body protested the additional weight of my pack, even on the short distance to the picnic table. I made a mental note to take a couple of ibuprofens after I ate. I had a thirteen-mile day ahead of me, and I needed to muster up some enthusiasm to get started.

Leslie made quick time of breaking down her tent. No doubt second nature for her after more than twenty years of experience. We set off together for Gooch Mountain Shelter when it was finally bright enough to see the trail markers on the tree trunks. Just before I rounded the bend out of camp, I turned back and captured a mental image of Stover Creek Shelter. My first night on the trail had been a good one, well, except for lack of sleep.

It was hard to believe that this would be my life for the next six months or so. Such a dramatic contrast to my former existence. Less than a month ago, I'd rarely walked across the local park and had never heard of long-distance hiking. Instead, I was focused on running a corporation. I had a car service on speed dial for the frequent work dinners at fine restaurants, where strongly poured cocktails were both appetizer and dessert. Every waking hour, I was glued to a myriad of electronic devices in order to keep tabs on all things both in and out of my control. I worked ten and twelve hour days in the office, only to come home and often work some more. Now, it would seem, my greatest goal was to put one foot in front of the other, over and over again, and do my best to not get lost off trail. I didn't mean to toot my own horn, but I was adapting to the striking lifestyle change pretty well so far. I'd only reached for my phone a few dozen times yesterday. Today was young and full of promise. Eventually, I'd wean myself off the habit.

The day started out cool and clear. The morning sun was still low in the sky, highlighting a few large fluffy clouds scattered about. When I was a kid, I was certain that rain from those sorts of clouds came down in the form of cotton balls. It was funny what I thought of when the chatter of modern life took a back seat.

We kept walking in a peaceful silence until we came to a spot where the trail crossed Stover Creek. The water was crystal clear and burbled along at a good clip. There was something tranquil about the sound of flowing water. The sun finally peeked above the horizon and bathed the landscape in a golden hue. We decided it was a perfect little place to stop for breakfast and each dug out our camp stove. My second time cooking on the trail. I made a large bowl of oatmeal. I added cream milk powder, walnuts, and raisins for extra calories and flavor. It was tasty and warmed me up from the inside out. After I ate, I filtered more water and made a strong cup of hot tea. Leslie had coffee. We sat on a log next to the creek and enjoyed the scenery while our stoves cooled.

Leslie bent and picked up a rock. While remaining seated, she skipped it downstream with an amazing ability. I counted nine bounces before it dropped below the water surface. "You never did tell me why you're hiking the AT." She bent and looked for another stone.

I choked on both the question and my tea. "Do I need a why?"

"Everyone has a why."

My chest tightened, and I felt called to the carpet. This was unfamiliar territory. In my world, vulnerabilities weren't willingly disclosed. I didn't want to admit my truth any more than I wanted to be cornered and dined on by that pack of coyotes. "What's your why?"

"You know mine. It's all about the scenic eleven." She got up and skipped another rock.

"If I'm honest with you, will you be honest with me?" I asked. "Please?"

Her shoulders stiffened, a telltale sign that she was leaving something out. "I am."

"I'm willing to bet there's more to your why." Something deep inside told me to take a leap of faith. It was time for my confession. "As far as my truth goes, you nailed it with your colorful commentary on the plane. One Friday afternoon, a few weeks ago, someone pulled the rug out from under me, and my world flipped upside down. Not only did I lose the bigwig job that earned me the diamond status membership, but I arrived home an hour later to find out that my girlfriend was moving out. She left me for a server from one of my favorite restaurants.

"Worst day of my life. I lost everything I've ever worked for. I am every bit the *Wild* hiker you accused me of being. I happened upon the movie later that Friday evening." I decided to omit the part about the profound effect it'd had on my soul. "Then, I purchased the movie and immediately watched it again. I bought the audiobook that same night and listened to it twice over the course of the following week. My friend, Sue, talked me out of the PCT because of drought and rattlesnakes. I searched for other trails and found the AT. More research and I purchased Bill Bryson's book. I listened to that and did a fact-finding deep dive. I spent the last two weeks researching and shopping for gear. Then, I spent several nights camping on my patio before I boarded that plane with my brand-new backpack stuffed full of brand-new gear. Go ahead and enjoy your *I told you so* moment."

Leslie was quiet. She didn't taunt or tease. After a long minute, she turned to face me. No smirk, no sneer, just the kindest expression I'd ever seen. "How about I clarify? My impression of you has shifted a lot since the plane. Your inspiration may have come from a movie, but from what I can tell so far, you're more like the unabridged book. There's a big difference. The women who stumbled into camp last night set off on the trail with a romantic notion of self-discovery based on what little content could be squeezed in an hour and a half. Bet your sweet ass they didn't do a bunch of research and test out their gear before last night."

She skipped another rock, then returned to the log and sat next to me. She patted my leg and left her hand on my thigh after the last pat. I felt the warmth through my pants. I didn't want her to pull her hand away. There was something about her touch that had a powerful effect on me.

"You set up your tent perfectly last night and broke it down equally well this morning. Your gear might be new, but you've tested it and know how to use it. You haven't asked anyone to do anything for you. You're tenacious. I have a feeling that you'll persevere, whether or not you lose toenails. Experience doesn't always make a good hiker, but determination does. I saw what you wrote at Springer. I hope you find both what you're looking for and what you need."

Her eyes were so sincere. I felt much the same way about what was gleaned from reading a book versus watching the movie.

Completely different stories. She saw me as an unabridged book. I'd take it. It gave me credence and depth. For reasons I couldn't yet explain, her opinion mattered to me. I wish I knew what she'd written back at Springer Mountain. A question for another time.

She stowed her cup and her stove and swung her pack up on her back. "Come on, we've got more miles to go."

We walked for a half an hour or so. The trail continued to follow Stover Creek. A gentle breeze carried the sweet scent of the dogwood trees. All around us, the forest was embracing spring and coming to life. The rhododendrons were covered in buds on the cusp of bursting wide open. The colorful petals protruding beyond the green husks already offered their distinct sweet and spicy scent, as if a carnation had been sprinkled with a grain or two of cloves. I hoped to come across more rhododendrons once they were in full bloom. The bushes put on such a grand display.

The sound of rushing water grew louder as we progressed. I looked around for the source, but the woods were already too dense with early spring undergrowth to see anything.

Leslie grabbed my hand and pulled me down a faint side trail. "I think I found it. It's this way."

"Where are we going? We won't get to Gooch Mountain if we keep stopping every half hour." I'd enjoyed being the first one to Stover Creek Shelter and wanted to turn that bit of good fate into a trail habit. Once I'd made it to camp and set everything up, I was able to relax and enjoy the evening by watching everything around me, the ultimate anti-procrastinator. I couldn't rest while there were things requiring attention, and hiking thirteen miles was definitely a thing requiring my full attention. Checking things off a list was how I managed my world. It was yet another thing instilled in me by my mother.

"Where's your sense of adventure? We have plenty of time. Come on, you'll see." She tugged on my hand. "Living in the moment and taking in the scenery, isn't that the point of hiking?"

I relented and followed her into the thicket. Shrub branches tugged on my pant legs and made scratching noises on my coat sleeves. After a bit, the trail spilled out into an oasis. There was a wide swath of flowing water, much wider than where we'd crossed Stover Creek earlier.

"Hey, this is it. It's really it. We found Long Creek Falls. It's one of a few attractions I've been looking forward to on this beginning stretch of trail," Leslie said.

The significance was lost on me. No doubt, the falls were stunning. Mossy covered glossy black rock beneath bright white, cascading water. There weren't words that I could come up with to adequately describe the captivation of the scene. That said, we'd already seen several settings that morning, each was every bit as beautiful, and none had garnered a reaction like this from Leslie. She removed her pack, pulled out her ground cloth, and spread it out in a sunny section of the sandy shore.

I set my pack on the edge of the tarp and stood next to her, taking it all in. The sight, scent, and the sounds of this hidden oasis captivated all my senses. After a while, Leslie lay on the ground cloth and tucked her pack beneath her knees. She patted the spot next to her, then folded her arms behind her head like a pillow. A short break couldn't hurt. The setting was far too irresistible to instantly turn and head back up to the trail.

"Relax, First Class, I won't bite, though, I might nibble if you ask nicely." She shot me a sideways glance that stirred a flurry of butterflies deep in my belly.

I settled next to her. A horizontal stretch on the sandy beach was exactly what my weary, sleep-deprived body needed. I tucked my pack beneath my knees just as she had done. The leg support felt amazing. "Be careful, I might get the impression that you actually like me."

"Would that be the worst thing in the world?" she asked.

"I suppose not." I tried my best to contain the giddiness tickling my insides.

"The sun feels good, doesn't it?"

"Hmm, it does." I closed my eyes and enjoyed the warmth on my skin. It made my eyelids heavy. A perfect place for a power nap.

Something nudged my arm. "Earth to Amber, did you hear a word I said?"

"What?" Crap, I must have crashed out.

"I said, everything I told you about myself on the plane was true, but you're right, it wasn't all of the truth." Her voice pulled me from my slumber.

There was a tap on the side of my leg. I lifted my head, squinting against the sun. Leslie held a photo between her thumb and index finger. I forced myself to sit up and took it from her. It was older, from sometime in the seventies or eighties, back when photographs were developed in three-inch squares because that was the format of the negative. The woman in the photo looked so much like Leslie, it was spooky, as if she'd traveled back in time for the pose. Same build, same incredible beaming smile, dimples and all, but whoever this was, she had a stellar head of hair: long, thick, wavy, and feathered back like Farrah Fawcett had done in her prime. She was standing beneath the arch in Amicalola Falls at the start of the Approach Trail. She had a beast of a backpack, complete with a big metal frame and a rolled up sleeping bag or something similar strapped high above her head. Thank goodness for the innovations made in hiking gear over the last forty years. Leslie's lookalike held a handwritten sign that read, "First of the Scenic Eleven."

"My *why*, at least for this trail."

I studied the photo a moment longer and then returned it to her waiting hand. "Is that your mother?"

She nodded. She looked at it for a moment before tucking it into a small, leather-bound book. "This is her trail diary." She pulled out another photo. Immediately, I recognized the location. No wonder she was so excited to find this spot. In this shot, her mom stood in the water at the base of Long Creek Falls. It would seem that Leslie was literally following in her mother's footsteps.

"Would you like me to take a photo of you in that same spot?"

"Would you?" She lit up. She dug out her phone before unlacing her boots and yanking off her socks.

I opened the camera app and laughed at her antics of tiptoeing into the icy water. She made the best faces, showing off a mixture of both shock and happiness. "Stop there. Give me your best *Rocky* pose." I took a couple of snaps. Both turned out great. "Perfect, just like the shot of your mom. Come on back before you get frostbite."

Leslie returned to the ground cloth and brushed the sand off her feet. She took her phone and swiped through the pictures. "These are great. Thank you."

"You should email them to your mom. Is the scenic eleven a family tradition? Did she finish all the trails too?"

"She made it almost halfway on the AT, to southern Pennsylvania, but she had to cut her trip short. She got sick and couldn't keep anything down. Turned out that it was morning sickness. She was pregnant with me. She never made it back to the trail, never finished the AT, let alone any of the others." Leslie brushed her feet off again before putting her socks and boots back on.

"How wonderful to have her diary and know where she stood at any given time, as if you're hiking with her. If you don't mind me asking, why *aren't* you hiking with her?"

"She was killed when I was ten."

"Oh, Leslie, I'm so sorry to hear that." I rested a hand on her arm. "What a horrible loss, especially since you were so young."

"Thanks. It happened when she was at work. Something was set up wrong, and she was electrocuted. My grandma took care of me after the accident."

"What about your dad?"

"Aw, ya know, it was the seventies. Free love and peace and all that. He was some random hiker dude on the trail. At least, that's what she said in the diary." She held up the small book before returning it to a pocket. "I found it when grandma and I packed up to sell the house. It was stuffed full of pictures. When I was older, I went through it and kept the photos of her at landmarks I could identify by comparing to pictures online. It'll keep me busy between here and Pennsylvania, that's for sure. I kept that beast of a backpack for the longest time, too, but the fabric disintegrated when I tried to pack for my first trail. There, now you know something about me that no one else knows. The whole truth of my why and why I saved the AT for last. This way, I'll not only finish the AT for her, but I'll have tackled all eleven of the scenic trails."

"You've dedicated more than twenty years of your life to accomplish your mom's dream?"

"I never thought of it like that. I always considered it to be my thing that was inspired by that first photograph of her at the Approach Trail. It was pretty wild, standing beneath that arch. I did get someone to snap a pic of me in that same spot. See, I told you, we all have a why."

I wanted to hug her, but before I could, approaching footsteps captured our attention. The distinct sound of boots crunching on rock and sand…and faint whistling, though I didn't recognize the tune. I heard the wolf whistle at the same time I recognized the bouncy light brown curls. Bobber, followed closely by Cricket.

"Ha. I told you we'd catch up with them at some point. Who knew it'd be this soon." Bobber shot us an exaggerated wink. "Once again, you're doing it wrong, girls. How many times do I have to tell you, clothes off, then you enjoy the snooky snooky."

I squeezed Leslie's hand, hoping she understood that our conversation about her mom would stay between us. She squeezed mine in return and held on for a moment longer. It was the realest, most honest conversation I could recall having with anyone other than Sue.

I'd mastered keeping people at a distance. In my world, communications were guarded because everyone was out for leverage or a tidbit they could use later. Much like what I'd done to Grayson to get Sue a better severance package. Even in my past relationships, girlfriends were kept at an arm's length for much the same reason. It was easy enough to do when being together was all about having arm candy for events and sex without the needy emotional ties. Whatever this was with Leslie, it wasn't anything like my experiences in Hartford. I'd confessed my truth to her, and I was rewarded with something very personal and honest from her in return. One thing was for sure, I was becoming quite fond of her.

We sat there chatting with Bobber and Cricket while they filtered water and filled their bottles. After that, Leslie folded up her ground cloth, and the four of us made our way back to the trail. We still had many miles to cover.

CHAPTER EIGHT

Sleep was much better the second night on the trail. It wasn't long after I set up my tent and ate a hot dinner that I crawled into my sleeping bag and gave in to the exhaustion of the last couple of days. I woke at the break of dawn feeling like I'd had way too much to drink the night before. It'd been a good long while since I'd had a hangover, but my, oh my, that was exactly what it felt like. If only I'd had the fun to go with the consequences. Head to toe, everything ached. If I were home, I'd shuffle out to the living room, curl up in the deep corner of the sofa with a blanket, and sleep through a couple of movies. But I wasn't home. I sat up and had to brace myself while I waited for the dizziness to pass.

My boots were in a pouch down by my feet. If I weren't feeling so icky, it would have been comical how far away they seemed to be, as if I'd left them on the other side of the house in Hartford. I extracted myself from my twisted sleeping bag and unzipped the flap to my tent. A deep breath of crisp morning air helped me muster the energy to crawl to the other end of my tent, retrieve my boots, and actually force them on my feet. I stood. The world swam wildly. I squatted for a lower center of gravity in case I toppled over. My legs screamed in protest, and I kept going backward until I was once again seated just inside my tent. Footsteps rapidly approached, then there was a hand on my shoulder. I kept my eyes closed because I was sure the world was still spinning madly out of control.

"Hey, what happened? Are you okay?" Leslie whispered.

"Worst. Hangover. Ever," I answered quietly because despite how horrible I felt, I had a feeling we were the only two awake this early. "I'd have to feel better to die." Damn Sue and her sayings.

"Were you drinking last night? You know you're supposed to pass the bottle, not drink it all yourself."

"I wasn't drinking."

"In that case, this might be a weird question, but do you feel the need to pee?" she asked.

"What? No. Why?" I tried to look at her, but the world started spinning again.

"Did you go at all last night?"

I had to think about it. I'd finally slept through the night, and I wasn't entirely sure I'd gone before bed. "No."

"You slept for twelve hours. Your bladder should be full. How much did you drink yesterday? How many water bottles?"

"I don't know. I'm guessing by your tone…" I drew in a deep breath and let out slowly to fight off the nausea. "Not enough."

Leslie pinched the skin on the back of my upper wrist. "You're right about that. You're dehydrated. Wait here."

Like I was going to go anywhere. I couldn't even stand. She returned a few minutes later.

"I hope you like salty tasting lemon-lime. Here, drink this… all of it." She handed me a water bottle and sat next to me. I felt her arm wrap around my shoulder and hold me. It felt nice. In fact, it felt very nice. I leaned into her because in that moment, I could get away with it.

Within fifteen minutes, I'd finished the water and felt surprisingly human again. "What's in this miracle juice?"

"It's called Electro IV. I keep powdered single serv packets in my food bag for moments just like this. It's like a sports drink on super steroids. I've been there myself. Some days, you sweat off more than you take in. Your color's already looking much better."

"I have electrolyte packets, too. I didn't even think of adding them to my water yesterday."

"You've pushed your body hard. Sometimes, water alone isn't enough, especially if you haven't taken enough in. Without the boost, it could take a day or two to fully recover. I'd recommend mixing a packet with your water at lunch, too. That is, if you feel up for hiking today."

How could I not? If I stayed back to rest and Leslie kept going, that'd be it. Same went for Bobber and Cricket. I'd never catch up to them. We were all getting along so well that I didn't want to risk losing our little group. Sure, there were other people that I'd meet, but I'd really clicked with these three. I'd push through. I'd find a way to continue.

I sat up a little taller. "I like hiking with you. I want to keep going."

"Good 'cause I like having you around, too. You should know, it's going to be a tough trek from here to Neel Gap. Almost all of it will be uphill, but there's a special reward when we get close to the end of our day." She stood up and held out her hand.

I grabbed my pack. She took it from me and again offered her free hand. The extra stability was welcome. This time, my legs were kind enough to support me. My muscles were still fatigued, but I attributed that to twenty-five miles of hiking in two days. At least the world wasn't swirling. I tested fate again by bending and zipping up my tent. Success. That was some seriously magic juice.

"Do you think you can make it to the picnic table?" Leslie asked.

"How about I meet you there?" I took my pack and swung it over one shoulder. "I want to clean up and grab my bear vault."

She shot me a questioning look.

"Really, I'm already feeling much better. It's my morning routine. I'll holler if I need you, okay?"

She smiled and nodded.

Her concern for me offered the warmth of a great big hug. We were figuring out a rapport. One that took much less effort than any relationship I'd ever had, personal or professional. For the second day in a row, we ate breakfast together in amicable silence. It was nice. Rather than make hot tea after, I mixed one of my electrolyte drink packets into another bottle of water and used it to chase down a few ibuprofen. The extreme effects of dehydration scared me just a bit. I knew myself well enough to know that I'd likely overcompensate, but better to be well hydrated than to risk feeling like that again tomorrow. Besides, I'd read about Neel Gap and more specifically, Mountain Crossings, an outfitter and hostel that was literally the only indoor part of the trail. Not to mention, there was the possibility of a hot shower, laundry, a cocktail, and pizza if all went well. *Count. Me. In.*

We each went about our tasks, silently breaking down camp. I knew it wasn't a race, but because I was competitive by nature, I made it one. My inflatable sleeping pad slowed me down, and she beat me by just under two minutes. Years of experience with her gear for the win. The sun was fully up, and still, no one around us had stirred. We hoisted our packs and bid farewell to Gooch Mountain Shelter. A checkbox for day two.

The climb was instant and relentless. At times, it was so steep that I found myself winded and had to stop to catch my breath. My legs burned with overuse and fatigue. How I wished for my trail legs. Would I constantly feel like this for the next eight to twelve weeks until my legs adapted to this new lifestyle? I wasn't sure if Leslie was feeling it too or if she was being kind and matching my pace. It was likely the latter. Her trail legs were more like hefty tree stumps. Either way, I was grateful to have her close by.

We stopped a few hours later for a second breakfast. At least, I wasn't the only one already hungry again. I remembered reading that hikers should consume about six thousand calories a day due to the physical exertion of the trail. I typically ate about thirteen hundred a day, a bit more if cocktails were involved, so I bumped my daily estimate up to about four thousand and planned for four days of food from my kickoff point in Amicalola Falls.

I opened my bear vault and was relieved that we'd be shopping later that afternoon. My trail gluttony had put a big dent in my provisions. I finished off my oatmeal, walnuts, and freeze-dried fruit, along with the milk powder for my fifth breakfast in three days. This left me with two high-protein granola bars for snacks, some turkey jerky, and a couple handfuls of trail mix for lunch, or I could break out my stove and cook up my last freeze-dried dinner of beef stroganoff. I wouldn't starve, but I definitely needed to resupply with this overzealous appetite in mind.

"Are you good to keep going?" Leslie asked between mouthfuls of her second breakfast extravaganza.

"I am." I scraped the last of my masterpiece from my cup. "Thanks again for taking care of me this morning. I didn't even consider dehydration. I thought for sure I'd had bad water or something."

"You're filtering all your water, right?" she asked with a stern facial expression.

"Oh, I am. I just couldn't think of another cause. It's not like I caught the flu out here in the woods."

"Trust me, if it was bad water, you'd have had a whole different set of issues." She winked, and I knew enough about the symptoms to be grateful for the lack of specifics, even if we'd already finished eating.

Leslie bent over and washed out her cup. I took a moment and admired her from this perspective. She had a nice ass. Toned and muscular, yet enough plumpness to grab a good handful. Would the past couple of days have been as enjoyable if we hadn't met, or would I be on the verge of tapping out, like the *Wild* ladies at Stover Creek, if I'd been out here all alone? Quite possibly the latter. Thankfully, Lady Luck was shining down on me at the airport. Hiking with Leslie had made the last couple of days an unexpected treat. I bent next to her and washed my cup out before I was caught ogling her ass.

We packed up and got moving again. The ibuprofen finally kicked in, and my legs were fighting through the weariness. Onward and upward, one foot in front of the other toward the summit. Hiking felt a little like existing in slow motion. I'd never done anything slow in Hartford. I was always going a hundred miles an hour. Nope, never, in a million years, would I have imagined myself a hiker. The reality of it still caught me off guard at times. Just three weeks earlier, I was perched in my fancy corner office and had people at my beck and call. Who knew that I'd lose the corner office and end up on a trail in Northern Georgia? *What a difference a day makes.*

We climbed and climbed, ate lunch, plateaued briefly, ate a snack, and climbed some more...relentlessly. Leslie made it to the peak first. She was in front of me by a hundred yards or so and stood stoically on the vast gray shale when I crested the summit. She turned and had that same emotional expression she'd had back at Long Creek Falls. I instantly felt an urgent need to hold her. I resisted and walked up beside her instead.

"The treat I promised you. The tippy top of Blood Mountain. The highest peak along Georgia's portion of the AT." She removed her pack, unzipped a pocket, and pulled out her mom's diary and her phone.

The vast mountainous terrain was breathtaking. Rolling landscapes below went on for miles and miles, as far as the eye could see. Leslie plucked a photo from the diary, stared at it for a moment, and handed it to me. The views were much hazier than the crystal clear atmosphere of the moment. In this picture, her mom stood with a trademark seventies man, including the Fu Manchu mustache. Two backpacks were on the ground, one leaning against the other. Leslie's mom and the male hiker had their arms wrapped around one another and their heads leaning into each other, touching at the crown.

"Is that your father?" I asked.

She shrugged. "Who knows? It could be him, or it could be one of countless others in photos along the trail. She left the trail in mid-June, and I was born in December, but I don't know if I was early, late, or on time. She likely became pregnant sometime in March, so it could be him. I stopped wondering who he was long ago."

I didn't know what to say to all of that. I wasn't close with either of my parents. Would I feel a sense of wonder if I didn't know who my father was? Truth be told, I wasn't entirely sure I was my father's daughter. He had a dark complexion, dark hair, and brown eyes, while I was blond, fair skinned, and blue-eyed like my mother. I'd looked up the odds of that happening, and it was less than ten percent. My mother never hid her trysts, and I never cared enough to ask for a DNA test. Much like what Leslie said, knowing wouldn't change much.

"Can I capture another photo for you?" I asked.

"Instead, would you be in this one with me? We can mimic the pose."

I nodded, smiling like a freshman being asked out to homecoming, and removed my pack. We stood arm in arm with our heads touching and cheesy smiles on our faces. Leslie snapped a few shots. Our pose closely matched her mom's. It was perfect.

"Would it be too much to ask to take one with my phone, too?"

"Not at all."

I opened the app and configured the settings. We posed, and Leslie took a few shots. They were fantastic with the vast views off behind us. I had decent signal, so I attached the photo and shot off a text to Sue, telling her that I was still alive and having fun. Her response was a smiley face with heart eyes. I wasn't sure if the heart eyes were for me or because she'd read more into the photo than what it was.

Thankfully, the rest of our hike was downhill. We made it to the infamous Mountain Crossings outfitters by five in the afternoon. On our way to the stone building, we passed a tree draped with used hiking shoes. I stopped next to Leslie to take it all in. We each pulled out our phones and took photos.

"The AT hiker's boot tree," Leslie read from a plaque. "This is the final resupply on the trail for southbound hikers. When they complete the trail from Maine to Georgia, they get to throw their hiking shoes up into the tree so there's always a part of them on the trail."

It was the most touching tribute I'd ever heard of. "Is there one in Maine for the northbound hikers?"

"We'll have to make it to Maine for ourselves and see, won't we?" She rested her hand on my shoulder. Her touch was becoming a craving, and I savored each and every fix.

We stared at the tree for a moment more before we walked up the sidewalk and into the outfitters.

"Hiya. I'm Steve. Welcome to Mountain Crossings," a man said from behind the cash register. There was a sign on the wall behind him that read, *Have a question, ask, we're all successful thru-hikers.*

"Hi, are there any bunks still available?" Leslie asked.

"Sure. You two are our first arrivals of the day. We've done some major renovations in the bunk room over the winter months, including all new mattresses. I think you'll find it very comfortable in there."

"Do you own this facility?" I asked.

"Sure enough. My wife, Rosie, and I bought it a year and a half ago."

"And you've both hiked the entire trail, like the sign says behind you?" Leslie asked.

"That's right. We hiked the trail in entirety six years ago. There's something about the AT that just gets into your blood. It's different than any other trail. When this place came up for sale, we ditched our corporate jobs and took a leap of faith. Best decision we've ever made." His smile said it all.

"You're literally living on the trail. How cool is that? Talk about being surrounded by trail magic all the time." Leslie spun slowly, her eyes darting here and there as if she was trying to take it all in.

"No regrets?" I asked.

"Not one. We have great staff, amazing customers, and there's virtually zero stress. Honestly, we've never been happier. I tell ya, it's a load of fun being at the thirty-mile mark. For the northbound folks, this is the first sign of life after Amicalola. It's a defining stop. Hikers are either loving the trail or they're in tears and trading in their gear for a ride home. Then, there's the southbound hikers in the fall who get to toss their boots up in the tree. There's nothing like living where people yearn to vacation."

"Interesting perspective." I wasn't sure I could consider trading my corporate paycheck to run a setup like Mountain Crossings, but prior to this trip, I hadn't even known they existed. He did look happy.

"Sorry, here I am talking your ear off, and you two are probably itching to get a shower before this place fills up. Rate's twenty-five dollars per person, and it includes a bunk, a shower, and a towel. Laundry is coin-operated if you need it."

"Sounds wonderful. Can I prepay for a couple who's trailing a bit behind? I want to make sure they each get a bunk, too. Trail names are Bobber and Cricket. That'll be four of us in total." I opened my wallet and added four twenties on top of Leslie's twenty-five. "I'll take the change in quarters, if that's what the laundry takes."

Leslie and I unpacked enough to claim all four beds in the two bunks along the back wall. I had saved a clean outfit, knowing I'd get a shower at Mountain Crossings. While Leslie was in the bathroom, I dug out my clothes and tossed my toiletries into my sleeping bag sack that was empty because my sleeping bag was currently calling dibs on the bunk above. The prospect of indoor plumbing had me absolutely giddy. I was about to feel like a brand-new woman.

The bathroom door opened, and steam escaped around Leslie's body. Wow, who knew the sporty physique was so incredibly sexy? Either I was seriously deprived, or I craved a new type because I couldn't look away. The damp T-shirt stuck to her skin, outlining the perfect swell of her breasts, and her shorts hugged her hips and strong thighs. She had a towel draped around her neck and looked like something out of a dreamy scene in a rom-com. Holy hell.

Without the bandana, her thick head of hair was on full display, all wet and wavy. No doubt a gift from her mother. She had an hourglass figure that started at her strong, broad, well-defined shoulders. Her waist was surprisingly trim without the multiple layers of clothes, and her legs were every bit as muscular as I'd pictured on the plane.

Was it my imagination, or did she have a mischievous glint in her eyes? I half expected her to beckon me into the shower, or perhaps that was wishful thinking.

"Sorry, I took so long. The water is superhot and the pressure is ah-mazing." She stepped into the bunk room.

"You should lose the bandana. You have a beautiful head of hair."

Color flushed her cheeks. "Thanks, the bandana does for me what your ponytail does for you. Keeps this mop from becoming an unruly mess and keeps it out of my eyes. You're in luck tonight, though. Much like everything I own, it needs to be washed. The shower's all yours. I'll get my laundry started. That way, the washer should be free when you're done."

I stood there like a smitten schoolgirl and had to force myself to move. My hope for an offer to help me out of my clothes was dashed. Without as much as a second glance, she scooped up her laundry and left. It was probably for the best. We were getting along great, and my track record with women wasn't all that. I grabbed my stuff and made a beeline for the bathroom.

She wasn't wrong about the shower. The water was blissfully hot, and the pressure massaged my sore muscles. I washed, rinsed, and repeated the process all over again. Never in my life had I gone so long without bathing. It felt incredible to get the three days of grime off my body. It occurred to me that, just like I'd only ever seen Leslie wearing the bandana, she'd only ever seen my hair in the ponytail so, for something different, I left it down and let it dry naturally, hoping she'd find it just as attractive as I found her natural looks.

I gathered everything that needed laundering and followed the signs. She was transferring her clothes from the washer to the dryer. Perfect timing. Once both machines were running, we grabbed our wallets and all but raced back to the store to go shopping.

Bobber and Cricket arrived an hour or so later. After they showered and had their laundry going, we took our pizza right out of the oven and our ice-cold beer out back to sit around the roaring campfire. For the time being, we had the little area all to ourselves. I'd never been much of a beer drinker, but after three days of extreme physical exertion, cold beer paired perfectly with a piping hot supreme pizza.

"Bobber, did you give them the cash? You two were sweet to claim the bunks for us. Thank you."

"Indeed, I did."

"Happy to do it. We have to keep our little group together." I held up my beer in a toast. Bobber, Cricket, and Leslie tapped the necks of their beer bottles against mine. I liked our little group and being a part of it felt good.

"So how long have you two been hiking together?" Cricket pointed to Leslie and I.

"Two days," I answered.

"No, not this trail. I mean, all added up," Cricket said.

Leslie swallowed her mouthful. "Like she said, two days. We met on the flight to Atlanta and shared a ride to Amicalola. Then, as you know, she totally ditched me on day one."

Bobber popped out of her chair. "Shut up. You two are so stinking cute together, like peas and carrots. You should totally hook up."

A pang of jealously popped up as an image of Leslie being whisked away by the rowdy crowd flooded my mind. "A correction is in order. If memory serves, I think it was you who totally ditched me the night before, like, the moment we arrived at the lodge."

Leslie bumped my knee. "Hey, I already said that I'm sorry about that, like, really sorry."

"Yeah, well, from what we've noticed, you haven't let her out of your sight since that first day. Munch is smitten on one Ms. Amber Shaw." Cricket wiggled her eyebrows and winked at me. "Munch has a First Class crush."

"Good one. Oh, I've got it. Munch is hoping for a First Class snack. Nom, nom, nom." Bobber made her arms into the Pac Man mouth.

Cricket laughed. "Munch wants to put her stamp on First Class." Cricket made a stamping motion.

"Keep it up, you two, and somebody's going to get stamped, all right." Leslie chuckled, and I wished I could read her mind.

"You could do worse." I flipped back my hair. "I am quite a catch."

"Yes, you are," Cricket said.

Bobber and I both looked at Cricket. She waved us off and rolled her eyes.

"You don't say." Leslie leaned over and rested her head on my shoulder. "Well, in that case, I'm in, especially if it means I get to curl up next to you on that cozy inflatable sleeping pad tomorrow night."

We all laughed.

Cricket pointed her pizza at me. "Is this your first trail, then?"

"It is." I kept my answer short, hoping Leslie wouldn't repeat her assessment of me from the plane. Thankfully, she remained quiet.

"Is the AT everything you thought it would be?" Bobber asked.

I chewed my mouthful and washed it down with the last of my beer. "I'm only three days in, and I'm still figuring out my rhythm. I'm not entirely sure I knew what to expect, but I'm really enjoying my time on the trail. For some reason, I thought I'd experience everything alone. Like I'd be isolated from the world, so in that respect, it's far better than what I anticipated. I had no idea there'd be so many people out here hiking, and I'm so grateful to have met and clicked with you two and the notorious Munch." I nudged Leslie with my elbow. "I've never, ever, experienced camaraderie like this before."

Leslie twisted in her seat to face me. "Really? Never? Not even at your big fancy—"

"Never." I cut her off but silently added, *it's lonely at the top*. I wasn't ready to discuss my recent disappointments. Out here, I had the chance to reinvent myself. I didn't want to lose that by being outed as a has-been CEO who was promoted beyond her skill set.

"We were just saying the same thing last night. How happy we are to have met you two. It makes it so much more fun to have friends to meet up with in the evenings and share this experience with," Cricket said.

Friends. I hung on to the word. I'd always wanted a group of close friends, but my all-consuming career hadn't been conducive to cultivating friendships, beyond what I had with Sue, and that existed solely because of the same all-consuming career. It was refreshing to be around people who were totally unguarded and were with me because they wanted to be and weren't being paid.

"I agree. Here's to new friends. I can't imagine a better beginning to the last of the scenic eleven." Leslie had the sweetest smile. She held up her beer to Bobber, then Cricket, then her expression softened when she looked at me. I melted.

"What's next, Munch? Are you going to tackle another series of trails, or are you hanging up your boots?" Cricket asked.

"I'm not sure." She leaned back in her chair. "Maybe I'll work for a place like this so I'm always on the trail."

Bobber popped up out of her seat. "That would be so frickin' awesome. Babe, we should do that. Ditch our jobs and run a hostel."

"What I'm hearing you say is rather than work long days with benefits and vacation time, you'd like to work twenty-four hours a day, seven days a week, with no benefits, and no paid vacation. You already put in ungodly hours at your restaurant," Cricket said. It was clear that Bobber was the dreamer, and Cricket was the one that kept them grounded.

"Yeah, but you could get away from the backstabbing office bullshit." Bobber spun in a circle with her arms extended. "Hello... life would be a vacation."

"Until the shelves need to be restocked, the floors swept and mopped, or the toilets back up. It's all fun and games until it's not."

"Buzzkill." Bobber plopped down in her chair.

The four of us continued to chat and laugh while we finished our pizza and the six-pack. Bobber and Cricket bailed on us to check on their laundry and restock their food bags. I was grateful that our tasks were already complete. There was a flurry of activity inside the hostel through the windows, and I'd never been a fan of shopping in a crowded space. Instead, I enjoyed the warmth of the fire, people watching from afar, and most of all, Leslie's company. That was, until someone new heard her trail name, and then everything was about the scenic eleven and the notorious Munch. It was fun, watching her in her element.

CHAPTER NINE

Knowing I'd have to hike in the rain at some point on the trail and actually doing it were two entirely different things. In my mind, I had this romantic image of walking along with the soft pitter-patter of raindrops dancing on my jacket. The reality was anything but that.

The plan had been to depart Mountain Crossings and traverse nineteen miles to Blue Mountain Shelter and then another nineteen the following day to Dicks Creek Gap, where a private room with a queen-sized bed and my first trail box from Sue were calling to me like a homing beacon.

We'd departed just after daybreak, our bellies stuffed with a hearty breakfast sandwich of egg, bacon, and cheese on a perfectly toasted English muffin. By midmorning, a dense fog had rolled in and blanketed the landscape. A couple of hours later, the sky had darkened to a deep mottled gray, and the winds had begun to whip, wildly swaying the tree branches high above. The air was heavy with the scent of pending rain.

Leslie had stopped and stared at the sky. "The storm's close. We should get our rain gear on." She removed her pack.

I'd trusted her knowledge and followed her lead. The ground was already damp from the foggy mist in the air. Dirt, dried leaves, and pine needles caked the soles of my boots. Not wanting that mess inside my rain pants, I'd leaned against a tree and removed one boot, fed my leg into the nylon gear, then stuffed my foot back into my boot. I'd repeated the process with the other leg, albeit, far less gracefully, almost toppling over twice. Why was balance so much easier on one leg than the other?

I hadn't thought to air out my rain gear before setting off on the trail. The pent-up plastic scent had reminded me of a brand-new beach ball being blown up for the first time on a hot summer's day. Hopefully, the wind would dissipate the overpowering fragrance once we were walking again. I'd pulled out a heavier weight rain cover and wrapped it around my pack. The sound of crinkly nylon snapping in the gusty wind was almost as bad as the *zzzzzt zzzzzt* noise it made with each step and each arm swing. It was unnerving and rattled my spirit.

When the rain fell, it hit hard and fast, assaulting us with a deluge of large drops that swirled with the wind and struck uncovered skin from every direction. I quickly pulled the hood of my rain coat up and dumped a captured pool of ice-cold water down my spine. Great, now I was both sweaty and chilled. Today was proving to be a miserable trudge.

"This is awful. Should we stop and pitch our tents?" The air was so cold and damp that my windproof gear didn't feel like it was living up to its name. I pulled my sleeves down around my clenched fists, trying to retain a touch of body heat.

"With this wind, it would be better to find a shelter. Never know when or where a tree limb could come down. This is looking much worse than what was in the forecast. Do you think you can make it another couple of miles to Low Gap Shelter? It's seven miles closer than where we planned to sleep."

"I trust you. I'll do whatever you think is best." I put my head down and forced myself to plod along.

She slowed her pace until we were side by side. "How about some conversation to pass the time? Let's see, how'd you word it back at Springer? 'I hope I find what I'm looking for, else, I hope I find what I need.'"

"Yeah, it was something like that." That was exactly how I'd worded it. Should I have been flattered or creeped out that she memorized my trail motto word for word? "What'd you write?"

"An epically original, 'Last of the scenic eleven,' followed by my trail name. That was all that I was willing to share with the public."

"What weren't you willing to share?" I asked, hoping she would answer, and the uncertainty in my life wouldn't be the topic of conversation.

"You first. Your words really stuck with me. What do you hope to find? What wasn't working in your life back home that a new job and a new girl couldn't fix?"

"You want to have that conversation right now? Out here in the freezing wind and rain?" I turned to look at Leslie. My hood slapped rhythmically against the side of my face.

"Why not? Do you have somewhere else to be?"

"Are you going to call me a *Wild* hiker if I say that, at this moment, another job and another girlfriend sounds pretty damn nice?"

"Everything sounds better than trekking when the weather is this cold and nasty, but we'd never finish if we only hiked on the nice days. How would you have answered if I'd asked you yesterday?"

"Can't you leave it be?"

"Come on, I really want to know. It's not a tough question."

"But it is if I don't know the answer." I stopped abruptly and threw my arms in the air. "I don't know, okay? I don't know what I hope to figure out. I don't know what it is that isn't working in my life. I don't know what I'm looking for or where to find it. I don't know anything. I just fucking don't know!" The urge to throw something was instant and overwhelming. I picked up an open pinecone, one that could adorn a festive winter decoration once dipped in sparkling glitter. I cocked my arm back and released it with everything I had. The wind caught it and whipped it right back at me with much more force. A direct hit to my chest. "Jesus. Apparently, I don't even know how to throw a fucking pinecone."

Instantly, I regretted my outburst. Definitely not the behavior of a seasoned executive. I was sure I looked and sounded as ridiculous as I felt. I half expected Leslie to turn and simply walk away. I certainly would have if I'd been on the other side of that tantrum, yet, she remained at my side and even reached for my hand. Her touch had an incredible grounding effect.

"I think that's the realest you've been since we met."

"What do you mean?" Thank goodness for the rain because I was on the verge of tears.

"You're edited. You think through every word that comes out of your mouth. Tell me I'm wrong."

I stared at her, trying to figure out what to say. Well, shit, that totally proved her point. "What do you want from me?"

"I want you to let me in. I want to know the you that no one else gets to know."

"I told you my why. I told you about my job and my girlfriend."

"You confessed to being called to the carpet, but you haven't told me anything real about what happened with your job or your girlfriend or anything else about your life. Come on, I want the raw, unedited Amber."

"I don't have a clue how to be raw and unedited. In my world, those are unacceptable traits."

"Why? Talk to me. Tell me more."

"Can we walk and talk? I'm freezing again."

"The shelter shouldn't be far." Leslie kept my hand in hers, and we pushed on.

I spent a few minutes trying to figure out how to explain my world to Leslie. We lived completely different lives. The conversation we'd shared on the day we'd met seemed the best place to start. "Do you remember on the plane when you said that it was easy to avoid expectations because you didn't have any?"

"Yeah."

"I can't relate to that, like, not at all. Expectations are the air that I breathe. My mother's affection has always been the proverbial dangling carrot, and to have a chance at capturing it, I had to exceed her expectations. That carrot has always been just out of reach. I had to be the best of the best. I graduated at the top of my class at boarding school because anything less was unacceptable. I thought, finally, she'll be proud of me. When the dean congratulated me on a 3.92 GPA, my mother said that it wasn't a 4.0. If I'd studied more and pushed harder, I could've done better. I graduated summa cum laude for both my undergrad and my MBA and still not good enough, not four point perfect. Do better. Be better."

I kicked at a stick in the path that turned out to be anchored at one end. I stumbled, and Leslie caught me, which was just as embarrassing as the pinecone. Physical attempts at emphasis were not my friend today.

I regained my balance and kept talking. "Nothing's ever been good enough. It's been that way all my life. I've pushed myself, hoping to at least meet her expectations. I've spent my life striving for her approval. You say you want to know the me that no one else knows? I say good luck because I don't know the me that no one else knows. I've been so busy trying to be someone my mother would be proud of that I don't know if I've ever had my own identity."

"See, that was raw and unedited. It's also totally screwed up. Your mom sounds like an impossible woman to please."

"She is."

"And yet, you're still trying?"

I nodded. Tears fell, and I thanked God for the rain.

"Boarding school? What, public schools weren't good enough?"

"Oh, I firmly believe that public schools would have been a fine education if the kids weren't dropped off at home every afternoon. Boarding school because I didn't fit into their world. I was only home for six weeks in the summer. Even then, I typically hung out with the housekeeper. Mabel made the best chocolate chip cookies."

"Wow, your childhood was kind of fucked-up."

"To me, it was normal. Sadly, everyone I went to school with had the same life. What was your mom like? Were you two close?"

"Yeah, she was the best. She worked two jobs and somehow always made time for me. Whether it was helping me with my homework or playing outside or cooking dinner together, she always included me. Back then, it was only us, and we were each other's everything, which made her death really tough to accept."

"It's so sad that you lost her at such a young age. It sounds like you have some great memories to look back on."

"Yes and no. I had my grandma to take me in. I'm grateful that I didn't end up in the system." Leslie tugged on my hand. "Come on, the side trail is this way. We made it. I almost missed the sign."

Fighting against the wind and the rain, we hurried up the side trail and scurried up onto the platform of the shelter. We were the only two there. The wind swirled with such force that it was raining just as hard inside the shelter as it was outside. Water dripped from the ceiling. The inside was soaked.

"Pull your ground cloth out." Leslie already had her pack open. She pulled out some rope and tied it up in the rafters at the front corner and then weaved the other end through grommets in her ground cloth, then around the front beam between each grommet. At the midpoint, she repeated with my ground cloth. It was an ingenious solution that created a fourth wall. We secured the bottom in a similar way with rope from my pack. Just a few minutes of being out of the relentless weather had already made a huge difference on my spirit.

"Hey, before you take off your rain gear, what do you say we bring the picnic table inside? It will give us a place to sit besides the cold floor."

"Good idea."

The picnic table was much lighter than it looked. With the two of us, we made quick work of getting it beneath the tarp and up on the platform without things getting soaked all over again. Other than being super dark, our little hideaway was shaping up quite nicely. Leslie wiped the standing water off the seats and the table while I hung up my head lamp as a light fixture and switched on the high beam option. It worked brilliantly. *See what I did there, brilliantly. Ha.*

Mimicking Leslie's trail ingenuity, I removed my rain gear and hung each item on my extended trekking pole to drip dry.

"In the spirit of raw and unedited, what weren't you willing to share with the public at Springer Mountain?" I asked. "I'd like to know the you that no one else knows, too."

"You already know more than anyone."

She pulled out her camp stove and started a mug of water to boil. She set a baggy of instant coffee and a plastic spoon on the table. I couldn't agree more; something warm to drink sounded wonderful. I dug for my stove and filled my titanium cup with water for tea. The two flames helped to take the biting chill out of the air. I draped the rain cover from my backpack over the picnic table bench, dry side up, as a barrier between my pants and the waterlogged wood and took a seat across from her.

My recent resupply offered a lovely assortment of teas to choose from. Holiday Chai seemed the perfect fit. It promised a hint of nutmeg, cinnamon, and gingerbread. Talk about something to warm your soul. I hoped it tasted half as good as it smelled and forced myself to be patient while it steeped.

"Do you remember how you said I nailed it when I called you a *Wild* hiker on the plane because you were hiking to get away from some shitty things that happened in your life?"

I nodded, hoping that we weren't back on that conversation.

"Well, you nailed it on your assessment of me, too." Leslie fiddled with the plastic spoon. "I haven't planned for anything beyond the scenic eleven. Truth be told, I'm scared to finish because I've focused on this one goal for so long that I have no idea what to do after I accomplish it. That's what I didn't share with the public, and that's what I hope to figure out over the next two thousand miles. I'm almost forty, and I'm literally no better off than I was the day after high school. Sometimes, I wonder if I haven't wasted the last twenty years. I mean, what's the point really? What did I really accomplish? All I know is that I have no idea what I want out of life. It's kinda like what you said in the trail journal, and maybe that's why it stuck with me. I hope I find what I'm looking for, else, I hope I find what I need. That's exactly how I feel."

Sincerity showed in her expression, and my heart melted for her. I reached across the table and held her hand. "Aren't we the perfect pair. Like two lost souls searching for answers. Each of us trying to figure out where to go from here."

Leslie stirred a spoonful of instant coffee into her steaming mug. "It's weird, isn't it? Such a fluke that we even met, and we're both struggling with the same kinda thing."

"I've never thought much about fate and all that, but maybe that's precisely why we met. Nothing says we have to figure it out on our own. Maybe, we're exactly what each other needs at this moment in time. We can help each other figure out what's next." I bumped the toe of her boot with mine. "I can't think of anyone else I'd rather be on this journey with. PS, I'm happy that you and Mr. Aftershave were assigned the same seat, and there was only one seat left in first-class. I'm grateful for the happenstance."

Leslie's smile lit up the shelter better than any headlamp. "Yeah? Even after I tormented you? PS, I'm glad your friend talked you out of hiking the PCT." She sipped on her coffee and stared at me. "So can we get back to the question that started all of this?"

"What's that?"

Leslie sipped her coffee. "Well, you still haven't told me anything about what happened with your job and your girlfriend."

"Why ruin a perfect conversation? You'll tease and torment me all over again."

"Come on, things are different between us now. This is a safe space. I swear, I won't tease you." She smiled, and I drank in her eyes like a tequila-soaked blue margarita. She was every bit as intoxicating.

"Fine, remember that you swore." I sipped my tea and took a moment to figure out what I wanted to say. "I spent the last seven years as the CEO for a large corporation. Over the last six months, my sole focus was on a huge merger, one that put the company in *Fortune 500* standing. It was a big deal. I knew some jobs would be lost, especially with overlap in upper management, but I never imagined that I would fall into that category. I mean, I was the one who proposed and secured the merger. The day it was finalized, I was escorted out of my corner office with my box of stuff. They felt I wasn't a good fit to move the new company forward. I'll spare you the gory details."

"I'm sorry you were let go. Their loss and my gain."

"It's still a loss to me. Being walked out still hurts."

"If you could go back to work today, would you?"

"I honestly don't know. My pride wants to say, fuck them, but every waking minute, I gave my heart and soul to that place. What do I do with that? Better yet, what do I do without it?"

"Maybe you have to find the next thing to put your heart and soul into? Luckily, you don't have to decide today. I can honestly say that you're the first bigwig CEO I've ever hung out with. No wonder you have diamond member status." She winked at me. "And the girlfriend? What happened there?"

"That same day, I arrived home, obviously unexpected, to find Tiffany and her new love interest packing up a U-Haul. She'd planned to be gone before I got home. She left me a note on the counter explaining all my flaws and why Bridget was a better fit for her."

"Bridget was the server at your favorite restaurant?"

"Yep, that's right. Good memory."

"That had to sting. What could Bridget possibly have that you didn't? You're gorgeous, successful, smart, and I'm sure a bunch of things I don't know yet."

"Right. See, that's why I like you." I drew in a deep breath and let it out slowly. So many snarky responses ran through my mind, but we were having an honest conversation, and as much as I wanted to avoid the truth, I answered honestly. "Love. Like, all in, head over heels, starry-eyed kind of love. Bridget gave her what I couldn't. She told Tiff that she was in love with her."

"Was she simply not the one, or are you a non-believer?"

"Your questions are crushing. Are you forgetting about my great big 'I don't know' tirade followed by the pinecone?"

"Remember, this is a safe zone. I bet you know the answer."

"We were only six months in. It hadn't had time to become love. It was still in the fun, bed warmer stage, and she made stunning arm candy at corporate events."

"Six months…that's the honeymoon period. If you were ever going to be all in, it's within the first six months."

"Have you ever been in love? Like, all in kind of love?"

Leslie stared into the distance with a soft smile in her eyes as if reliving a magical moment. "Once. Her name was Steph. She transferred to my high school in the winter of my senior year. We hit it off, instant friends, then instant everything. She was a free spirit, willing to try most anything. We made plans to hike our first long-distance trail right after graduation."

She picked at a splinter in the table. Sadness washed across her face. "Second day out, she connected with this group of guys and gals and wanted us to join them. Personally, I wanted to hike alone with Steph, ya know, like what Bobber and Cricket have. Anyway, I woke up on the fourth morning to an empty tent. I freaked. I thought something had happened to her, like maybe she'd gotten up in the night and wandered off or lost her way. I called out for her over and over until she finally answered. She'd been in the camp the whole time, sleeping in a different tent with three other naked people."

"Ouch. That had to sting."

"It stung plenty." She continued to pick at the table. "Despite being hurt and angry, I begged her to break away from the group and come with me. She said that I needed to be more open-minded and experience all that life has to offer. I knew myself well enough to know I only wanted experiences with one person, and that was Steph. I packed up my gear and bolted. I never saw her again."

"Anyone besides Steph ever capture your heart? Have you found love again?"

Leslie sighed and stared at her hands. "I'd love to have that, but over the years, I've found that casual works better. I don't think it's in the cards for me."

"Why not?"

"Because I'm not like you. In fact, I'm the exact opposite. I don't have anything to offer, nothing to contribute."

I stood, grabbed my bench cover, and walked around the table. I covered the bench next to her and sat. "What do you mean? You have lots to contribute. You're smart, sexy, dedicated, determined, and you're about to accomplish one hell of a goal. I could go on and on."

"Don't let me stop you." Leslie leaned over and bumped me with her shoulder. "I'm calling Vegas rules."

"What are Vegas rules?" I asked.

"What's said at Low Gap Shelter stays at Low Gap Shelter."

"Sure, I can support Vegas rules. How about our entire conversation falls under that?"

"Yeah, okay." Leslie nodded. "I want to back up a bit. On the plane, you asked me about work and money, and I got pretty upset with you. It was a little intimidating sitting next to you in your first-class world, especially with your comments about assets and financial security and planning for whatever. I don't remember ever feeling more out of place."

"Probably every bit as out of place as I felt when we arrived at the lodge and we were surrounded by your people." I rested my hand on her arm. "We're each experts in our areas. For me, it's the corner office, and you're the expert out here. I mean, you made us a wall."

Leslie rolled her eyes. "Anyone can hang a tarp."

"I'm not sure I would have thought of it or secured it so well. I probably would have pitched my tent way back in the woods and been crushed by a falling limb."

Leslie stared at her coffee spoon. "I didn't know you felt out of place at the lodge."

"We're all good at hiding what we don't want others to see." I'd had a lifetime of practice.

"I suppose so. I'd never guess that you'd need to hide anything."

"Isn't it funny? We look at each other and think, wow, she's got her shit together, when really, we're all treading water in our own way. I've got my stuff just like everyone else. Please, keep talking. I interrupted your thought. We were on the plane and talking about work and money."

"Yeah, I played it off like everything was just like I wanted it, but my life's not as carefree as I made it out to be. I do work during the offseason, but all I qualify for are minimum wage jobs, and they have to be close to wherever I'm living because most of the year, I have no use for a car, so I need to be able to walk or ride a bike. No one wants to pay premium for someone who can only commit to four months or so, and there's no guarantee I'll be in that area the following year. Aside from the offseason jobs, I've been living off the proceeds from the sale of my grandma's house, and I get a monthly distribution check from some settlement fund that was set up for me after my mom's accident. I can cover my expenses, but trust me when I say, I'm not rolling in dough."

"What does any of that have to do with finding love? Love and money are completely different topics."

"Not when you consider the fact that I've pretty much been a hobo for the last twenty years. I don't know where I'm going to end up or what I'll end up doing. That's especially true when I finish this hike. I won't even have another trek to start planning for. No one wants to jump on this train. So, no, no love, no relationships, not since Steph. I've had my fair share of casual fun on the trail, but I haven't let anyone close enough to risk falling in love." Leslie stared at me and started to say something else but shook her head and remained quiet.

"What? What were you going to say?"

She paused long enough that I thought she was going to tell me, but she shook her head again. "Nothing. How about you? Same question. Have you been in love?"

"It was something. Please? I really want to keep talking about this."

"Another time. Your turn." The look on her face told me that she was done talking. It would have to wait for another day.

"I'll answer, but I want to say this one thing first. A friend recently told me, if you don't like your adjectives, change them."

Leslie quirked an eyebrow. "I don't even know what to do with that."

"You call yourself a hobo with nothing to offer. Your words, your adjectives, not at all how I'd describe you. When I look at you, I see someone entirely different. Trust me, I have my own adjective problem. Again, we all have our own stuff."

"What do you mean? What's your adjective problem?"

"When we got to the lodge in Amicalola, I called Sue to let her know I'd arrived safely. The conversation you and I had on the plane really stuck in my craw." I rolled my eyes, damning Sue and her sayings. "Anyway, I asked her if she thought I was judgmental and condescending because I'd certainly made that impression on you during our flight."

"I shouldn't have said—"

"Stop. Apparently, you weren't wrong. Not only did Sue agree with you, she also added to the list. Then, she told me that if I don't like an adjective, I should change it. Wasn't that what my big hike was all about? So I share that bit of wisdom. We have two thousand miles to work on new adjectives."

"I really need to meet your friend."

"I'd like that."

"Okay, I'll work on my adjectives. Now, back to the question. Have you been head over heels in love?"

"I don't normally share like this. Your wish for raw and unedited may have created a monster. Fine. As we've established, I've enjoyed my fair share of bed warmers over the years. I'm not a robot. I can appreciate a beautiful woman. I embrace desire and lust, but I'm not sure I've ever been in love. I'm not opposed to it. I'm just not sure it exists. Then again, it wasn't like I had the best role models. My parents literally describe their relationship as a mutually beneficial arrangement, and both have always had a playmate on the side for as long as I can remember. I also think that my career was so consuming that I didn't have the time or desire to add anything more to my plate, as evident with Tiff saying she felt like an afterthought. So I don't know if I haven't met the right person or if I'm broken and incapable of love."

Leslie swung one leg over and straddled the bench, facing me. She traced her finger over the back of my hand. "Hiking might prove to be a less consuming career, and you should totally erase everything you've ever learned from your parents. Who knows, maybe you'll get your chance to experience that all in kind of love when you find your answers out here. In the meantime, there's always good ol' lust to fall back on."

I gazed into her eyes, consumed with a desire I could no longer resist. I cupped her face and leaned in. She met me halfway with a kiss that warmed me from the inside out. Our lips touched, then parted, and our tongues teased one another in a passionate first dance. She pulled me closer, our kiss deepened, and one or both of us moaned. She was an incredible kisser.

"Hey, everyone, look, we found a shelter," a voice said from somewhere outside.

I broke our magical kiss. No. No, no, no. I wasn't ready to share this evening with anyone except Leslie.

"If we turn the light out, do you think they'll go away?" Leslie whispered in my ear.

"I wish." I leaned forward and nibbled her lower lip. "I was just getting started."

"Don't tease me. If it weren't still pouring outside, I'd suggest we set up a tent."

"Hey, Munch, First Class, are you in there?" I recognized Bobber's voice. "How in the hell do we get inside? Everything's tied off."

"Munch? Seriously? Are you talking about the Munch who's hiked the scenic eleven?" a male voice asked.

Here we go again. It was going to be another evening of Leslie surrounded by her admiring fans. She got up and untied enough to create an opening. "Yep, it's us. Sorry, we were trying to keep the rain out."

"Get decent lovebirds, we're coming in." The ground cloth wall flipped back, and several hikers rolled up onto the platform. So much for our quiet evening alone.

"It feels so good in here." Cricket removed her pack.

Things shifted between us that stormy night. I'd found someone I could be raw and unedited with, and she rewarded me with the same openness. The amazing kiss aside, something developed between us unlike anything else in my life.

CHAPTER TEN

The heavy, relentless rains continued for the next three days. I'd developed a serious love-hate relationship with my rain gear and was becoming immune to the *zzzzt zzzzt* noise that came with every movement. The trail, now beyond saturated, was a path of red-tinted, squishy muck infused with leaves, twigs, and pine needles. Often, my boots became so heavily caked in glop that I'd have to stop and scrape what I could onto a log or a rock. This made for exhausting miles. Mud, it would seem, was every bit as invasive as beach sand kicked up in gale force winds. It got everywhere. *Everywhere.*

Another note on top-end hiking boots, they were only waterproof when not submerged in a deep puddle of soupy red pancake batter. Waterproof leg gaiters and Frogg Togg rain gear were no match for a back-jarring, shin-deep submersion. I didn't want to know what my socks and insoles looked like. What I did know was that it was squishy between my toes with each step from that point on. Yuck. Even the most aggressive laundry soap would have met its match, of this, I had no doubt.

Hiking in the rain and muck wasn't at all what I'd expected when I'd planned for this trek. While I'd purchased rain gear on Kit's strong suggestions, I'd never expected to really need it. I pictured myself a fair-weather trekker, hiking on mild sunny days with a gentle breeze. This was not that. Merely thinking the words, "It wasn't what I thought it would be," conjured up an image of

Leslie tagging me as a *Wild* hiker all over again. Throughout my first week on the trail, I'd never felt more like a *Wild* hiker than I did that day because, as I kept repeating on an internal loop: *This wasn't at all what I'd expected.*

We were on day four of our two-day plan to get to Dicks Creek Gap and running low on provisions. With any luck, we'd make it to US Highway 76 by lunch and could call for a ride into town. I'd never been so excited for a hotel room, a hot shower, and a piping hot feast that required serious molar action. Maybe a scotch on the rocks. Yes, I was definitely ordering at least one of those. *And dessert, oh, maybe chocolate cake.*

Backpacking had turned me into a foodie of sorts. I couldn't recall a time in my life when I've had such vivid food fantasies like I'd developed over the last few days. Insatiable cravings for monstrous chef salads with all the glorious fixings, or steak, oh, and potatoes loaded with butter and sour cream. I'd just finished a nutrition bar and was starving already. If I never saw another nutrition bar in my life, it would be too soon. They left me with a weird aftertaste. *A cheeseburger wouldn't have a weird aftertaste. Oh, with bacon and extra cheese and french fries, no, onion rings.*

A change of topic was needed.

"What do you love most about hiking?" I asked.

"Can anyone answer, or was that a question for Munch?" Cricket asked from behind me.

Bobber and Cricket had woken up when we'd removed the tarp wall at Low Gap Shelter and had hiked the day with us. Given the relentless weather, we'd had to create tarp walls the last couple of nights, thus creating a similar situation each morning. I enjoyed their company, and in the same breath, missed hiking alone with Leslie. That wasn't to say that Bobber and Cricket weren't great people and stellar conversationalists, but Leslie and I hadn't had a moment of alone time since that incredible kiss. Hmm, just thinking about it brought back all of the spine-tingling feels.

"Hello, earth to First Class...you're daydreaming again," Bobber said.

"Sorry, anyone can answer."

Leslie shot me a smirk. Mud was smeared across her cheek, and there was another plop of it on her forehead. She was a soaking wet hot mess and couldn't get any sexier.

"I don't love anything about hiking at the moment," Bobber said.

I held my arm to the sky to emphasize her point and felt seen. "Hallelujah, can I get an amen?" Damnit Sue and her sayings.

"Personally, I started hiking for weight loss and ended up falling in love." Cricket appeared at my side and matched my pace.

"I definitely need to hear more of this story," I said.

"I'd tried everything. Weight Watchers, meal plans, keto, you name it. I'd lose some and regain more. It was a vicious, depressing cycle. I have an office job and sit at my desk all day, only to come home and flop on the couch in the evenings, too tired to think about going to the gym. Then, I won a fitness tracker at our company Christmas party. I started taking short walks on my breaks and longer walks at lunch, trying to get my ten thousand steps every day. One Saturday, walking around the park, I literally bumped into Bobber. She was big into walking. We finished that walk together and met there the next day to walk again and again the following day after work. Soon, I was hooked on both Bobber and walking, and I've never been in better shape."

"You look fantastic. Do you still diet?" I asked.

"No. That's the best part. Now, I eat anything I want to."

Leslie spun in front of us. "Including Bobber," she said with a wink and spun back around.

"You know it, sista," Bobber called from behind us.

"What's your why, Bobber?" Leslie asked.

"Why do I hike, or what do I love about it?"

"I'd like to hear both," I said.

"My parents were big into backpacking when I was a kid, and hikes with them are some of the best memories of my childhood. We'd trek into some remote lake and camp for the weekend. While there, we'd catch fish and cook our food over the campfire. We'd also spend two weeks of summer vacation hiking each year. My favorite was the Bighorn Mountains in Wyoming. Always an adventure somewhere. What do I love about it? I love how bright the stars are at night. It's like I can reach up and pluck one out of the sky, and the conversations around a campfire are the best ever. The pace out here is different, too. Everything happens when it happens, which is typically at two miles per hour. Who's next?"

"Your turn, Munch. Same questions," Cricket said.

"For me, it's all about the freedom to do what I want, when I want. That and trail magic. It's fun to both give and receive. I'd live on the trail year-round if I could carry a sturdier house for the winter."

"What's trail magic?" I'd seen the term online but had never really dug into it.

"Small acts of kindness that have a huge impact for hikers. Bottles of water in a spot where water sources are scarce or a trail angel cooking up a feast at a road crossing for any hikers who happen by. There's nothing like a completely unexpected meal of a couple of hotdogs, a bag of chips, and a soda or a beer to rejuvenate the spirit."

"And people just do this for free?" I asked.

"Yep, out of the kindness of their hearts. Hence, trail angels," Cricket said. "Finish your answer, Munch."

"Every trail I've been on has had touches of trail magic. I think that's what's kept me going all these years. I keep hiking because for me, it's a way of life. I love the ability to sit still and enjoy a beautiful setting instead of having to rush off to work so I can punch a time clock. Each spring for the last twenty years, I've been super excited to get back on the trail and super sad in the fall when my trek is over. I love finding little trail towns. Dots on the map that have decided to embrace a hiker's needs. Even if they don't have what I need, over the years, I've learned to improvise and make do with a few simple items in my pack and have survived just fine. I've snacked on wild berries. I've made soup with early spring fiddleheads, wild onions, and oyster mushrooms. I've watched spectacular sunrises and sunsets, and like Bobber said, stared up at night skies filled with billions of stars. I can't begin to describe all the wildlife I've seen over the years. That said, I've also trudged through some nasty ass weather, and I'm looking forward to a hot shower and an equally hot meal tonight."

"Hear, hear," Bobber hollered out from behind us.

"How about you First Class?" Cricket asked.

"No way. Nothing I say is going to compare with the prose of the three of you, and with a boot full of glop, I'm not loving anything about this trudge at the moment, company excluded."

"Amen, sista," Bobber hollered. "I also have goopy glop sloshing in my shoe."

"Sing it, Dr. Seuss," Cricket said.

We all laughed. Before we knew it, we emerged from the woods, crossed the highway, and stood dripping and giddy in the AT parking lot just outside of Hiawassee, Georgia. We'd hiked seventy miles since the kickoff at Springer Mountain. Before I had a chance to pull my phone out and call for a ride, headlights crested the hill coming from town. The van slowed and pulled into the parking lot. "AT Shuttle Service" was stenciled on the door.

A stocky woman wearing a ball cap rolled down the driver's window. "You gals lookin' for a ride into town?"

"Yes, please." I smiled to fend off the emotion that welled up. She sounded so much like Sue with her thick Georgia accent that I wanted to wrap myself up in her arms and sink into an awesome, Sue-style hug.

"Please tell me there's a couple of hotel rooms left," Bobber said.

"With this weather, the town's definitely chock-full of hikers. I know of a hotel that has a couple of rooms left. It's on the pricey side."

"I don't care what it costs. At this point, I'd pay most anything to get out of the rain and to sleep in a real bed." I meant my statement with every fiber of my being.

"Same," Cricket said.

"Well, climb on in. Don't worry none about the mud. It's been a nasty mess for days. I'll give the van a good scrubbin' when things dry out some."

"Thank you."

We scurried into the open seats. Ten miles up the highway, she pulled into the hotel parking lot and dropped us off at the lobby doors. I tried to tip her, but she refused, saying it was a service provided by the town just for AT hikers. I thanked her again and followed the others onto the pavement. There was no way that I was walking into that lobby with all this mud caked on my boots. I spotted a hose hanging on the side of the building and walked over to spray a layer off before we went inside. Bobber, Cricket, and Leslie joined me. I felt ten pounds lighter by the time we made it up to the check-in counter.

"Do you have a king suite available?" I asked the clerk when it was my turn.

"Actually, yes, it's the last one. Two thirty-five per night," he said.

"I'll take it." I slid my credit card across the counter.

"I want a hot shower, food, and sleep, in that order. What do you gals say about being on our own tonight? We can connect tomorrow at breakfast and decide which shelter to meet at next?" Bobber asked with her room key card in hand.

"I was going to suggest the same thing," Leslie said and tapped me on the shoulder. "Hey, it'd be less expensive if we split a room. What do you say?"

The chill I'd been fighting off all day dissipated in an instant. Warmth emanated throughout my body. I was just about to suggest the same thing. I didn't care if she was trying to conserve money, I was all in on sharing some one-on-one time. "Okay, sounds good." I tried for nonchalant, but based on the smirk on her face, I failed to pull it off...miserably.

"Do you still want the suite? I'm out of rooms with two queens. I can get a rollaway bed." he asked.

I turned to the clerk. "Let's keep the suite, and a rollaway bed won't be needed."

When vacationing, getting settled in the hotel had always meant the beginning of calm and relaxation. When hiking, getting settled meant the beginning of a lot of work. I had no idea how much trouble the rain would cause. Most everything in our packs was damp or outright wet. We draped our tents over the couch, strung our damp ground cloths and rope over the curtain rod, and spread our sleeping pad and bags on the floor. Our rain gear, packs, and covers—all now rinsed off—hung on hangers in the closet. That left the bed and a small table available to use. Still chilled, we kicked the heater in the room up to seventy-five, which not only warmed us but took some of the humidity out of the air.

"Would you like to shower first, or should I?" Leslie asked. "Or, we could—" She wiggled her eyebrows. The mud chunk on her forehead broke free and fell to the floor. "I'm so sick of mud." She bent and picked up the mess.

Did I have the strength and energy for shower sex? It was a question I'd never thought I'd ask myself. Pre-AT, I'd always had the energy for shower sex, but I wanted to savor her with every cell in my being. Hiking for four days in the muck had me standing on exhausted, trembling legs. Better question, when was the last time I'd brushed my teeth? I ran my tongue over my front teeth, and they felt furry. Mornings became less routine when trying to clean up in the wind and rain.

"You shower first. I haven't brushed my teeth in days. I'm too gross to feel sexy."

"Now that you say that, I'm not sure when I last brushed my teeth either. Rain check?" She winked.

"Rain check." I nodded. "Do you have anything clean and dry to put on after your shower?" I asked Leslie.

"No. Everything is filthy, but I can wear my rain gear to do laundry. It won't be the first or last time."

"But your rain gear is dripping wet inside and out now that we've cleaned the mud off. You'll be chilled all over again. Go get in the shower. I'm going to walk up to the post office and get my box from Sue before they're tempted to send it back. There's an outfitter just up the block that'll have something for you. I'll be right back."

"You'd do that for me?" She looked surprised. "There's some cash in my jacket."

"Yeah, okay, but let's go with trail magic." I had no intention of taking her money.

She walked into the bathroom. "That's not how trail magic works."

"Oh, but that's how it's going to work today."

"Clearance rack works, it's where I shop," she said from behind the door.

Anyone else in my life would accept money or gifts without a second thought. Then again, Leslie wasn't like anyone else. She'd proved that over and over again. I put my rain gear back on, grabbed my wallet and phone, and made my way back to the lobby. At least there was decent phone reception in town. I tucked one of my Bluetooth earbuds in and dialed Sue's number before tucking my phone inside my raincoat.

"Well, hello," she answered on the second ring. "How's my favorite hiker?"

I stepped out the lobby doors into the rain. "Wow, it's great to hear your voice. I'm doing pretty good, all things considered. It's been raining for the last four days, which has been less than pleasant, but we just got into town and checked into a hotel for the night, so it's not all bad. I wanted to call you and let you know I made it to the first box stop. Seventy-eight total miles under my belt."

"Look at you, crushing it. You sound good. Did you get your box?"

"I'm headed there after I finish up at the store. How are you doing? How are things in Hartford?"

"Everything's fine. I have to tell ya, I've heard from a few gals from the office, and it's a good thing that we're no longer there. The new management's a clusterfuck, and there's talk of an exodus."

"If we were still there, there wouldn't be a managerial clusterfuck. We had a great team."

"You had an epic team. Douchebag Turner is fighting off a mutiny."

As petty as it might have been, hearing that made me smile. I might not have been what the board wanted, but the retention rate under my tenure was stellar. "That's too bad. I bet the veins are popping out on Grayson's forehead."

"Girl, you know it." Sue laughed.

Talking about the office felt weird. I kind of missed it, but at the same time, I didn't, and I felt the loss less and less each day. Did that mean I needed to consider a new career or just a new company?

"Say, who was the cutie in the photo you texted me?" Sue asked.

"Her name is Leslie. She's one of three I've been hiking with this week." I loved that Sue called her a cutie. She'd never said anything like that about Tiffany.

"I'm glad you found some friends. From the look on your face, she's someone special."

"She's one of a kind." One of a kind who was waiting for some clean clothes. I stood in front of the outfitters. "Listen, I've made it to the store, and I want to get out of the rain. I'll call again in a few days, okay? It was great to hear your voice."

"It was good to hear yours, too. Take care of yourself and let me know if you need anything."

"I will. Thank you for sending the box. I'll call again soon. Bye."

"Bye now."

Shopping for Leslie was both fun and easy. A far cry from past experiences shopping for say, Tiffany. I found everything I'd hoped to, paid for my purchases, and made my way up the block to the post office. Thankfully, they still had my box. Now, we'd both have something not covered in red mud to wear tonight. I all but skipped back to the hotel.

I expected Leslie to be sitting there, waiting impatiently, but when I keyed back into the room, she was curled up beneath the covers, sound asleep. I left the bag of treasures on the floor next to the nightstand, pulled my clothes out of the box, and headed into the bathroom to scrub the last four days off my body. I brushed my teeth twice and flossed before stepping into the shower. The hot water felt amazing. If there'd been a tub, I would have filled it to the brim and soaked until it started to cool.

I emerged a new woman. My boots were disgusting, so I shoved my sock clad feet into my Keen sandals. *Lord help me.*

Someone needs to call the fashion police, stat. I looked ridiculous, but it would work for now.

Somehow, Leslie's boots felt dry inside. She had a mound of dirty clothes next to them on the floor. I stuffed all of our laundry, including my boots, into a plastic bag from the closet and set off in search of a commercial washing machine and extra-strength soap.

There was a restaurant in the hotel, kitty-corner from the laundry room. It was just one in the afternoon, and we hadn't eaten lunch yet. I was starving, like "I could eat at least one of everything on the menu" kind of starving. When the laundry was almost dry, I ordered two bacon cheeseburgers with all the fixings, side salads, fries, onion rings, jalapeño poppers, and two tall bourbon and Cokes, light on the Coke. I matched the bartender's tip to the bourbon pour; both were excellent.

I procured two clean laundry bags from the sweet guy at the front desk and returned to our room with my haul on a luggage trolley. Leslie was still sleeping when I entered. I set the two bags of clean clothes on the foot of the bed, propped my clean boots upside down on the heater, and finally opened the food containers one by one. I smiled when I heard Leslie inhale deeply.

"Oh my God, what smells so good?" She rolled over and faced me.

"Sure, I climb out of the shower smelling like a rose and you sleep right through it, but bring a deep-fried potato into the room and you're salivating like Pavlov's dog." I smiled over the top of my Beam and Coke.

She lifted her head off the pillow. "Do I have clothes?"

"On the floor next to you." I was eager to see if she liked what I'd picked out for her.

Like a bashful kid at a slumber party, she grabbed the bag and pulled it under the covers. Plastic rustled, and the covers flipped around from her feet up to the pillows. All of a sudden, the covers flipped back. She'd chosen the long-sleeve, tie-dye shirt that matched her bandana and the purple underwear. The new hiking pants were in her hand.

"Do you like it?" I held out a jalapeño popper for her. She stuffed it in her mouth, chomped twice, and swallowed.

"Yum. That was so good. Thanks for taking care of everything. I crashed." She stuffed her legs into the dark gray pants. "Hey, these are great. Thank you. No one's ever picked out clothes for me before. I love these." She stood and pulled the pants the rest of the way up.

"They fit you perfectly. I found socks to match your shirt."

She dug through the bag and pulled out the thick wool socks. She put them on. "Ah, happy feet. Oh, and you got cheeseburgers. If I'm dreaming, don't wake me up."

She pulled the covers back up and propped up pillows. We sat next to each other on the bed with the myriad food containers spread out between us. I told her about my adventures around town and my call with Sue while we stuffed ourselves with gloriously greasy food. It was perfect. Spending time with Leslie was easy, no matter what we did.

CHAPTER ELEVEN

Thoroughly stuffed, I leaned back against the headboard and extended my legs. Being inside, like, really inside, with four walls, a locking door, and a bed, was such a luxurious treat. Rain continued to pelt the large window in our room, making me even more grateful for our current surroundings.

"Since you cooked such a gourmet meal, I'll do the dishes." Leslie folded the last onion ring into her mouth and carried the empty containers to the trash next to the microwave.

"How many non-hiking days do you plan for on a long trip like this?"

"Well, not many. It took us four days to get here, so we've already used up two, and we're not even a hundred miles in. Why?"

"That's a non-answer, and the two extra days here don't count because they weren't non-hiking days. We hiked, and it sucked big time. We should get bonus days for hiking in shitty weather. I ask because I vote that we stay here until it stops raining and the trail dries up some."

Leslie flopped onto the bed next to me, her head on the pillow as if she was calling it a night. "Whatever would we do with all that free time?" She reached up and tugged on the shoulder of my shirt.

"Oh, I'm sure we could think of something." I slid down and snuggled next to her, propped up on my elbow.

There'd be no rain-soaked hikers interrupting us tonight. No discussions about the scenic eleven. I'd been daydreaming about this for the last three days, ever since that epic kiss. Oh, that kiss. I stared at her lips, still wet from the last sip of her drink. She ran her tongue along the bottom edge of her front teeth, and I shivered in anticipation. She was simply irresistible.

I bent and grazed her lips with mine. She lifted her head slightly and closed the gap. Any inhibitions I might have had dissolved when her lips parted, and our kiss deepened. She was unlike anyone I'd ever been with. She cupped the back of my head, wrapped her other arm around my waist, and pulled me half on top of her.

I didn't need to be asked twice. Without breaking our magical kiss, I swung my leg over her hips and tucked my other knee up so I could straddle her. I liked being on top, a position of control, and she felt oh-so good pinned between my legs. Her hand moved from my waist, down to my hips, and cupped my ass. She lifted her hips into me and applied pressure in just the right spot. I gasped and circled my hips counter to hers. She pushed harder. I shuddered. Her moves were blissfully effective, and in that instant, I understood that I'd have no control when it came to her.

Leslie slowly moved her hands back to my hips, then slid them beneath my shirt and teased the skin of my lower back. Her hands were strong and commanding, yet tender and delicate. I wanted to feel her touch me everywhere, all at once. My body trembled with excitement. Finally, I had an excuse to bury my fingers in her thick mane of hair. Her breath caught, and our kiss intensified, if that was even possible. She ran her hands along my ribs and teased the sides of my breasts with her thumbs, then her touch was gone. The clasp of my bra released beneath her expert fingers, and my breath caught when her hands fully cupped my bare breasts. My skin tingled everywhere she touched.

With my previous partners, I was typically in the driver's seat, exploring my lover's body without competition for control. Being with Leslie had me in the opposite position. She was doing all the exploring. This was new territory for me. An entirely new experience. Having an assertive lover was an erotic affair. I immersed myself in the moment. She lifted my shirt, and I broke our kiss long enough for her to tug it over my head. She guided my bra straps down my arms and tossed it off to the side. I was so taken with her, my desire was so great, that I'd have done anything she asked of me.

"You're beautiful," she whispered.

The way she looked at me made me feel beautiful. She brushed my forehead with her fingertips, caressed my cheeks, and tickled the sides of my neck. Then, I felt the heat of her hands cover each breast again. My eyes closed, and I drew in a quick breath. I arched my back and pressed into her touch. She sat up, wrapped an arm around my waist and took one of my nipples into her mouth, flicking the tip with her tongue. I captured her head in my hands and savored being the focus of her attention. When she switched from one nipple to the other, I tugged on her shirt, but my efforts were blocked. She kept her arms wrapped around me and her attention on my breasts.

All of a sudden, she shifted and rolled me onto my back. Her eyes were dark with desire that made her even sexier. She rose to her knees, positioned between my legs, and reached to the waist of my pants. I was all in for the removal of another barrier between our bodies. She freed the button and lowered the zipper.

Storm-darkened daylight filtered into the room from above the blackout curtains while the lamp cast the room in the golden glow of an incandescent bulb. I was grateful for the bit of light because it was erotic to watch her drink up my body with her eyes. I lifted my hips for her, and she worked my pants and underwear down my ass. My legs trembled uncontrollably. She guided my pants off each leg and removed my socks. Completely naked, I quivered beneath her gaze.

"Are you cold?" She traced her fingertips along the inside of my leg. Goose bumps erupted everywhere.

I shook my head. "No, but you have way too many clothes on. I need to feel you, too." I pinched the hem of her shirt with my toes and tugged on it. "I'm not accustomed to being naked first."

"See, I'm already different than anyone else you've been with." She lifted my leg and kissed my ankle.

"What you are is too far away." I wrapped my legs around her and pulled her to me.

She caught herself in a push-up position and had a confident glint in her eyes. Her arrogant cockiness was such a turn-on. I tucked my hands beneath her shirt and raked my nails across her bare back teasingly. She squeezed her eyes closed and licked her lips. I teased the sides of her breasts and smiled when she inhaled a quick breath. She was so expressive, it was such a treat to watch her respond to my touch. She held herself up, probably expecting me to take her breasts in hand, but instead, I slid my hand into the waistband of her pants and beneath her underwear. Her eyes opened. She stared at me with a smoldering expression and pushed herself into my hand. She was so wet. She bit her lip and spread her legs apart slightly.

I shimmied beneath her for better access and smiled when she circled herself over the heel of my hand. "That's it, I want to make you feel so good."

"Believe me, you do." She pushed into me again, and my fingers slid inside her. She tightened, then quickly pulled away until my hand slid out of her pants.

I resisted the urge to be insistent. Her strong arms shook as she lowered herself on top of me. She kissed me with such passion that my toes curled. Her hand that wasn't supporting her weight explored every inch of exposed skin within her reach. She broke the kiss and worked her way down my neck.

I'd never been with anyone who'd made me feel so thoroughly savored, cherished, and adored. I guess that was what I'd missed all those years by not giving up control. I closed my eyes and embraced the experience. Leslie brought out a desire in me that I didn't know existed. I dug my fingers into her hair and gave in to her completely.

My breasts were lavished with delicate nibbles, attentive caresses, and firm flicks for so long that I squirmed beneath her with an unrelenting desire to be wholly satisfied. Even the word desire seemed so understated because in that moment, I was utterly consumed with cravings, with needs, with a thirst that, at that moment, didn't seem like it could ever be quenched.

She pulled away and worked her way down my body. Her lips teased one hip, then the other. She shifted lower on the bed and tickled the inside of my thighs with her fingertips. Silently, I begged for her touch by bending my knees and opening myself to her. She granted my request by kissing up my inner thigh and exploring between my legs with her talented tongue. It took all the control I had not to wrap my legs around her head and hold her against me while I rocked myself into oblivion.

She slid a finger inside me and asked if I wanted more. I did, definitely more. I nodded breathlessly and lifted into her. I'd never begged for anyone or anything in my life, and yet, I found myself begging for everything she suggested. I begged her to go deeper. I begged her to not stop whatever she was doing that made me feel *so very good*. "Oh, oh yeah."

I begged her to keep doing that thing with her tongue that made my head spin. She brought me right to the edge—"Oh holy fuck"— and then slowed and found an entirely new way to make me squirm beneath her touch. I was hers for the taking because everything she did to me felt so incredibly amazing.

She thrust her fingers inside and sucked me into her mouth, then there was more pressure...deep pressure, from everywhere. "Oh my God." It wasn't enough, and it was too much all at once. I wanted more. I begged for more. I wanted the feeling to last all night long but craved the blinding, pulsating relief that would cause it to stop.

She granted me everything I asked for and so much more.

Climax hit me like a tidal wave, such a rush that I knew I'd soaked the bed. Another first. The initial power of it swept me out to sea in an out of body experience. I'd never been a vocal lover, yet there I was crying out, moaning, and begging for her not to stop. She didn't stop, either. It was the longest, most intense orgasm I'd ever had.

The aftershocks were fierce electrical waves that pulsed throughout my body. Leslie kept the pressure right where I needed it. She remained inside me, wiggling her fingers just so, while I convulsed and quivered and rocked beneath her touch.

She stayed with me until the pulsing subsided. I desperately missed her when she withdrew. She lifted her head and looked at me from between my legs. Her cocky expression was now outright swagger, which made her even sexier. She worked her way up my body, teasing my skin with sweet trailing kisses. When she kissed my lips, I could taste myself on her. It was a turn-on greater than any aphrodisiac. I tugged on her shirt, and she finally let me lift it over her head. I hooked my leg behind her thigh and rolled her onto her back. I hoped I could make her feel even half as good as she'd done for me.

I captured her wrists in my hands and guided her arms up to the headboard. "Hold on and don't let go." I barely recognized my own voice.

She smiled and curled her fingers around the posts. "I can't promise anything, but I'll do my best."

No wonder she could suspend her pack directly out from her body. She was ripped. Her arms and shoulders were lean and muscular. She pulled on the bedposts to adjust and revealed an entire upper body every bit as defined as her sculpted arms. Without a doubt, I had a new type and a need to see all of her. I maneuvered down the bed and released the button and zipper on her pants. She lifted her hips for me, and I caught a glimpse of a six-pack on her belly. It would seem that hiking for twenty years was stellar for the physique.

I slid her pants and underwear down and removed her socks. Positioning myself as she had, up on my knees between her legs, I admired the totality of her sexiness. "Stunning." It was the only word my brain could come up with.

Her face flushed, and she smiled almost bashfully up at me. "The view from here is equally amazing."

I lay my naked body on top of hers. I felt her arms move toward me and then return to their spot on the posts. I smiled and kissed her passionately. My body responded immediately to the talent of her tongue. I ignored my already urgent needs and focused on fulfilling hers. Her back arched, pressing her breasts against mine, and her hips undulated beneath me. She was so wet earlier that I wondered what she felt like now. I resisted the urge to find out and decided to tease her instead.

Nibbling on her earlobes and kissing down along the sides of her neck, I worked my way to her breasts. I listened for a response to tickling her skin with my unrestrained hair. I swayed, allowing it to caress her as light as a feather. She inhaled a sharp breath and held it when I repeated the tease. Before she could let the breath fully escape, I bent and captured her nipple in my mouth. It was already so firm and erect that I couldn't resist flicking it with the tip of my tongue. I felt her hand capture the back of my head firmly and instantly disappear. Her breath came into her lungs just as quickly.

Oh, this was going to be fun. I savored and teased until I felt her restlessness grow. She lifted her hips in a request for attention. I couldn't deny her if I wanted to, and I didn't want to deny her anything. I worked my way down her sculpted body and teased each hip as she'd done to me.

"Oh yeah." Her moan was a wonderful reward. "Just like that."

She spread her legs and opened herself up to me as I had done for her. I kissed her inner thigh on one side and the other, then wrapped my arms around her legs, resting my hands on her hips. At first, I teased her with just the tip of my tongue. Her scent was addictive…a total turn-on, and made it difficult for me to take my time. She lifted into me, and I could no longer resist. I stole one hand from her hip and slid three fingers inside her while circling her clit with the tip of my tongue. She bucked her hips into me and moaned loudly. I matched my rhythm to her pace.

There wasn't time for any more teasing, and I'd lost the moment for seductive questions like she'd asked me. She tightened inside, and I felt her legs start to shake. She was on the edge and begged me not to stop. I had no intentions of torturing her. I covered her with my mouth, continuing to encourage her with my tongue, and pushed into her like she'd done for me. She called out my name, adding to the excitement that already had me on the edge, and wrapped her legs around my upper body, holding me against her. I felt every shudder and pulse. Her response had me right there with her all over again. I matched her movements until she relaxed her legs and asked for a kiss.

Leslie wrapped me up in her limbs the moment our lips met. Our next climax was together, each of us on our knees, facing one other, slightly offset. We rode each other's hands into a gloriously vocal explosion, then collapsed into a tangle of arms and legs, absolutely breathless and our hearts pounding wildly. Most of the bedding was on the floor. I couldn't get enough of her. I couldn't get enough of how she made me feel. I hoped I made her feel just as good. Once we'd recovered, she put me on my hands and knees and pleased me from behind. Another first for me. Just before I came, I rose to my knees and leaned back into her, screaming out her praises. She came with me, all the more erotic. I wasn't sure I ever wanted sole control in the bedroom again, at least never with Leslie. We'd connected in a way I'd never connected with anyone before.

Exhausted and sated, we snuggled beneath the retrieved covers. I laid my head on her chest and listened to the beat of her heart. My eyes grew heavy, and one blink was a little too long. I drifted off to sleep.

I woke groggy, as if I'd slept way too long. There was still a touch of daylight above the curtain in the room, and I wasn't sure if it was still the same day or if it was the next morning. Leslie sat next to me, fully dressed, leaning up against the headboard with a mountain of pillows behind her back and her smartphone in her hand.

"Did you have a good snooze?" she asked and pushed the hair out of my eyes.

"How long was I asleep?"

"A couple of hours or so."

"That's all? It feels like I slept for days. What time is it?" I asked.

"Just after seven in the evening. You woke up just in time for dinner, and guess what, it's finally stopped raining."

No rain meant more hiking. I glanced at her phone. It was a map. "Are you already planning tomorrow's trek?" I dreaded to hear her answer. I really wanted another day with her all to myself behind a locked door.

"Wasn't planning on hiking at all tomorrow. The trails could use a day or so to dry out, or at least, that's what I heard." She smiled down. "This…" She held up her phone. "Is a ridiculous, unrealistic, pipe dream. While I waited for you to wake up, I did a search for hostels for sale, and one just listed in Pennsylvania. It's a great setup."

"Yeah? Let's see what ya got there."

Leslie tapped on the green diamond in the center of the map on her screen. The listing popped up to the right. She tapped on it, and the small screen of her phone filled with the property's details. The AT passed through town less than two blocks away, at the edge of the woods. The complex sat on five acres, close to the halfway point on the trail. It included the main lodge, which was both an outfitter and a resupply post. Also on the property was a large bunk house with two bathrooms, as well as four small cabins, each including a kitchenette, bed, bathroom, seating area and a small porch. Similarly sized to the private cabins sat a building with several coin-operated washers and dryers. All of which surrounded a pavilion and firepit area. The main residence sat off in the distance, back behind the lodge.

The listing description went on about how the tiny town had reinvented itself to cater to hikers after the steel mill in a neighboring town had closed down. There was even a diner next door that offered oversized platters just for the hungry hiker. In fact, it was called the Hungry Hiker.

"Leslie, this is incredible." I sat up, wrapped the covers around me, and flipped through the pictures on her phone a second time.

"Isn't it?" Her smile beamed.

"What is it about running a hostel that calls to you?" I asked.

She sighed heavily and flipped through the pictures again. "I keep thinking about Mountain Crossings, about how Steve and his wife bought that place and have never been happier. I also wonder what I should do when I've finished the scenic eleven. Living on the trail, running an outpost, is the one thing I keep coming back to. Something about it feels so right."

She turned and looked at me. "What Bobber said about how every day could be a day on vacation? I want that. I want to do something that isn't work, not because it's easy, but because I love it so much." She held the phone up. There was a drone shot showing the five acres from above, with the buildings and a dotted red line depicting the Appalachian Trail at the town's edge. "Does your career make you feel like that? Work that isn't work because you love it so much? Do you love what you do?"

The words "I don't know" popped into my head, and I almost started laughing. The tantrum I'd had in the storm replayed in my mind. It seemed the more time I spent with Leslie, the less certain I felt about anything from my Hartford life. "I think I was good at it. I thought I loved it, but anymore, I really don't know. That's why I'm out here, trying to figure it all out. Let me ask you this, if the hostel is something you keep thinking about, why do you call it a ridiculous, unrealistic pipe dream?" I took her phone and set it beside me on the bed. I wanted to see her eyes when she answered the question.

With hands no longer distracted by her phone, Leslie picked at the hem on the sheets, but before she answered, she gifted me with that transparent window into her soul through her emotional, sky-blue eyes. "Because even if I cashed out the settlement fund from my mom's accident, I'm not sure there's enough to pay for something like that and get started. Besides, hiking's what I know. I wouldn't have the first clue about running the business side. That's not to say I couldn't learn, but I wouldn't even know where to start."

I reached for her hand. "You could always work at one and learn the ropes from the owners. Doing something like that keeps your options open, too, in case it isn't what you expected."

"Here I was hoping that you'd volunteer to teach me or better yet, take on that side of the business for me." She winked and smiled.

I didn't have a clue as to how to respond. Was she asking me to go into business with her? We didn't know each other well enough to consider anything like that. That was a commitment even more binding than marriage. While we'd enjoyed incredible conversations and equally amazing sex, we were barely getting to know each other.

My reaction on the outside must have matched the shock I felt on the inside.

"Relax, it was a joke." She leaned over and shoulder bumped me. "I'm sure that someone like you wouldn't be the least bit interested in running a hostel with someone like me." Her face didn't make it seem like it was a joke. Disappointment, hurt, sadness, so many emotions were revealed with a forced smile and a stolen glance.

I cupped her chin. "Hey, both of us have more questions than answers right now. We've got two thousand miles and six months to figure out what to do after the trek, right? Anything's possible."

"Anything's possible," she said quietly and nodded.

She wrapped her arms around me and kissed me. I ordered room service, and we made love again before curling up in each other's arms and giving into the exhaustion of the past few days. The rain had finally stopped, and we had a bit of time to let the winds take the moisture away from the trail. I'd take all of the time with Leslie that nature would gift me.

CHAPTER TWELVE

We woke up the following morning and enjoyed pleasing each other before and after room service delivered breakfast. Each time she tipped me over the edge was more powerful than the last. I'd always enjoyed my ability to thoroughly satisfy my sexual partners, but never before had I been pleased like Leslie was able to please me. I'd also never been so insatiable. We'd shared so many orgasms that I was starting to get a little sore from my unrelenting need to feel her inside me, and yet, I wasn't ready to get dressed and share her with the world. Not yet. I wanted more time. Hell, I needed more time. I wasn't sure what was coming over me, but everything about being with Leslie, from our conversations to our time in bed, felt so unbelievably wonderful.

"Wait, pose just like that. I want a picture of you inside the tent, naked, with that look that you only give me," Leslie said and snapped the photo.

"That's for your eyes only." I collapsed on top of her. "I think we're going to need a larger sleeping pad," I said while trying to catch my breath for the third…or was it the fourth time that morning? I'd lost count. My body was splayed on top of hers. "And a larger sleeping bag to go with it."

We'd rearranged furniture and set up my tent inside the room to see how it would fit the two of us and our gear. The tent was fine. I'd always loved space and had started out with a nice, two-person tent. The one-person sleeping pad, however, not so much. If I straddled her, my knees scraped the nylon floor of the tent. If we tried to snuggle, side by side, half my body was on the floor. I was sure half of hers was hanging off the other side of the pad, too. If we turned the pad sideways, it was too long for the tent width and wasn't wide enough to support us from the hips up. That and her foam pad was so much thinner that the transition, that hit just below our ribs, was extremely uncomfortable. It simply wasn't going to work. We needed two-person gear that could hold both of us and allow for some play room.

"Oh, I don't know. This position's pretty comfortable. You'll just have to sleep on top of me every night. Where there's a will, there'll be never ending orgasms. We'll make it work." Leslie ran her fingers through my hair. Her heart was still beating wildly in her chest.

"I'll never sleep if your naked body is between my legs all night long." I rolled over and lay on top of her, facing up. My head was next to hers, hanging down off her shoulder. I purposefully bent my knees and splayed them apart. She quickly wrapped her arms around my body, and one of her hands explored between my legs. "See what I mean? The distraction is real."

"No doubt," she whispered. "A certain, extremely sexy, naked distraction." She teased my skin everywhere she touched.

"Hmm, you make me feel so good. This position, however, isn't at all comfortable. It's quite literally, a pain in my neck."

I flipped back over and kissed my way down her body. I tried to slide down between her legs and ran out of space. The tent was too short to enjoy her in that way without some serious contortion. "How heavy would a tent be that allowed us to do this without having to be twisted up like a pretzel?" I maneuvered myself between her legs, tucking my knees beneath me, and still had a difficult time kissing her inner thigh.

"Let's save that for the nights we get hotel rooms. That way, we'll always have something to look forward to." She reached for my arms and pulled me back up on top of her. "Seriously, we don't need to buy new gear. I can put my pad next to yours. It'll be fine."

"It won't be fine because you'll be too far away, especially if we're in separate sleeping bags. If we're sharing a tent, I want to be in your arms and feel your body right next to mine. Besides, the two pads will separate, and we'll end up on the floor in the crack. At the very least, let's pick up a new pad and bag."

"I think the tent test is over." Leslie sat up and unzipped the tent. Her stomach growled loudly.

"Sounds like someone needs food." I wrapped my arms around her and kissed her lower back. "How about we order room service, and I'll do my best to distract you from starvation until the food arrives. Then, maybe a shower and a trip to the outfitters."

Leslie stiffened in my arms. She twisted out of my embrace and exited the tent.

"What's wrong? Was I not supposed to notice your growling stomach?" I scurried out behind her and tugged on her arm. "Leslie, hey, what's going on?"

"Don't worry about it." She started to put clothes on. "Do whatever you want. It's not like what I say makes any difference."

I stood there completely baffled. If it was anyone else acting that flippant and snarky after such a lovely morning, I'd have shown her the door and done exactly what I wanted, but it wasn't anyone else, it was Leslie, and she was different. I actually cared about how she felt.

"Don't worry about what? I don't know what just happened. Talk to me." Begging her to open up to me while standing there completely naked felt weird. I quickly put on my shirt and hiking pants, not bothering with anything else at the moment. "Hey, come on, what's going on?"

"Forget it, you won't understand." Fully clothed, she bent and started pulling everything out of the tent.

"You're not giving me the chance to understand."

"It's this." She stood up, held her arms out, and spun around in a circle. "And this." She lifted the hem of her tie-dye shirt and pulled on the waistband of her pants. "And now it's talk about a brand-new tent and sleeping pad and a bigger sleeping bag."

"Forgive me, but I don't know what you're trying to say. I thought you liked the clothes, and if we're moving too fast and you don't want to share a tent with me, just say so. Trying it out was your suggestion." Me, moving too fast? What the hell? I'd never been the hare in that race, choosing instead to be the tortoise when it came to the pace of a relationship. What was happening to me?

"I know it was. That's not what I'm trying to say." She pulled the last few items out of the tent and started breaking it down. "I didn't think…look, I can't keep up with you."

"I don't understand. Keep up with what? Sex? You're doing a fine job, believe me. Being with you is—"

"It's not the sex. The sex is incredible. Being with you is incredible." She released the air in the sleeping pad and started rolling it up.

"Then what is it? I don't understand." I kept busy by shoving the sleeping bag into the stuff sack.

"How could you? There's no way you can relate. I must have been kidding myself to think it wouldn't matter, and we could actually work."

I stood there motionless with the stuff sack in my arms and stared at her. Still not entirely sure what she was getting at. "Try me." I finally managed to find words. "At least give me a chance."

"Do you realize that I can eat for an entire month on what it cost to stay in this room for two nights? And that's just my half. Then, there's all that food we ordered for dinner last night. It was a second feast from the restaurant downstairs, and both times, you accepted twenty dollars from me as if I'd covered half. I didn't think anything about it until I saw the slip from breakfast this morning. I barely covered the tip. I don't even want to know what you really spent yesterday if breakfast was thirty dollars per plate. Thirty dollars for a tiny piece of toast, two eggs, and two paper-thin slices of bacon. Coffee and juice were extra, the small plate of hashbrowns was extra, not to mention the tip you gave the guy that delivered it, but I decided not to worry about it because we were having such a great morning. I mean, splurging on this room and all the food will make things a little tight for the month, but I'll figure it out. Except, now you also want to order in lunch because, hey, what's another hundred?"

She dropped whatever she was holding, threw her arms in the air, and stepped closer to me. "Oh, and after lunch, let's go and buy a thousand dollars' worth of new backpacking gear. Well, I can't do that, Amber. I can't because unlike you, I don't have an endless supply of money. I can't keep up with you. Remember, I'm the one with nothing to contribute. Like it or not, we're too different for this to work. I'll always sit in the economy seat on the Greyhound bus, and you'll always fly first-class."

I stood there dumbfounded. *Too different for this to work.* Her words sunk in, and my heart tightened in my chest. We hadn't even had a chance to see what this could become. Tears welled in my eyes. Okay, when did I lose my edge and become a crier? I needed to get a grip on all of these emotions. Never before had money been an issue with anyone I'd been interested in. Any woman prior to Leslie was all too happy to see me pull out my credit cards. Why was it that the one woman I'd actually been daydreaming about, the one woman I would have loved to buy the stars and moon for, was the one who had a hang-up about money?

"The clothes that you picked up for me are a perfect example. I know these brands, top-of-the-line. I don't have anything with these labels because they're never on the clearance rack, which is where I asked you to shop from."

In all of our talks, I'd never seen her upset like this, and now that I had, I didn't like how it made me feel. Hurting her was like stabbing myself in the heart. It was a pain unlike anything I'd ever experienced. "The clothes were a gift. I said as much before I left." I felt like a rug was being pulled out from under me all over again.

"The brands I wear are just fine."

"I never said—"

"I didn't ask to be your charity case."

In an instant, I'd had all I was going to take of being yelled at. "You need to hold on a minute. Who says I see you as a charity case? Just so we're clear, I didn't buy the clothes because of any goddamned label. I picked out that shirt because it reminded me of a much-loved bandana, and quite honestly, that's what caught my attention, not who made it. All I could think about was whether or not your face would light up when you noticed how well the colors and pattern matched. Same thing when I saw the socks. And as far as the pants go, I asked the salesperson for help because the amazing woman that I was shopping for has these monster strong hiking legs. She suggested that pair of pants because, and I quote: 'Nothing sucks more than pants that are too binding when you're trekking.' Look, if you hate the clothes because of the labels, then throw them in the goddamned donation box. You want to know the sad part about all this? I actually had fun shopping for you. I guess that's what happens when you really care about the person you're shopping for. I apologize if my splurge insulted you because I really wanted it to show you how special you are to me."

Leslie's squared-off shoulders deflated. The tension in her jaw released. "You picked out these clothes to show me I'm special to you?" She sat on the end of the bed and stared at the floor. "I don't hate them. Actually, it's the opposite. The pants are the most comfortable I've ever had, and the shirt is super cool. Amber, you're special to me, too. That's what makes this so hard."

"Makes what so hard? Are you saying we won't work because I have money? Or are you saying we won't work because you think you don't have enough?"

"I don't know."

I knelt in front of her and took her hands. "I'd pick on you and tell you that I've already used that argument, but I'm thinking now's not the time."

Good, a hint of a smile. We were getting somewhere. If there was ever a time for me to choose honest and well-thought-out words, this was that time. I wanted to explain how I felt without insulting her pride or having her think I was trying to buy her affection because nothing was further from the truth. Not with Leslie. I really didn't want to screw this up. Whatever this was, whatever it could become, I didn't want to blow it over money.

"When we got to the hotel yesterday, I wanted out of the rain so badly that I couldn't have cared less what a room cost. I also wanted a do-over on that amazing kiss. In fact, I was trying to figure out how to ask if you'd stay with me when you suggested we split the room.

Leslie, I wanted you to stay with me because I wanted to spend time with you. It had nothing to do with half the hotel bill. I planned to pay for a room regardless. As far as breakfast is concerned, yes, it was overpriced, and yes, the portions were ridiculously small, and neither of those things has anything to do with why I'd do it all over again given the chance, and why I now want to order in lunch."

I bent until I was able to look her in the eye. "Raw and unedited, I ordered room service because I wasn't ready to share you with the world. I wanted to savor our time alone in this room for as long as we had it." I touched my forehead to hers. "I'm not asking you to go halves with me on everything. I admire the fact that you've budgeted your trip, and you know when and how you want to splurge. What I am asking is that you not fault me when it comes to the same thing. If I want to splurge so we can have this time together, and it's within my budget, then, please, don't begrudge me for doing so. Money shouldn't have anything to do with whether or not we work."

I hoped my words got through to her. It was difficult to know. Our foreheads were still touching, and I couldn't see her eyes.

"I know this might sound crazy, but out on the trail, I feel like we're equals, then we get to this place, and I see you sign your name for a hundred-dollar tab like it's nothing, and I don't feel much like your equal. I can't pay my fair share when our spending habits are so different."

"I hate to break it to you, but we're not equals out on the trail. Not even close. My signature on a room service tab will never elevate me to your skill. I bow to your expertise and admire you so much. Can't we each contribute in our own way? Isn't that considered fair?"

"I don't want you to think less of me for not being able to spend like you do."

Something inside me clicked, and the words were out before I even had a chance to think it through or really understand them myself. "Leslie, you've become so special to me. The spend that I ask of you is your time, not your money. You've managed to do something that no one else has done. You've captured my heart, and no matter what we're doing, I can't seem to get enough time with you." I cupped her face and looked into her eyes.

"I know the feeling. I was so excited to see you that first night at Stover Creek. Bobber and Cricket weren't wrong when they said I haven't let you out of my sight since. I can't imagine not having you with me on this hike." She wrapped her arms around me. "You must think I'm nuts."

"Not in the least. I'm so glad you told me how you felt. Maybe it's you who thinks I'm nuts."

"Nah, I hear what you're saying, and now that you've explained it, I think it's sweet. You're the first person who's ever spent a fortune just to have some alone time with me."

"I know it was selfish. I know we'll have to go out today at some point, but I'd finally gotten some uninterrupted time with you, and I wasn't ready to give that up just yet. We won't get this kind of time out on the trail."

"I like that you didn't want to share me." She kissed my forehead. "And I do like the idea of sleeping with you on the trail."

"Wait, does that mean that you won't mind if I splurge a little at the outfitters? My request, my credit card."

"I've never been with someone like you." She squeezed her arms around me.

"I've never been with anyone like you, either." I wrapped my arms around her and held her close. "Is that a yes?"

She shrugged and smiled. "A bigger tent will be too heavy, but I wouldn't refuse to curl up next to you with a wider sleeping pad and bag."

"Yes. I'll savor you in other ways when we have a hotel room." I had no idea how Leslie agreeing to the purchase made me feel like I'd won the lottery, but it felt wonderful.

"I won't fight you on lunch, either. Can we get onion rings again?"

Excited, I pulled back and looked into her smiling eyes. "Absolutely, as many as you'd like."

After lunch, which was a thousand times better than breakfast, we took our lovemaking into the shower and didn't rejoin civilization until midafternoon. Hand in hand, we decided on a stroll along the city sidewalks. The small town was completely overrun with weary, waterlogged hikers. I was grateful that we'd arrived when we had and thought to extend our stay before our hotel, the last with any vacancies, had filled to capacity. Neon signs glowed in various colors up and down the main thoroughfare, touting the lack of availability. The park at the top of the hill across the street from the post office was covered with tents and hammocks with rain covers tied up between trees. Wet gear, along with dripping clothes and sleeping bags, hung from lines strung beneath the pavilions to air out and dry.

It felt odd to walk outside without a pack. The wicked weather, much like our monetary misunderstanding, had shifted off to the east, taking the storm clouds with it. Temperatures rose enough to pull out a short-sleeved shirt, and the warmth of the sunshine felt good on my skin. We meandered around the little shops and even stopped to enjoy an ice cream cone; Leslie insisted on paying for the treat. She called it her kind of splurge, and it was one that I loved accepting. I went with black cherry, and she opted for the bright, multi-colored Superman ice cream. It matched her new shirt and her personality. We were figuring out a way to make it work.

Slowly and quite enjoyably, we made our way up to the outfitter supply. We picked out the perfect sleeping pad and bag and headed up the main aisle toward the food.

"Hey, Crunch-n-Munch, First Class, over here." Bobber's voice was unmistakable.

"Crunch-n-Munch?" Leslie had a questioning expression on her face.

Bobber and Cricket waved at us from the far end of the main aisle that was packed shoulder to shoulder. We held up a thumbs-up in acknowledgement and followed the slow-motion traffic toward our friends.

"I kinda like Crunch-n-Munch. It's like she disguised your trail name because you know if someone shouts out Munch in a crowded room, everyone will be over here asking you about the scenic eleven. It's happened all week, at every shelter. Face it, you're a celebrity. I might as well be hiking with Ruby Rose or Megan Rapinoe. All you're missing is the purple hair, although your bandana is as distinctive."

"Ruby Rose is a badass. I remind you of her and Megan Rapinoe, the soccer star? She's awesome, too. Do you think I could pull off purple hair?" she asked.

I dug my fingers into her hair, which was much longer than Megan Rapinoe's, and tussled it. I liked the fact that she hadn't worn the bandana since we'd arrived. "There's nothing you couldn't pull off."

"Does the Munch thing bother you?"

"It doesn't bother me that you're famous. I admire all that you've accomplished. I like the way you light up when you talk about your experiences." I rested a hand on her shoulder and leaned in close to her ear. "Trust me, I'll let you know when my needs are overwhelming, and I don't want to share you with others."

I felt her shiver when my breath tickled her ear, and her grinning sideways look was the perfect response. Being able to tease Leslie and not having to worry about how my words came across, our misunderstanding earlier aside, was refreshing. She was so much fun to be around. We continued to snake our way through the bodies milling around the store until we met up with Bobber and Cricket at the edge of the shoe department.

"Hey, you two. Are you all recovered and ready to hit the trail tomorrow?" Leslie asked. "I was thinking we could meet at Carter Gap Shelter tomorrow night. It would be a twenty-four-mile day, but we could make up some miles that we lost to the storm if we pushed it."

"Yeah, Carter Gap, whatever, where have you two been?" Cricket had her hands on her hips as if we'd missed curfew.

"We get the text last night about staying an extra day, but you're a no-show for breakfast, and we didn't see either of you at lunch. Believe me, we lingered for a long time waiting, too." Bobber looked from me to Leslie, then at our joined hands. She nudged Cricket in the side. "Are you seeing what I'm seeing?"

"Oh, I see it. I'd have to be blind not to see it, and somehow, even if I was blind, I'm sure I'd still see it. It's all over their faces."

"See what?" I asked and looked for whatever it was I was missing.

"It's distinctive. The glow. The inability to keep their hands off each other." Cricket shook her head. "It's the FFL"

"What are you two, twelve?" Leslie wrapped an arm around my shoulder. "I haven't heard it called that since middle school." Her cheeks flushed red. She was sexy even when she was embarrassed.

"Definitely the FFL." Bobber nodded. "Oh, and look at what's in the basket, Cricket. New sleeping gear…for two."

"I'm afraid to ask." The conversation was lost on me, other than the fact that it had to have something to do with sex. It was Bobber who'd initiated it, after all.

Leslie half laughed and half snorted. "She went to boarding school and probably doesn't know what that is."

"Hey, what happened to Vegas rules?" I playfully slapped her arm. "I'm sure I'll regret asking, but what is the FFL?"

"Freshly Fucked Look and sweetheart, I'm afraid you've both got it bad." Bobber smiled as if she'd cracked a great mystery. "We couldn't be happier. It's about time you two hooked up."

Cricket grabbed Bobber's hand and batted her eyelashes. "Oh, Bobber, remember when we used to stay up all night long having mind-blowing sex?"

"Our sex isn't mind-blowing anymore?" Bobber faked a shocked expression and covered her heart with her hand.

"Oh, it's still mind-blowing, baby, but last night, sleep was more so." Cricket kissed her on the cheek.

"Truth." Bobber wrapped an arm around Cricket's shoulder. "So now that you two have finally consummated your inevitable relationship, could we be your first double date? The town's overflowing with hikers, and we hear that the bar cried mercy last night, so they brought a few bands in to set up at the park like an impromptu block party. There'll be dancing, and they're bringing in some food and beer trucks. You two wanna go?"

Truthfully, I wanted to get our supplies and take Leslie back to our hotel room for a few more rounds of pleasure. It would be several days before we could get another hotel room, and I could have her all to myself again. But Leslie's eyes lit up, and I melted, more than willing to do whatever made her happy. God, what was happening to me? I'd never felt so needy or in the same breath, so selfless, when it came to a woman. I sighed on the inside, nodded, and matched my smile to hers. I could wait a few more hours to once again be naked with her. We'd have the entire night after some fun food and music.

"Sounds like fun," Leslie said. "We have a few more things to pick up and take back to the room. Where should we meet you and at what time?"

"Don't worry about a specific time. Maybe Munch still needs a little First Class attention." Cricket patted Leslie's shoulder. "You both tried to hide it with enthusiasm, but I've got you. You gals get your stuff and find us in the park whenever it works for you two. We haven't been married that long. We get it." She winked.

Leslie smiled, and I felt understood. Bobber and Cricket were proving to be wonderful friends.

We found everything we'd gone to the store for. Once we'd restocked our food bags with items from my home box and what we'd purchased, we once again set up my tent inside our room and tried out the new sleeping pad and bag. It worked perfectly for our afternoon lovemaking. We tried it twice, just to be sure. I hoped I could still my requests when we were in the silence of the woods, but for now, I didn't worry about holding back and begged for everything I wanted her to do to me.

Once again, Leslie didn't disappoint. I loved the fact that she begged too and wasn't shy about telling me when I was in just the right spot. Her ability to please me kept getting better and better. Based upon her vocal explosions, I'd guess it was the same for her. We were very compatible in the bedroom, of that, there was no doubt.

Knowing that Bobber and Cricket were waiting at the park, we reluctantly got dressed, broke down the tent, and arranged our packs for the next morning. My pack remained status quo with all of my original gear. Leslie insisted on carrying the extra ounces, swapping the new gear for her old pad and sleeping bag. We could do one final load of laundry later that night if we felt like it, and collect our charging cords in the morning before we hit the trail. It was time for some fun with our friends.

There were still a few hours of daylight when we started up the hill to the park. The strum of a guitar and the beat of drums could be heard from blocks away. I couldn't recall the last time I'd been to a park party; actually, I couldn't recall ever having gone to a park to listen to music and eat from food trucks. In my corporate world, events and receptions occurred in convention halls or resorts, not outside in a park with bugs, and I'd never really had friends outside of the workplace. This entire trip had been about trying new things, and this would certainly be something new.

We ordered a six-pack of tacos and frosty margaritas in red Solo cups. Provisions secured, we set out into the sea of people in search of Bobber and Cricket. They had claimed a picnic table and saved us seats. We chatted, we laughed, we ate, and we even danced. It was an amazing few hours that I didn't mind sharing at all.

CHAPTER THIRTEEN

I swear, every hiker who'd been drying out in that fiercely overcrowded Georgia town departed on the same day we did. Despite covering twenty-five miles on still soggy trails, Carter Gap Shelter was so packed—easily double what I'd seen that first night at Stover Creek—arguments broke out, and the peace and tranquility of the evening was replaced with frustration and tension.

Later that night, while camping at the edge of the woods, far from the chaos, the four of us decided to push ourselves and put in several twenty-plus mile days to break away from the congestion. Four days later, we made it to Fontana Dam Shelter in North Carolina, also known as the Fontana Hilton, and pitched our tents in the primo spots with amazing lake views. It was one of the few shelters on the trail with hot showers and actual restrooms instead of an outhouse. We arrived early enough to take advantage of the kayak rentals for the afternoon. We'd earned a few hours of play before we called for a ride into town to do laundry, resupply, and enjoy dinner at an actual restaurant.

Rather than order two tandem kayaks, the group decided it would be better for each of us to have our own. I was the only reluctant one of the bunch, having never been in a kayak. I kept that tidbit to myself and watched what everyone else did so I didn't make a fool of myself. Bobber and Leslie were already taunting each other before we'd even pushed away from shore.

"Munch, I'll race you to the other side." Bobber adjusted herself in the seat and dipped one side of her paddle in the water.

"Oh, it's on." Leslie clicked the last strap on her life jacket and readied her paddle. "I'm taking you down."

"Cricket, give us the ready, set," Bobber said over her shoulder.

"On your mark, get ready, get set, get double set…"

"Cricket!"

"Go."

Water sprayed off the paddles as they set their sights on the far side of the lake. Wake from the race lapped gently on the sides of our kayaks. Taunts, jeers, and laughter echoed off the steep rock walls close by. Leslie had the best laugh. Bobber's laugh was pretty great, too, but Leslie's was full and rich and hearty, like a hug.

"Look at those two goofballs. I'm so glad that Bobber has Munch to play with," Cricket said, as if we were chatting about children and not the women we crawled into bed with each night.

"Me, too, otherwise I'd be forced to race across the lake, and my skinny arms would be no match. Not to mention the fact that I'd end up upside down, stuck in this tube, drowning."

"Right?" Cricket laughed. "I've gotta say, we are so glad to have connected with you two. Who knew when we set off on this adventure that we'd end up besties with the AT power couple. We can't tell you how great it's been."

"I'd hardly call us the AT power couple. Munch holds all the trail glory. Seriously, we feel the same way. The four of us click. It's really been great." Besties. No one had said that about me, ever. It might sound silly, but it warmed my heart to be considered someone's bestie. Maybe this slowing down, living life, and letting people in stuff wasn't so bad after all.

"And, oh my God, you and Munch make the cutest couple. Is she your one and only? Do you think you'll stay together after you've finished the trail?"

I used my paddle to turn so I could better watch the antics of the race. Leslie was ahead by half of a kayak length. I tried to picture a life with Leslie off the trail. What would we do? Would I return to corporate America and resume my dawn to dusk work schedule? I couldn't see how that could work with my new, all-consuming need for time with Leslie. Luckily, I didn't have to decide at this moment and had many more months to enjoy what we had.

"I'd like to think we'd stay together, but we haven't talked about it," I answered honestly.

"I find it hard to picture Munch domesticated. How do you think she'd adapt to being a kept woman, living in a penthouse in downtown Hartford? Oh, I bet she'd look hot in a suit. Was she living in Connecticut when you two met on the plane?"

"She was staying in a place north of Hartford, up near the Massachusetts border. Domesticated, huh? Are you implying that, at this point, she's feral?" I kept my response light but scoured my brain for a conversation I'd had with Cricket about where I lived and what my life in Hartford was like. Nothing came to mind. I'd purposely avoided the topic.

Cricket laughed. "Good one. She has spent the last twenty years living in the wild. Come on, you know what I mean. Even though I haven't known either of you for very long, I feel like I've known both of you forever. Munch because of Bobber's obsession with her and the scenic eleven. We've read every article and listened to every podcast that she's been on, and one thing I know for certain is that she's not a fan of big-city life."

"Cricket, how do you know I'm from Hartford? You said you feel like you've known both of us forever, but as far as I know, we've never talked about where I'm from or that I live in a penthouse. Certainly, you didn't come across any details about me from listening to podcasts about Munch and the scenic eleven."

She looked like a deer caught in the headlights. "You signed your real name back at Springer Mountain, and Munch made such a fuss about you being top-shelf and first-class, but if I'm being honest, I've been a fan of yours for years. It took a second to recognize you at Stover Creek. I mean, you had your hair back in a ponytail, and you weren't wearing your corporate designers, but I've watched your TED Talk, like, a hundred times. The moment you spoke, I recognized your voice."

I turned my kayak so I could look in her eyes. "I need you to keep talking because at the moment, I'm a little freaked out."

"No, don't freak. Shit, I'm not a creepy stalker, even though I knew it would sound that way when I got the nerve to confess my admiration. I have no agenda other than to tell you that to me, you're what Munch is for Bobber. You see, I went back to college seven years ago for my MBA, though I didn't go to Stanford like you. I'm a Wharton grad. Anyway, you'd just made the cover of *Fortune* during my course on corporate finance. I was so impressed with your story in the article that I used you as the case study for my class project and again in my Foundations of Leadership course."

Her voice kind of trailed off. I think she forgot to breathe. She visibly swallowed and drew in a huge breath and kept right on talking.

"I kept following your career all through my MBA. In the end, you were the focus for my thesis project. I titled it, "Career Advancement Barriers Faced by Women." You, Amber Addison Shaw, aka petrified tree sap, aka First Class, became my star subject because you were one of the few women who'd smashed those barriers and wouldn't take no for an answer. You graced the cover of *Fortune* at the age of thirty-nine. Youngest, as of my research, for a female in your field. I still have three copies of that issue, by the way." She balanced her paddle in her lap, held out her hand, and held down her index finger as if ticking off points.

"A few years after college, you accepted a job at a lackluster, underperforming corporation, and over time, brought it into the spotlight by working your way up the managerial ranks. As the CFO, you streamlined their financials and used future financial projection data as insight for strategic decisions that strengthened their position in the market. While at the same time, you positioned yourself to step into the role of CEO, which you landed at thirty-eight with a starting annual salary of twenty million.

"No small feat, and it made you the youngest female to achieve that title at the time. Your direct reports raved about your leadership style. Turnover was all but nonexistent. Profits shot through the roof. You created a company that made people take notice, and you did all of that while earning ten percent the salary of your male counterparts in similar-sized corporations. Or at least, that was the case when I finished my thesis.

"I googled you again when I realized who you were at Stover Creek. *Forbes* now cites your net worth at over two hundred and fifty million. Your wealth is ranked fifth in the top ten US-based female CEOs. Amber, not only are you a role model of mine, but you're a frickin' legend to boot. You carried that corporation into the *Fortune 500*, and how'd they thank you for all of your hard work? They walked you out the door and gave your replacement four times your final salary."

I sat there floating in whatever direction the current took me because my paddle sat on my lap. How could I respond to that? Flattered or even more freaked out than I was before? "Cricket the creeper. You know exactly how much money I have, and I don't even know your real name."

"God, you're right. Totally creeper. I'm Marie Hamilton. Bobber is Rebecca Gains. She goes by Becca. We kept our own names when we got married. We live in Port Clinton, Pennsylvania, just a little past the midpoint of the Appalachian Trail. I'm a finance accounting manager, thanks to my MBA, and Becca owns a small restaurant. Her crew is running it while we're on this hike."

Port Clinton, Pennsylvania...now, why did that sound familiar? It didn't matter at the moment. Knowing Cricket's real name helped me feel marginally better, but the level of detail she had about me was still slightly unnerving. I knew it was entirely my fault for agreeing to do all those articles. At the time, I thought it would help my career. Who knew I'd end up unemployed, floating in a kayak, in North Carolina...alone...with my number one fan?

A moment from Stephen King's novel, *Misery*, flashed in my mind. I shook the vision from my thoughts. Nothing about Cricket or Bobber screamed psycho. Then, her comment about Carl clicked. "Carl's really making four times my salary?"

Cricket grimaced and nodded.

"Dick."

"Right." She smiled. "Can I just say that it's been an honor to get to know you. I mean, who gets to call their hero a friend? You're, like, a real person. Not at all what I expected."

"Thanks, I think."

"I mean, seriously, what big-time multimillionaire would be out here trudging through the mud with us like it's any other day of the week? I'm not sure what I expected, ya know, like if we ever met, but I'm certain I never expected you to be out here hiking or digging a cathole so you can pee in the woods, let alone splattered with mud, drinking beer, and eating pizza with the likes of us."

I had to laugh. "The mud was the worst."

"Right?" She maneuvered her kayak next to mine. "Amber, I hope I didn't make things weird. I just wanted you to know that your career really impacted me and helped me keep going when doing so, while working full time, was difficult. Your story inspired several women in my class."

"Thanks, that helps. It's getting less weird by the minute." I smiled.

"Good. I'd tell you about the Amber Shaw Fan Club at Wharton, but then I'd have to kill you." She winked and smiled. "Too soon?"

"Yeah, a tad. Why didn't you say anything sooner?"

"I tried a few times. I've tossed out questions, hoping to open up the conversation about your life off trail or why you were hiking, but you avoided answering them, and I never really had an opening."

"Sorry about that. Being walked out the door was hard on my ego. I'm still wrestling with what's next."

"Does Munch know who you really are?" Cricket asked.

"Well, it's not like I'm a secret superhero or a celebrity. Yeah, she knows. She doesn't know my bio quite as well as you do, and I doubt she bothers with *Forbes*, but she knows I was a CEO. She knows that I lost my job after the merger, and she knows I arrived home that same day to find my girlfriend moving out. She even knows about my motivation behind this hike and what my childhood was like. One of the things we do really well is talk."

"I bet I know the other thing you two do really well. It prompted a sleeping setup for two." She tapped my paddle with the tip of hers and wiggled her eyebrows.

"The sex is pretty amazing. Honestly, I'm not entirely sure anyone else knows me like she does, not even you, creeper." I winked and smiled at that last part so she'd know I was teasing. Kind of.

APPALACHIAN AWAKENING

"Well, I really hope we can remain friends long after the hike." Her expression was sincere.

"Me, too," I said and realized I meant it.

Bobber and Leslie were making their way back across the lake. I'd been so taken aback by Cricket's intimate knowledge of my life that I hadn't noticed who won.

"Does Bobber know the details of my life?"

"She knows you were a big wig CEO. She thought I was crushing on you by the time we reached Mountain Crossings and didn't realize that I was fangirling, so I explained my thesis all over again. She's not interested in the world of corporate finance and couldn't really care less about who did what to bring a company into the limelight. Her eyes glaze over when I get into specifics."

"Can we keep my net worth between us? I came out here to figure out what I want out of life, and I can't do that if I'm the millionaire hiker. Inevitably, someone will ask me to help them start a business or ask for a loan. I hate it when money is all they see when they look at me."

"Yeah, totally. After reading all those articles, I thought I knew you, but I now realize I only knew about you. It's pretty cool, ya know, getting to know you, the person."

"I'm enjoying getting to know you, the person, too. Well, since you seem to know everything about me, any suggestions on how I can tell Leslie about the money? Our only disagreement so far has been about that. I haven't denied having it, but I wasn't up-front about quite how much I have."

"You'll know when the time is right. Unless you two become more than a trail romance, does it really matter?"

She had a valid point. "No, I guess it doesn't. Thanks."

The conversation stuck with me all evening. Part of it had to do with Cricket knowing almost everything there was to know about me, but I'd set myself up for that by agreeing to open up to reporters. What was really gnawing at me was what I had with Leslie. What were we to each other? Was this just a trail romance, or could there be more to us? What was happening to me that had me even worrying about that?

We returned from our trip to town, and once our food bags were restocked and laundry was put away, we sat on the benches in the gathering area just below the shelter. There was a view of the lake from the bench Leslie and I were sitting on. Someone had started a fire, and a few more hikers were trickling into camp.

Leslie stood and held out her hand. "Come on, let's go for a walk."

Her hand was warm, and I loved the way her fingers fit with mine. We walked along the trail that crossed over the top of the dam. The views were breathtaking. There was a deep gorge of the Little Tennessee River almost five hundred feet below on one side and Fontana Lake, where we'd kayaked earlier, on the other. All of it was surrounded by the Great Smoky Mountains and the mountains of the Nantahala National Forest. The air was clear, and the sky a perfect blue with a few far-off floating clouds in the late day sun. It was picturesque and so peaceful. Due to the stillness of the evening, the water was glass, mirroring a reflection of the clouds in the sky and the shoreline on the far side. The air was sweet with the fragrance of spring.

Leslie tapped the side of my leg. I looked at her hand and noticed the two photographs. In the first, Leslie's mom was standing with that same guy from Blood Mountain. They had their arms wrapped around one another, and Leslie's mom's head was nuzzled into his neck. The gorge was visible in the distance behind them. The second photo was in the same spot but with the lake and the mountains behind them.

I wrapped my arms around Leslie's waist and tucked my head into her neck. "Is this okay, or would you prefer to nuzzle into my neck like your mom's pose?"

"This is perfect. I love how your head fits perfectly. Like my body was made to hold you." She extended her arm and took a couple of pictures.

I swooned, and my heart melted for her. "That's the sweetest thing anyone's ever said to me."

"I mean it. We fit together perfectly."

Part of me wanted to dig into that last statement a bit more, but I was emotionally spent from my conversation with Cricket. Who we were to each other could wait for another day, especially since I had more questions than answers on what I even wanted. We pivoted our bodies one hundred and eighty degrees and took the same shot with the mountains and the lake as a backdrop.

"Next photo, Clingmans Dome, at over sixty-six hundred feet, it's the highest point in the Great Smoky Mountains. It's only thirty-two miles away, but it's more than a four thousand foot climb in elevation. It will likely take us four to five days to get there. Are you up for tackling it tomorrow?"

"If I say no, can we head back into town, get a hotel room for the next four nights, then take an Uber over to meet Bobber and Cricket?" I was only half joking. I nuzzled in closer and kissed that sweet spot behind her earlobe.

"I like the ingenuity of your plan, but it will ruin our claim to being AT thru-hikers. The point is to hike the trail, not play hopscotch."

"I know. I'm in."

I stood there, cuddled in Leslie's arms, and stared out at the lake. I wasn't in any hurry to rejoin the group at the campfire.

"You've been unusually quiet this afternoon. Is everything okay?"

Leslie was so perceptive. Another thing about her that made my heart swell. Part of me wanted to avoid answering, brush off the question, and just enjoy snuggling close, but I already knew her well enough to know she didn't ask a question that she didn't want an honest answer to.

"I had a weird conversation with Cricket while you and Bobber were racing the lake. She knows about my life back in Hartford. Turns out that I, too, have a fan. She admires me like Bobber admires you. I was her case study in college." Rather than pull away to see Leslie's expression, I remained curled up against her body. Her breathing didn't change a bit, which meant that nothing I'd said surprised her.

"I know. I overheard Cricket talking to Bobber about it while you were in the shower. Did she really call us the AT power couple?"

"That's what you got out of the conversation?" I squeezed her a little tighter, then relaxed my grip.

"Hey, I'm not the one who did a multipage spread in *Fortune* for the whole world to read."

"No, your multipage spreads were in *Hiker's Life* and *Backpacking Adventures*. Have you read the *Fortune* article?"

"Oh yeah, back at Amicalola Falls. You looked hot in the pictures. I like you in corporate clothes and heels. There're several articles out there about you. So you googled me too?"

I turned my face into her neck and smiled. I'd totally googled the famous hiker of the scenic eleven. "Busted, and you looked hot in shorts and a tank top on the trail. I read all the articles about you, too. I might have saved a couple of pictures to my phone."

"Nothing that Cricket and Bobber talked about surprised me. I also happen to think you're pretty impressive." She gave me a little squeeze.

"So you've known everything all this time? But you asked me about my why and acted like you didn't know anything."

"I didn't know your why. I only knew what you let them print in the articles, but I've learned a whole lot more about who you are from our conversations. There's so much more to you than what was in those magazines. PS, I like our talks a whole lot better. I get the real you."

"I like our talks a whole lot better, too. You'll always get the real me, just like I get the real you. Raw and unedited, right?"

"Right."

We sat on top of the dam and watched the sunset. Ours wasn't a deep conversation that night on the dam, but what was said left me feeling at peace, and I'd never felt more understood.

CHAPTER FOURTEEN

The hike up to Clingmans Dome was no joke. After the first day, my legs were on fire. The second day, my legs ached as if I'd severely overdone it at the gym. The third day was pure misery, and ibuprofen was no longer helpful. By the fourth day, I was nothing more than wobbly rubber from the waist down. I held Leslie's hand for the last of the climb simply so I wouldn't give up, sit on the nearest log, and cry, begging and pleading for helicopter rescue. Thankfully, the skies were picturesque and clear on the day we made it onto the half mile path up to the concrete observation tower. The views of the Great Smoky Mountains were spectacular and brought about emotions that I couldn't begin to put into words, a visual treasure that made the torture of getting there somewhat worth it.

Leslie's photo of her mom on the dome forty years ago included a small group of hikers. Luckily, Bobber and Cricket had made the climb with us. Without reason, and at my suggestion, we posed at the railing, just as Leslie's mom had done with her friends so long ago. We asked a nearby stranger to snap several shots on each of our phones. It was perfect. Leslie's smile aimed in my direction was the absolute best reward. The secret of her AT why would always be safe with me, no matter what.

When we came down from the dome, the trail ran parallel with Clingmans Dome Road for a few miles. Faint whiffs of meat cooking on a grill began to tease our senses. Starving, I once again had a little pep in my step and hoped that whoever was cooking would be willing to share. The heavenly aroma grew stronger and stronger, and we heard laughter and voices. We were all eager to investigate.

A sign indicated that the trail crossed through Newfound Gap parking lot and picked up on the opposite side. We emerged from the woods to find the closest end of the parking lot covered in pop-up awnings. Long tables were set up beneath, piled high with an assortment of buns, chips, and condiments, along with potato and macaroni salad in large bowls sitting in bins of ice. A sign taped on one of the tables encouraged AT thru-hikers to stop and enjoy a hot meal provided by a few businesses in Gatlinburg, Tennessee. Another sign indicated options of hotdogs, polish sausage, hamburgers, chicken, and veggie burgers: the heavenly scent that emanated from four different grills sitting in the parking space beyond the covered tables.

My stomach growled with anticipation. "Trail angels?" I asked.

"Trail angels. Come on, let's eat." Leslie tugged on my hand.

"Where'd you gals start your trip?" a woman standing behind the first table asked.

"Amicalola Falls," Leslie said.

"Well, then, this is your two hundred and seven mile reward. Congratulations on making it this far. Grab a plate and help yourself. There're beverages in the coolers underneath those trees over there." She pointed to a shady spot behind the grills.

I followed Leslie's lead by wrapping up my plastic fork and spoon into a couple of napkins and tucking them in my pocket and then picked up a hefty paper plate. Everything looked so, so good. I accepted scoops of both potato and macaroni salad and selected a bag of barbecue potato chips. I couldn't recall the last time I'd had a hotdog. It very well might have been my early boarding school days. It sounded incredibly good, so I opted for one with mustard and a touch of dill relish, then added a chicken leg slathered with barbecue sauce for my second meat option, even though I wanted at least one of everything.

"You all are sincerely angels for doing this. Everything looks and smells so good," I said to the group of volunteers.

"Our pleasure." Their collective smiles led me to believe it was, indeed, a pleasure for them.

"Do you have a donation jar or anything? I'd like to make a contribution."

"We don't accept donations from hikers. This spread's been paid for by businesses in Gatlinburg. A way of saying thank you for supporting our town. Don't forget to grab something to drink."

One of the coolers had a variety of beers, and the other had canned sodas. I found a Country Time Lemonade and snagged it. Leslie went for an ice-bathed beer. Bobber and Cricket followed her lead. None of the picnic tables had enough open space for the four of us, and I was two hundred miles past worrying about sitting on the ground or sharing my space with tiny ants. We settled off to the side beneath a shade tree.

Everything looked so good that I wasn't sure what to eat first. I opted for the two mayo-based salads. Whoever had made them used just the right amount of red wine vinegar and stone-ground mustard because both flavors were present while not overpowering. I finished almost everything on my plate, including my barbecue chips. Then, having saved the best for last, I savored each and every bite of my hotdog. It was absolutely divine.

"Have I stuck around long enough to learn how you managed to get the trail name of Munch?" I asked. "You said you'd tell me if I made it to North Carolina. Now, here I am in Tennessee, and I still don't know."

Leslie tapped my boot with the toe of hers. She had the most adorable smile on her face with a glint of mischievousness in her eyes. "I like to imply that it has something to do with my ability to please the ladies, but the truth is that when I first started hiking, I couldn't consume enough calories. I was starving all the time, to the point that I kept baggies of trail mix in my pockets and ate constantly, hence…Munch. But if anyone else asks, it's all about my abilities in the tent."

I burst out laughing. So did Bobber and Cricket. "There was a lot of hype back in Amicalola for that. Although, you do possess that tongue teasing talent, so we'll keep the story alive." I tapped her boot, too.

Bobber leaned around Cricket and tapped my shoulder. "Well, First Class, now your trail angel cherry has been popped. I'm afraid you're about out of firsts."

"It was almost orgasmic, too." The words were out before I could stop myself. Leslie half laughed and half coughed next to me. Apparently, I was spending too much time around the three of them. "Seriously, this was pretty spectacular and perfectly timed. A simple beef hotdog has never tasted quite so good," I said.

"Nonsense, Bobber. Don't tell her that. There's still nineteen hundred miles of firsts," Leslie said and drank the last of her beer. "Every step is someplace new. Don't you dare give her a reason to call it quits."

"Spoken like someone who had to walk over twenty-three thousand miles to find her heart's desire. Don't worry, she's totally into you, too. Besides, she's no quitter. She's not going anywhere."

"Um, hello, she's sitting right here." I leaned over to Leslie. "Hey, I'll follow you anywhere. Mostly because you're carrying our bed."

"Uh-huh, keep it up." Leslie shook her head and rolled her eyes. Her sweet smile was on full display.

"I still find it hard to believe that after this season, there'll be no more articles about Munch and her pursuit to conquer the scenic eleven. No more podcasts. Your story's almost over, my friend. A great big, fat, *the end*, with nothing left but the rolling credits. Shit, I'm already going through withdrawal. Who will I fan over now?" Bobber leaned back against her pack and lifted her forearm over her forehead in a motion of fake anguish. "I'll have to find someone new to put into my Google Alerts."

"What? Really? You have a Google Alert on me?" Leslie asked.

"Duh. How else would I know when and where to tune in? But now, your travels are over, and I'm gonna have to follow someone like Steve, the one-legged hiker, or some shit. I'm telling you, your fanbase is at an epic loss. It won't be the same."

Cricket and I laughed.

"Babe, you'll always have a fan in me," I said and kissed her on the cheek.

"Me, too," Cricket said with too much enthusiasm and a few seconds too late. That made all of us laugh all over again.

I collected our four empty plates and took them to the trash. When I returned, my overstuffed belly was begging the rest of my body to take a sunny snooze, but Leslie, Bobber, and Cricket were already up and donning their packs.

"We should get moving. I overheard someone say that the shuttle heading up to Gatlinburg is here and only has six spots left," Cricket said.

Just hearing the word Gatlinburg lifted my spirits almost as much as the surprise lunch had done. Things that I'd once taken for granted back in Hartford now stirred up extreme and abundant joy. The simplicity of my time on the trail had brought so much of life into focus. A perfect example? The act of showering. Once considered a mundane activity at home, now it was something I looked forward to like some people looked forward to a trip to Disneyland or a tropical beach vacation.

It had been almost five days since I'd last showered at Fontana Dam. A much needed, yet not entirely private experience, so Leslie hadn't been there to help me rinse off. Tonight promised not only a private shower but also laundry, a box from Sue, and the first real hotel room in quite some time, which meant uninhibited, extremely vocal sex. Win, win, win, in my book. I ached for Leslie's touch as if I'd been deprived for years, and the mere thought of the two of us together behind four walls already had my body on fire. I'd become an obsessed fiend. Perhaps both of us had since we literally ran across the parking lot hoping that plenty of seats were still available.

The shuttle hadn't traveled for more than a mile or so when the driver slammed on the brakes. Leslie's quick reaction kept me from sliding right out of my seat.

"Sorry about that, folks. Looks like a momma bear and a couple of cubs have decided to play tag out in the middle of the road," the driver said over her shoulder.

We all stood, trying to get a peek of the bears. The cubs kept going in opposite directions, causing the momma bear to run back and forth, trying to corral them. I'd never seen anything like it. Hell,

I'd never seen a bear that wasn't safely secured on the screen of a TV, period. The trio finally made it across the road. Momma bear followed her two cubs over the railing and ran off into the woods. We were once again on our way.

"I read that the Smoky Mountains have one of the largest bear populations for a national park, but until now, I hadn't thought about how that might impact us as hikers. I really hope my bear vault lives up to its name," I said to anyone who was listening. "Especially considering that the next resupply is seventy miles away."

The shuttle driver looked into the mirror and nodded. "For those of you with food bags, if you don't have carabiner clips, pick some up. You'll need to secure your bags to the hooks on the suspension cables at the shelters. The bears have figured out how to shake the lines and pop the bags off. I'm hearing all sorts of stories from folks who come back hangry with a need to resupply for the eight-day trek, then start that hike all over again. Make sure you pick up some bear spray, too, if you don't have any. With over sixteen hundred bears in the park, you're bound to see them. Better safe than sorry. They've been a bit of a nuisance this year."

"Thanks for the info," Bobber said and looked over to us and mouthed, "What the fuck?"

I must have had some kind of terrified look on my face because Leslie wrapped an arm around my shoulder and leaned in close. "Don't worry. It'll be fine. I've camped in bear-dense woods before. Trust me, I know how to keep us safe."

"I trust you." I looked in her eyes and realized that without a doubt, I completely trusted her, which was huge for me. All my life, I'd been guarded, keeping people at a distance. Trust didn't come easy.

I was grateful to be hiking with the three of them and not taking the Great Smoky Mountains on all by myself as I had first envisioned. Had I tackled it alone, I could only imagine the headlines: "Ex CEO Mauled by Bear Family, Remains Consumed by Coyote." And without my small tribe, Sue would be the only person at my funeral. Even my parents would find a reason not to attend. I snuggled a little closer to Leslie, silently thankful for her protection.

Our overnight stay in Gatlinburg was blissful. We scratched every itch, so to speak. A lovely steak dinner out with our friends, then a stroll around town that included resupply shopping, followed up by a passionate evening in. Really, anytime behind a locked door with Leslie made up for anything and everything we couldn't do in our tent.

We set off early the next morning with clean bodies, clean clothes, eight days of food, and renewed spirits. Arrangements on where to meet Bobber and Cricket on our first night in the park had already been made, so we had the entire day to ourselves. I was in heaven.

The first couple of hours of our hike were quiet, unusual for us. Anymore, it seemed we always had something to chat about. But that morning, ever since we'd been back on the trail, Leslie seemed distracted and lost in thought. So much so that her stride changed, and she pulled a couple of hundred feet in the lead.

"Hey, Speed Racer, give me a second to catch up, would ya?"

She stopped and waited for me. "Guess I got in a groove, sorry about that."

I hooked my arm into hers, hoping to set our pace. "Do I hold you back? Would you be farther along if we weren't hiking together?"

"No. No, not at all. Why would you ask me that? I just got lost in my thoughts." She pulled me to a stop. She took both of my hands and stood directly in front of me, staring into my eyes. "Having you with me makes this last trail a thousand times more special. Without you, I'd be questioning everything." Tears welled in her eyes, and her chin quivered.

Seeing her like that broke my heart. "Questioning everything? Like what? Talk to me."

She stole her eyes and looked at the ground. "It sounds dumb in my mind, and I'm sure it will sound worse if I say it out loud."

"Didn't you say something about a safe zone? It still applies. Come on, out with it."

"With all the other trails, there was always something next to plan for. With this one, I don't have a next thing to think about when everything's quiet, and I'm not sure what I'm supposed to do when it's all done. What if it's like Bobber said yesterday, and after I finish this trail, I become a has-been with zero followers? Who's gonna care about Munch and the scenic eleven? What do I do then? I can't help but to think I've wasted twenty-one years of my life. All this effort, and I have nothing to show for it."

I grabbed her shoulders. "Hey, you're not a has-been anything, and you'll never be a has-been. You've done something awesome, incredible, and amazing, and everyone, and I mean everyone, who steps foot on any one of the national scenic trails will forever remember and know your name. That, I can promise you. I admire you so, so much."

"Really? You admire me?"

"I admire you with every fiber of my being. I admire you. I—" Whoa, I almost said the one thing I hadn't said to anyone, ever. What was happening to me?

"I admire you, too. I can't imagine a moment on this trek without you."

Warmth filled my heart. "Ditto." I tucked my head into that special spot against her neck. "I can't imagine a moment on this trek without you, either. There's still time to find your next thing. What kind of stuff interests you?"

"Let's walk and talk. I'll mind my pace." She tugged on my hand.

We hadn't walked more than a couple of hundred yards when a rustling noise in the underbrush stopped us in our tracks. I swear my heart stopped beating for a moment and then resumed in an ear-pounding overdrive. The underbrush wiggled again, closer this time. We were maybe five miles into the Smoky Mountains, and here we were, face-to-face with our first wildlife encounter. I prayed it wasn't a bear. Especially not a bear with cubs.

Leslie unzipped a pocket on my pack. I was frozen in place. She held out my can of bear spray. A twig snapped. Jesus, we were going to die.

Then, the cutest little critter came out onto the trail. It was black with white dots and a white-tipped tail.

"Back up slowly." Leslie lowered her arm. "Amber, back up."

"It's so cute." The little critter spotted us. It turned to go up trail, then it did a handstand and held that pose like an acrobatic squirrel.

"Back up, back up, back up." Leslie tugged on my hand.

"Why? It's just a squirrel."

"Not a squirrel, skunk."

"Skunks are bigger with stripes, not spots."

"It's a spotted skunk, and the handstand is how they spray."

"Oh shit." I turned and ran with everything I had.

Eventually, I only heard my own footfalls. I stopped and spun to see if the little critter was still there. All I saw was Leslie, doubled over, laughing.

"You're quite the sprinter," she said, wiping tears from her eyes. "It left. You can come back."

"Was it really a skunk? Or were you just messing with me?"

"It really was a skunk. Spotted skunks are about half the size of a regular skunk, but they can still spray a good fifteen feet."

"Good to know. I swear, sometimes, I feel so inept. If you hadn't been here, no doubt I'd have been sprayed by the cute little squirrel."

"There probably aren't too many spotted skunks in downtown Hartford." She held her hand out for me. "Told you I'd protect you."

"That you did, and I'm forever grateful." I accepted her hand, and we continued our stroll.

"Have you thought at all about what might be next for you?" she asked.

"It's funny, I would've expected my answer to be yes. I'm an obsessive planner. At home in Hartford, I typically have my week planned to the minute, and I'm always working on a master plan. But surprisingly, I haven't really thought about it much these past few weeks. I've had so much fun spending time with you that I'm content to know which shelter we're stopping at and how many days of food to buy before the next resupply. Beyond that, I haven't thought about anything that far in the future."

"Do you plan on returning to Hartford?" Leslie asked.

"Of course, it's where I live." We were walking side by side, and I noticed Leslie kick a stone mid-stride. It sure seemed like I was missing something. "Have you been to Hartford?"

She shook her head. "I typically avoid big cities. Everything feels so claustrophobic, and they stink like the black exhaust from buses. Have you ever lived anywhere else?"

"Boarding school but even that was in Connecticut. We have electric buses now, so the city smells much better, and nothing about my place is claustrophobic. Maybe you'll reconsider? You could come and check it out?"

"Is that an invitation?"

"Yes, absolutely. I'd love to show you around. Maybe I could change your mind about city life." I felt giddy at the idea of having Leslie in Hartford.

Other than my brief conversation with Cricket at Fontana Dam, I hadn't seriously given any thought to what would happen to us as a couple after the hike. Could Leslie really find any kind of contentment in Hartford, or were we on two different paths that would diverge at the end of this adventure? One thing was certain, she was becoming more and more important to me by the day.

CHAPTER FIFTEEN

The hike through the Great Smoky Mountains was strenuous and spectacular. The vast views of far-off valleys blanketed with a smoky blue haze were unbelievable and made the physical exertion of climbing up and up and down and back up some more—because nothing was simply flat trail—tenfold worth the effort. Leslie and I captured two more Mom photos and several shots of our own. It was becoming our thing. We managed our entire eight days in the park without a bear encounter, although we came across mangled evidence of past successful food bag raids. The trail exited the park directly into the small town of Hot Springs, North Carolina, leaving us feeling proud and accomplished, or at least that was how I felt. The prospect of clean bodies and clean clothes once again had me elated. Eight days was a long time when using a washcloth to clean up and even longer once I'd run out of clean clothes.

There must have been some kind of local event since every hotel we checked on had no vacancies. Reluctantly, we paid twenty-eight dollars for a tent site at a campground along the French Broad River.

"Maybe I can find us an Airbnb or a VRBO." I pulled out my phone. "What's the point of hiking for eight days if we don't get a hotel room as a reward?" I tried to keep my profound disappointment in check. I didn't mean to sound like a spoiled brat, but damnit, I wanted what I wanted, and at that moment, it was a hotel room with a cozy, comfy bed.

"This isn't so bad. We have a spot right on the water's edge, and we've already paid for it. Let's go take a shower and do laundry. You'll feel better once you're clean. I'll even take you out for dinner, then we can go grocery shopping. Come on, hashtag best date ever."

"Maybe you're right." I tried to stay positive, but all I really felt was positively disappointed. Still, I didn't want to be the pissed off princess who didn't get her way.

We showered, changed into our rain gear, and did laundry. Being clean, with clean clothes, did brighten my spirit. The washing machines were even robust enough to tackle our stinky sleeping bag. At least we'd sleep in a clean bed, even if it was in our nylon home away from home.

Cricket and Bobber arrived and snagged the spot next to us. We set up our campsite and purchased a few bundles of firewood while they showered and did laundry. We'd all developed an easygoing routine, and it worked. Finally, the four of us were clean and ready to go into the heart of town. Apparently, everyone else who was visiting Hot Springs had the same idea. The restaurants were packed and had an hour-long wait for seating. I even attempted bribery with a crisp hundred and couldn't get bumped up in line.

"This absolutely sucks." I was annoyed and hangry. "I'm not eating at McDonalds, but I want something hot that I can chew, and I don't see any other option."

Cricket looked at Bobber. "Campfire steak and foil packet surprise?"

"Oh, I'm in. You know how I love a campfire steak and foil packet surprise." Bobber lit up.

"Me, too. That's the best," Leslie said.

"I'm all in on eating steak, but what is a foil packet surprise?" I asked.

"Potatoes, onions, and other fresh veggies with a pad of butter, sealed in tin foil and cooked over the campfire. It's amazing," Cricket said. "Bobber, you three hit the store, don't forget plates. I'm not eating steak out of my tin cup. I'll head back and get the fire going. I know how you like the coals, and this way, I won't pick out the wrong steaks like last time."

Bobber and Leslie walked incredibly fast when they were on a mission. I had to speed walk just to keep pace. They took charge of the shopping, and I let them. I ordered steak; I didn't buy it, and certainly didn't know how to cook it. Given time to research, I was sure I could have figured it out, but I'd never needed to; that was what restaurants were for. Soon, the cart held meat wrapped in white paper, potatoes, two sweet onions, a stick of butter, asparagus and zucchini, tinfoil, hefty plates, and a small bottle of scotch. The scotch was my contribution to dinner. Since they were willing to cook, I insisted on buying.

Cricket had the fire roaring when we arrived. Leslie took off to buy a few more bundles of wood for later.

"What can I do to help?" I asked.

"You can cut up the onions." Cricket pushed them in my direction.

I retrieved my multi-tool and unfolded the knife option. Cricket walked to the water spigot with the bag of potatoes and a plate. She turned the water on low and used her hands to wash potatoes. Did that mean I should have washed the onions first? I swapped my knife for the onions and followed her to the water, hoping to mimic her movements.

"What are you doing? They need to be diced," she asked after washing her last potato.

"Washing the onions. Am I not supposed to do that?"

"It's not necessary. Onions get peeled, potatoes get washed." She was kind and stifled her giggle. "You don't cook, do you?"

"Is it that obvious?" I kept my voice low.

"I forgot who you are."

"I think that's the nicest thing you've said to me." I smiled.

She cocked her head a little sideways.

"It means I'm becoming more your friend and less your idol."

"Definitely my friend." She motioned to the onions. "You really don't know what to do with those? Didn't your mom cook?"

I shook my head. "Mable, our housekeeper, cooked, but I wasn't allowed in the kitchen most of the time."

"But you've cooked all your meals on the trail and use your stove like a pro."

"That's because I did a boatload of research and practiced before I left home. I don't like to look foolish. Trust me, my first cup of tea was a colossal effort in the making." Confessing my ineptitude was a little scary.

She patted my forearm. "Come on, I'll show you what to do. You'll be an expert in the kitchen before you know it."

Before long, she and I had potatoes and onions cut into bite-size pieces, then she showed me how to cut up the zucchini and snip the asparagus. I had to admit, it was fun to have my hands in the activity. We spread out four pieces of foil and divided up the veggies equally, adding salt, pepper, and a few pats of butter to each pile. Then, we tore off similar-sized sheets and covered our pile of vegetables. Cricket showed me how to seal the four sides to make a pouch. As silly as it sounded, I felt very accomplished in my creation of a foil packet surprise. Almost as accomplished as having hiked through the Great Smoky Mountain National Park. Meanwhile, the fire had been reduced to a heap of coals.

"The fires almost out. I'll add more wood," I said, certain my efforts would be helpful.

"No," Bobber, Cricket, and Leslie said loudly in unison. "It's perfect. We'll add more after dinner."

Leslie grabbed a metal grate that was leaning up against the water spigot. She rested it on two steel pipes that straddled the fire. Cricket showed me where to place foil packets over the coals. This was all very interesting. Bobber and Cricket unwrapped the steaks and dusted them with a baggie of spices that Bobber had ordered from the meat counter. They smelled amazing and made my mouth water.

Leslie picked up the small bottle of scotch. "How about I pour?"

Within twenty minutes, we were seated at the picnic table with a beautifully cooked steak on one plate and a steaming foil packet on another. I mimicked the others on how to best open my packet and free my vegetables from their steamy cocoon. Everything was seasoned perfectly and tasted incredible.

"This is so much better than any restaurant," I said and stuffed another forkful of food in my mouth.

"You haven't eaten at my restaurant." Bobber winked.

Beyond that, there wasn't much conversation. Apparently, everyone was just as hungry as I was, and I could not overstate how wonderful each bite tasted. I never would have guessed that cooking over an open flame would produce results like that.

Cleanup was easy. Leslie used the stick that they'd used to flip the steaks to slide the hot metal grate off to the side. We tossed our paper plates into the fire and took what couldn't be burned to the dumpster by the bathrooms. The only items to wash were our knives and forks. Afterward, we sat at the picnic table, sipped scotch, and watched the fire. I enjoyed it when it popped, and a few sparks floated up in the air. The sounds of the water babbling over rocks in the river completed the peaceful evening. Perfection surrounded in simplicity. There were just some things that money couldn't buy, and I felt grateful to learn what a few of those things were.

I lifted my glass. "I'd like to thank you all. Tonight turned out to be stellar. I can't imagine being on this journey without each of you. Here's to great friends."

"To great friends," everyone said, and we tapped our cups together.

❖

We broke down camp the next morning and kept walking because that was the whole point of the journey. Four days later, we found ourselves in Erwin, Tennessee at the Nolichucky Hostel Cabins and Camping. We arrived early in the day and agreed on a much needed splurge, renting one of the four largest cabins. Bobber and Cricket rented the one right next door. Each included a kitchen, private bath, and a queen-size bed. Finally, a private evening indoors with Leslie. We had four walls, a roof, and an epically wonderful locking door. The best part, Bobber and Cricket craved an evening to themselves as much as we did.

After our showers, we stepped outside with our bundle of laundry and noticed that most of the other hikers, including Bobber and Cricket, were climbing into the shuttle van for a trip into town. I all but ran back into the cabin, dropped the bundle of dirty clothes, and grabbed my wallet. Leslie was still in the same spot on the small porch.

"Come on, let's go. We're going to miss the shuttle." I pulled the cabin door closed behind me.

"Would you mind if we didn't go to town? What do you say we get laundry started while everyone's gone, resupply here, and take a look around?" Her eyes were pleading. Given her expression, I would have done anything she asked.

Once our laundry was started, we scouted out the property hand in hand. The layout was similar to that of the hostel Leslie had drooled over on our first night sleeping together in the hotel at Dicks Creek Gap in northern Georgia. The building that housed the outfitter and resupply shop was a large log cabin sporting a deep front porch, complete with chairs and porch swings. It had reasonable hours of operation posted on a sign in the window and a handwritten note from the owner taped below about an honor system box on the porch for late arrivals. What a neat way to provide a service and not have to staff until all hours of the night. The bell chimed above the door when we entered. I watched Leslie take in the setup. She was like a kid in a candy store with a pocketful of birthday money.

Hiking wares took up two thirds of the building. Backpacks, ground cloths, food bags, water filtration systems, stoves, metal food cups, water bottles, and the like. The packs hung from floor to ceiling on pegs protruding from the wall. Tents, sleeping pads, and sleeping bags lined another wall with a ten-by-ten square of fake grass spread out on the floor. A small sign read, Tent Tryout Zone

"That's an ingenious idea." I pointed the area out to Leslie.

"You're not kidding. What a great way to know what you're buying and how to set it up."

The store didn't have the vast selection of an REI, but they carried a little bit of everything, and what they had appeared to be quality gear at decent prices. There were a couple of aisles dedicated to hiking boots and another couple for clothing and rain gear. It was an impressive setup.

"What is it about this that speaks to you?" I asked.

"I don't know how to explain it. It's the one thing that keeps calling to me. Like, I'd get to stay on the trail and still earn some money. I don't want to end up like my mom and my grandma."

"Hi, can I help you?" someone asked from behind us.

Leslie spun around. "Are you the owner?"

"I'm one of them. My husband, Charlie, is driving the shuttle into town. I'm Faith, how can I help?"

"I've been looking at a hostel that's for sale up in Pennsylvania and wonder if you wouldn't mind answering some questions?" Leslie said.

"Lucky for you, everyone's in town. Whatcha got for me?" Faith asked.

"Well, what's it like, running a place like this? Is there enough time in the day? Are you glad that you did it?"

I had plenty of questions of my own, but this was Leslie's vision, and I didn't want to take over.

"Most days, it's pretty easygoing. We place orders for the equipment as needed, and it all comes from the same supplier to keep costs down. The fresh vegetables and eggs I get from local farmers, and the lunch meat comes from the deli here in town. I spend a few hours in the morning making sandwiches and such. Let's see, what else? We have a few employees. We own six acres in all. There's an acre out back that two of our employees have campers set up on. We give them a break on the rent in exchange for some extra help cleaning up the bunkhouse, cabins, and emptying trash cans. Charlie does the mowing and keeps the place looking nice. All in all, we're glad we did it."

"Do you get any time off? Vacations?" I asked.

"Oh sure. The employees cover if I have errands to run or things I need to do, and each year, we take a week here and there to get away. We're closed for a few months in the winter, too, so we use that time for some fun and some projects that otherwise don't get done."

"And is it lucrative? Would you be comfortable sharing any rough numbers?" I asked. Leslie looked over at me and smiled. I hoped she wasn't upset that I'd jumped in on the conversation.

"We make a nice living. We could probably make more, but we try to keep the prices reasonable for the hikers, especially the thru-hikers. They're a different breed, and while they're strangers when they arrive, much like you gals, they're still part of the AT family, so we try to treat them like family." The bell chimed over the door, and two hikers came in. Faith looked over in their direction, then back to us. "Anything else you need, just let me know, and feel free to take a look around the property. The door codes for the bunkhouse and the big bathrooms are all the same: five, two, three, four."

"We'll do that. Thank you," Leslie said. After Faith stepped away, Leslie turned to me. "How about a sub and something to drink while we walk around?"

Not so long ago, during the days of my corporate life, I typically ate a small salad every day for lunch. I had to keep my calories in check since my only exercise occurred each morning on the treadmill while sipping my strawberry and kale smoothie. My how my life had changed while out on the trail. The thought of a hoagie roll stuffed with ham, hard salami, turkey, and provolone, then topped with lettuce, tomato, and Italian dressing made my stomach rumble and my mouth water in anticipation.

We each picked out a spectacularly overstuffed sub and decided on a drink. Leslie chose fresh-brewed Lipton sun tea, and I opted for a lemonade. I folded the wrapper down around my sub so I could cradle a treasure in each hand. My food obsession was going to have to get under control when this hike was over. Else, I'd need to be rolled wherever I might need to go.

Once we left the outfitters with food and drinks, we walked out the back, behind the big store, and swapped our laundry from the washer to the dryer. From there, we spotted the large bunkhouse that was easily the size of the store. We peeked inside. It was a rectangular building with bunkbeds perpendicular to the walls and spaced about three feet apart. Each bunk sported hooks for packs, and the top bunks had canvas pouches on the side rail for shoes or other items that would otherwise typically be stashed beneath a bed. The bathrooms, complete with shower, toilet, and a wide, one sink countertop and mirror, were just inside the entrance, one on the right and another on the left. Again, it was well-thought-out and efficient. More and more, I was beginning to understand Leslie's pull to running something like this. It seemed manageable, and watching her excitement added to my enthusiasm.

There were trash and recycle cans scattered everywhere along the paths of the property. We tossed the sub wrappers in the trash, and after dumping our ice into nearby bushes, we put our wax-covered cardboard cups in the recycle bin on our way to the bathrooms and showers for the RV area.

"This is just like the shower setup at big campgrounds," Leslie said when we entered the building.

I had to take her word for it since I'd never been to a campground in my life. The structure was a huge concrete block, rectangular-shaped, with a gender on each side and a gender-neutral space in the center. The women's side had four stalls, five showers, two changing areas, and a long counter with three sinks spaced far enough for each person to have room for a bag, hair dryer, or anything else. There was a mirror from splash guard to ceiling, the full length of the countertop. The floor was texture-coated concrete with drains strategically spaced throughout. It was shiny and clean, without the icky grout lines of similarly tiled spaces. Again, the owners did an amazing job planning for wear and upkeep.

"If you were at boarding schools and stuff, you've probably never been to a big campground, have you?" Leslie asked.

"Having not camped had nothing to do with being at boarding school. I've never been to a campground until this year and this hike. My youth never included Girl Scouts, there were no summer camps, nothing in my past that required parental interaction. My parents were more about tuition and avoidance."

"I'm glad you're here, but your parents suck, big time." Leslie snagged my hand and pulled me out of the camp bathing space.

We walked the RV loop. Each gravel pad included a picnic table, firepit, water, and electricity. The tent area was a separate loop, with level sand spots and included water, a picnic table, and a firepit. Finally, we made our way to the cabins: the four large ones that included a queen bed, kitchenette, small sitting area, and a private bathroom. The other eight shared a nearby community bath and shower house similar to the campsites. Each loop had a small pavilion with four to six picnic tables. All in all, it was a very well-thought-out design.

"This place is amazing." Leslie stood off the side of the trail and looked around. "Thanks for hanging back to check it out with me."

"It really is quite the setup." I wrapped my arm around her waist. There was something she'd said at the store, just before we'd met Faith, that had stuck with me, begging for an answer. "What did you mean earlier when you said you didn't want to end up like your mom and grandma?"

She was quiet for a moment. I felt her draw in a deep breath, then she finally spoke. "My mom worked two to three jobs to pay for our tiny apartment and keep food on the table. The jobs were hard on her body, hard on her spirit, and she hated them. Sometimes, she'd come home and I knew she'd been crying. She never complained to me, but I had ears, and I heard her talk to Grandma about how hard it was to just survive day to day. She worked first shift at a factory for the main job and cleaned office buildings on the weekends or some nights after dinner when my homework was done. She was always so tired. Then, after my mom was killed, my grandma had to go back to work until the settlement came in. Working was hard on her, too, and she was always tired and sad. She died a few weeks after everything was settled. They said it was a stroke. It hit her when she was sleeping. I don't want to live like that. I don't want to hate life. I don't want to die miserable."

It was the most Leslie had really shared about her mother. I wasn't raised with money issues and couldn't relate, but I certainly empathized. Sue had talked about money struggles when we'd first met and how she'd had to work two jobs when her kids were younger. I worked my one job day and night. I couldn't imagine having two, let alone with children.

"If you don't mind me asking, how was your mother killed?"

"At the factory. Grandma filed a civil suit. They'd installed some new equipment on the line, and it wasn't working right. The vendor sent someone in, and it was supposed to be fixed, but the electrical part wasn't installed properly. She had her hand on some part of the machine, the floor was wet from a tank leak on the line next to her, and when she pressed the power button, she got all the juice. The kill switch wasn't installed right, either, and they couldn't cut the power right away. She died right there on the line."

"That's awful." I pulled her into a hug.

She held me close. "When I found her trail diary, it was like meeting an entirely different person. She looked so happy when she was on the trail. The exact opposite of the exhausted person I grew up with. I mean, she was a good mom and did help me with my homework and let me cook, but she never looked happy, at least, not like she does in those photos. I think that's why I got so into hiking after Grandma died, and I rediscovered Mom's diary when I was cleaning up. I also think it's why running a hostel like this speaks to me. I'm miserable in the offseason, working for minimum wage just like my mom and grandma. I don't want to live like that. I need a life that doesn't work me to death."

I understood what she was saying. I'd certainly noticed the difference in my health since I was no longer in the office each day. At work, I was always stressed. I was pulled in twenty different directions and dealing with this crisis or that. My chest felt tight and my face flush from elevated heart rate and adrenaline. I'd never thought anything about it until it disappeared. I hadn't felt any of those symptoms since the start of my hike. Now, I could draw a full breath and rarely heard my heartbeat, and when I did, I was usually recovering from an epic orgasm.

If I'd thought she'd accept it, I would have bought the hostel in Pennsylvania for her, but after our argument over clothes and the hotel bill, I was certain I knew the answer to that idea. "You've mentioned your mom's settlement a few times. Have you had an attorney evaluate it to see what your options are?"

"No, I figured I'd dig into it once this hike is over."

"I have no doubt the right hostel will be waiting when you're ready." I nuzzled against her.

"Crap, I didn't think about that. What if the Pennsylvania one sells? Do you have someone you trust who could look at my mom's stuff?"

"Most of my career was in finance and contracts. I'd be happy to take a look. Or if you'd rather it not be me, then, yes, I do have others that I trust."

She pulled back. "You'd do that for me?" Her face lit up. "The documents are in a safety deposit box, but I have pictures of each page on my phone."

"Well, if something like this feels right, let's take a look and see what your options are. And if owning a hostel ends up not being what you thought it would be, it's an asset you can put back on the market and sell."

She beamed. Her eyes sparkled, and her dimples were on full display. I would have done anything to see her that happy every single day. She deserved it. "I could definitely find happiness at a place like this, but if one ingredient is missing, it will throw everything off-kilter."

A breeze blew my hair across my face. Leslie hooked the flyaway strands with her finger and swept it back where it belonged. "In case you didn't catch that, the one necessary ingredient would be you." She caressed my cheek. "I want a future that includes you."

The moment her words were spoken, my breath became lodged in my chest until I felt the crushing need to exhale. I did, then sucked in another lungful. How on earth was I supposed to respond to that? I wasn't sure what I wanted for my future.

One thing I did know, more and more, was that I saw Leslie as a part of it, but… "We talked about this. My life's in Hartford."

"Is it? Sure, you have your house and your friend, Sue, but do you really have a life in Hartford?"

I listened to her words. Swam in them. Mulled them. Exhaled and sucked in another gulp of air. Sadly, she had a point. What did I really have in Hartford now that my career was gone? "Could you ever see yourself with me there?" I asked, hoping she'd thought more about it since our conversation earlier.

"Without a doubt, I can see myself with you, but I doubt I could be happy in Hartford. Amber, cities suffocate me. It's only in the woods, on the trail, that I feel like I can breathe. Could you ever see yourself with me in the biggest, grandest city I can offer? It would be a trail city like this, with small stores, trail magic, and a setup like here. I'd cash in every penny of my mom's settlement in a minute if I thought buying something like this would keep you with me."

Her eyes were so sincere, and I already cared for her more than I'd ever cared for anyone. I'd buy the hostel in Pennsylvania in a minute if I thought I could live in Tiny Town, USA. Could I let go of my big-city life for life in a one-stop, Appalachian Trail town? Sure, they were all friendly enough, but my social life started after seven or eight in the evening and involved a town car and high-end dining while most of these towns rolled up the sidewalks at five or six. Where would we go for a fine meal or drinks or dancing?

Were those things more important than being with Leslie? That was the million dollar question, wasn't it? Would living a small-town life with Leslie be enough? The mere thought of taking a leap of faith like that was absolutely terrifying.

"Being with you sounds wonderful. Can you accept a firm maybe? Let's not force a decision today."

"We have more than fifteen hundred miles for me to convince you. I'm all in on a definite maybe." She squeezed my shoulders. "As long as you're not saying no, there's hope for a future."

"There's hope." I squeezed her waist and leaned my head into her shoulder. "Of that, I have no doubt."

She leaned into me, too. Leslie was as understanding and as graceful as I needed her to be. In the same breath, I hoped I was as encouraging and as honest as she needed me to be. I couldn't flip my world on its axis and claim to be all in on her boondocks world any more than she could claim to be all in on my city life. I cared enough about her to compromise, and she seemed willing to do the same. We just had to figure out what that compromise was.

We collected our laundry, shopped for the next four or five days of hiking, snagged something we could cook for dinner, and then retired to our cabin. I needed some alone time with Leslie, away from the future hostel, away from the RV and tent pads, and away from anyone close enough to hear me beg her for what I wanted her to do to me.

CHAPTER SIXTEEN

Daytime temperatures had been in the low seventies, which sounded perfect for hiking, but carting around twenty-some pounds on my back, often uphill, made seventy feel like eighty-five, and it was humid. Awfully humid. It'd been three days since we'd restocked, and I'd last showered—an anticlimactic event that occurred in a small campground instead of a hotel—and with the still, humid air, I felt like the character Pigpen from *Peanuts*. The only difference was that his stench floated around him, whereas mine stuck to me, inviting more dirt and bugs to add to the layers of sweaty, greasy grime. It was so bad that I'd run out of wet wipes, and my deodorant was no longer helping.

We'd traversed one hundred and twenty-five miles over the seven days since we'd departed the hostel in Erwin, TN, and today we'd be rewarded with a hotel stay in what was known as the friendliest town on the Appalachian Trail.

Damascus was a small town tucked away in the hills of southwest Virginia. At just over eight hundred locals, there were as many residents as in some decent sized, multi-story apartment complexes in larger cities. It was known as Trail Town, USA because five different trails intersected on the edge of town. Luckily, there were vacancies at one of the hotels that boasted about their perfect reviews. I reserved us an affordable room with nearby laundry and food options. Leslie was all in. Bonus, the post office was close by, and with any luck, there was another box from Sue waiting for me.

The four of us emerged from the woods and made our way onto a wood-chipped path into the park on the edge of town. Midway through the well-kept oasis, the path made its way beneath a wooden arch with "Damascus, Virginia" carved into the uppermost board. Bobber had made some crude, off-color remark, and we were all laughing. I'd no sooner walked beneath the arch when I froze in my tracks to the point that Cricket walked into me from behind.

"Hey, First Class, warn a girl before hitting the brakes. Come on, step it up," she said.

Still, I stood there, staring ahead. I would have recognized that round face framed with bottle red hair anywhere. "Sue? Is that really you?"

"Amber? Wow, honey, you look different. Not sure I've ever seen you dressed like that." Hearing her say my name as Amburr nearly had me in nostalgic, homesick tears.

One of my trail boxes was on the bench next to where she'd been sitting. I shed my pack and all but fell into her arms. "What are you doing here?"

"I decided to deliver this box in person." She wrapped her arms around me. "Um, sugar, I hate to say this, but you's a little ripe. You seriously need a shower."

I half laughed, half choked on tears. "You're telling me." I released her and stepped back. "Come here, I'd like you to meet everyone."

"You mean I actually get to meet that little cutie who makes your face light up?"

I beamed. I couldn't contain my excitement. My dear friend and my everything person were finally meeting. Yes, Leslie was definitely my everything person. I was overjoyed for my two worlds to collide.

"Sue, this is Leslie, trail name Munch." I had to release her hand so she could shake Leslie's. Bobber and Cricket stood off to the side. "And this is Cricket, also known as Marie, and Bobber, aka Becca. Everyone, this is my friend, Sue, from Hartford."

Hellos were exchanged. Leslie tucked her left hand in mine and used her right to shake Sue's hand. "It's very nice to meet you, Sue. I've heard wonderful things."

"It's nice to meet you, too. You've given my friend a new smile. Anyone who can make her light up like that is all right in my book." Sue patted our joined hands and then let Leslie's go.

"I'm over the moon happy to see you, but you didn't travel all the way to Virginia just to bring me a box. What's going on? Is someone sick? Was there an accident? How are Cass and the girls?"

"Slow down, everyone's fine, just fine, but you're right, I didn't come to Virginia simply to bring you a box. Our services have been requested. Specifically, your skills are needed, and let's just say they know you need me. Something's happened at the off—"

"Hello, Amber." I spun in the direction of the voice. Grayson, decked out in his corporate best, was making his way across the grass. There was a shiny black Suburban parked on the street behind him. A driver stood next to the rear door, at the ready. "What are you, training for the Ironman or something? Not exactly what I expected you to be doing with your free time. I've never seen you quite so sweaty."

I ignored his comment. "Grayson."

"We need to talk," he said.

"There's nothing to talk about. In case you've forgotten, I no longer work for you." I hoisted my pack over one shoulder. "If you don't mind, we have reservations, and I'm told I need a shower."

Leslie, Bobber, and Cricket all followed my lead. Sue wrapped her hand around my forearm and gave me a little squeeze. I turned back to look at her.

"Sugar, Kelly walked out and took her entire team with her. Stan left, too. I know that you know the merger was timed to the fiscal year-end, so the quarterly and annual reports on the old books are due. You're the only one who can pull all that together in the time that's left for reporting before fines are levied." She kept ahold of my arm.

Cricket leaned in close. "Who are Kelly and Stan?" she asked quietly.

"Kelly was the CFO and Stan the COO. They'd each been on my team for more than five years." I aimed my eye daggers at Grayson. "I was walked out before I knew who'd made the cut. I take it they don't care for Carl's management style? Is the misogynistic asshole still sitting in my chair?"

"Ho-lee shit," Cricket said, "the entire accounting department walked out without filing the year-end earnings reports? That's a great big, giant fuck you if I've ever heard of one." Leave it to my fellow MBA to understand the impact of what had happened.

I turned to her, smiling. "Right?"

Grayson stood next to Sue. "As of now, Carl's still at the helm. I can't lose the entire C-suite in the same week, not right after the merger. It sends the wrong message to our investors. You know what will happen if they pull out."

"I'll say it sends the wrong message. The message being, you picked the *wrong* CEO to lead the way after the merger," Cricket muttered, and I couldn't help but grin.

Grayson turned to her. "You seem to have a lot to say. Who are you?"

Thankfully, she ignored him and just stood there staring with her arms crossed. I bet she was a force in the business world.

"If Carl's still holding the reins, I'm not the least bit interested in stepping in to save your ass," I said to Grayson.

Leslie huffed out a half laugh and wrapped her arm around my shoulder. "Take that, suit."

The vein in his forehead popped out, and he glared at me. "Goddamn it, I fought for you, Amber. I was outvoted, but I fought for you."

"Is that supposed to make me feel better? Apparently, you didn't fight hard enough. I exceeded every goal, and you replaced me with Carl Turner. Not only that, you signed him on at four, *that's four*, times my salary. You can go straight to hell."

"I can't believe you'd turn your back on the company that made you," he said. "You were a nobody before I took you under my wing."

"Don't you dare." I stepped forward and shoved my finger in his face. "I did the work. I made my name mean something. I made that company mean something, and I didn't turn my back on it, I was all in. I gave you everything I had. You repaid me by walking me out the door."

Anger flared in his eyes, and his face turned deep red. Sue tugged on his arm until he turned to face her.

"Hey, you're not being helpful. I thought you were going to wait by the car and let me handle this," she said sternly. "She'll never help if you get all red and puffy."

He sighed, and his shoulders dropped. "You're right. I'm sorry. Amber, I regret not fighting harder. Yes, Carl's proven to be a challenge. He's an asshole, okay? Is that what you need to hear before you'll help us out? He's made a mess of things, and a lot of good people have walked out the door. I'm begging you. Financials are due, and I have no idea what's been done to complete them. You're the only one I could think of to come in and know what the numbers should look like. You're the only one who can meet the deadline."

"Kelly and I had everything ready before I submitted the merger packet. Did you try to talk to her? She's a reasonable person," I asked.

"She slammed the door in my face. I'm telling you, just having you in the building will calm things down. Amber, everyone's pushing the board to bring you back." He ran his fingers through his graying hair. "I can't fix what happened, but I'm hoping you'll help us out of this mess. Please, tell me what it will take, and I'll make it happen. Sue's in. What'd ya say?"

It was a mistake. Everyone's pushing the board to bring you back. How I'd longed to hear those words. I turned to Sue. "What did he promise to get you back? I thought you were happily done."

"Money, what else? My baby girl's asked for a few more months in rehab, but the insurance won't cover it. It's eight thousand dollars a month. Amber, she's doin' real good. Cass and the girls have even gone up to see her. If we do this, Grayson offered to cover the costs for up to six months and add enough to get her set up when she's done."

"I knew you wouldn't consider coming back without Sue. Name your price. I'll get you whatever you want." Grayson stood tall.

Leslie leaned closer. "If you ask for a million, we could buy that hostel."

He perked up. "Done. Amber, I need your help."

"I was kidding," Leslie said. "Don't go."

"I'm not kidding. You know what it says about a company when they're fined by the SEC. Too much has happened in too short of time, and we need to stabilize. I have the corporate jet waiting on the tarmac thirty minutes away, ready to go. Please, say you'll help."

It'd been a long time since I'd seen him plead for help. Cricket squeaked behind me. I turned to her, and she gave me a grimace. I wished I knew what that meant.

"Take a moment to talk it over. I'll be waiting by the car." Grayson turned and walked toward the Suburban.

I sighed. He had hit the heartstrings. "Sue, why didn't you say something? I'd have covered anything you needed. We're a team. I've got you."

She leaned in close. Grayson wasn't far enough away not to overhear, so I understood when her words came out a hushed whisper. "Honey, you done already played Santa Claus. I can pay the bill, but if he insists on doing so to say thank you, then let him. Sugar, if you do this, I'll be at your side no matter what. In your heart, you know you'll have regrets if you don't see this thing through. You were sitting at the head of the table for that last quarter. You're the CEO on file. Besides, you didn't put all that work into the company, then the merger, just to stand back and let it all fall apart. Pettiness like that's beneath you. It's time to choose your path, and doing this might just help you figure out where it goes."

I kept my voice low. "I'm so angry. They don't deserve my help."

"I know you're angry. Do it anyway. Like Michelle Obama says, 'When they go low, we go high.' Do it to show them what real class looks like. Do it because you're Amber fucking Shaw."

Sue knew how to get to me. She knew how to push my buttons and motivate me. She also knew how to make me see reason. Grayson was smart to bring her along. Without her, I would have told him off and been on my merry way. She was right about the filing, too. I was the CEO on record. Not only could it harm my name with the SEC, but I'd also regret being able to help and not doing so, especially if it harmed the company I'd worked so hard to build up.

"Could you all give me a minute?" I swung my pack over my shoulder and tugged on Leslie's hand. "Come here."

I pulled on her until we were a hundred feet or so away from the group. When I stopped, I turned to face her and took both of her hands.

"You're doing this, aren't you?" Leslie asked. "Why would you help him? He tossed you out the door like a sack of trash."

"Leslie, I need to go. Sue's right. Cricket's right. I took a nothing company and turned it into a titan. That merger was my baby. If the investors pull out and it all falls apart right now, it'll have all been for nothing. This is about my name and my reputation. It's my legacy."

"Fuck them. Stay with me. This…is your legacy. You're a thru-hiker now. Amber, we have more photos to take. There's almost five hundred and fifty miles in Virginia alone. What about Tinker Ridge and Brush Mountain and Apple Orchard Mountain? What about Wind Rock, Cove Mountain, or Angel's Rest? What about the incredible McAfee Knob. You'll miss those shots." Leslie dug into a pocket in her pack and pulled out her mom's diary stuffed full of the old photos. "This has become our thing. There are more photos for us to take. Please, I'm begging you. Stay."

"I'll come back, and we'll get those shots. I'll meet up with you somewhere ahead on the trail. It would just be for a few days…a couple of weeks at most. The deadline to file is coming up quickly."

Leslie turned away. "You say you'll come back, but I'm worried that if you go, you won't want to. You'll go right back to your fancy diamond membership life, and I'll never see you again. Don't go, I don't want to lose you."

My chest tightened, and tears stung my eyes. "No, that's not true, that's not going to happen. You won't lose me. They don't want me back. This is a onetime gig. Hey, what if you came with me? Hell, we can all go, if that's what you want. The jet seats eight. Don't you have a year to accomplish a thru-hike? Come with me, and we'll come back together."

"I can't, and you know it. Your legacy is important to you, just like my legacy is important to me. People are charting out my hike. I can't just fall off the grid for two weeks. My legacy is here. I'm thru-hiking the last of the scenic eleven. I'm working to join an elite group of people. I can't up and leave the trail. If I do, I'd feel like a section hiker, like Bobber and Cricket. It's not the same accomplishment."

"You can't take a few days? No one would know. We'll come right back and pick up at this exact spot."

"I'd know, and besides, you'll be working around the clock. It's not like I'd get to see you. And what happens when they beg you to stay longer? What happens when they offer you your old job back at four times the pay? You'll decide to stay, and I'll lose everything I've worked so hard to achieve."

"I promise you, that won't happen."

"You really shouldn't make promises you can't keep." Her jaw muscles were tense, and there was a harsh look in her eyes.

"I need to do this one thing to keep it all from falling apart. Please understand."

"I understand perfectly. You want your Hartford life more than you want a life out here with me, and Amber Shaw doesn't compromise. It doesn't matter what I want as long as you get what you want. Tell me I'm wrong." She bent down, put the diary away, and started removing items from her pack. "Go if you're going to go. I need to swap the big sleeping bag and pad for the ones in your pack. The new gear won't fit in my old tent." The guarded Leslie from the airplane was back in full force.

"Would you rather keep the larger tent?" I asked.

"Only if it comes with you in it." She stood and held out the two items.

Tears fell, and there was nothing I could do to stop them. I opened my pack and exchanged the single pad and bag for the double. Leslie stuffed them in her pack and zipped it closed.

"It looks like Sue and the suit are waiting for you at the car." Leslie swung her pack up on her shoulder.

"I don't want to leave things like this. Please, come with me."

"I don't want to leave things like this, either. Please, stay. We have a king-sized bed calling our names. We could spend the night making love."

"If it were only that simple." I leaned forward until our foreheads touched.

"It is that simple. Amber, you can't go back, only forward." She pulled away. "I really hope I see you in a couple of weeks. If not, I'll know what you chose." She stared at me for a moment, then simply turned and walked across the grass toward town.

"I'll call you tonight."

She spun, walking backward. "Only if it's to tell me you're coming back." She brushed tears off her cheeks and spun back around and kept going. Bobber took off after her.

Tears streamed down my cheeks while I stuffed our inflatable double bed into my pack. I felt a hand on my shoulder. I popped up, hoping Leslie had come back. It was Cricket.

"Are you leaving the dream team?" she asked.

"Just for a week or so. I'll keep in touch so I know where to meet up with you when I'm done."

"Munch won't take your leaving well. Don't worry, we'll take care of her." Cricket took my hand and tugged on it twice. "Can I just say how fucking cool is it that you have a private jet waiting for you on the runway? God, I wish I could come with you."

I pulled her into a hug. "I wish you were coming with me, too. I have no doubt that we could knock out the reports in record time."

"Amber, they were fools to let you go in the first place," she said in my ear.

"That's kind of you to say."

"That said, make sure that you do come back. If you don't, you'll break her heart. Without a doubt, she's in love with you."

Leslie and I hadn't talked about love. I didn't know what to say.

"Hey, what are you going to ask for, ya know, for going and doing the favor? Do you think he'd really pay you a million dollars for one week's work?" She released her arms and stepped back.

"I'm not sure yet. It depends on what's involved," I answered honestly.

"Well, whatever you decide, make sure to multiply that number by four. Hell, make it six. It serves them right."

I nodded and forced a smile, even though I didn't much feel like smiling at the moment. Cricket hooked her arm in mine and walked with me to the car. I tossed my pack into the back and climbed inside. Grayson could choke on how awesome I smelled. When we passed the hotel, I caught sight of Leslie standing outside talking to Bobber. She was still wiping tears from her eyes. Fresh tears of my own threatened to spill over. I blinked them back. I was not going to cry in front of Sue and Grayson. My mother had taught me better. I could be strong when I needed to be.

The flight took about an hour and a half, and within another half hour I was standing in my foyer, backpack in one hand and elevator keys in the other. I dropped everything and tried to call Leslie. It rang five times and went to voice mail.

"Hey, it's me. We landed safely, and I'm home. I miss you so much already. I wish you'd answer. I was hoping to hear your voice. Call if you'd like. Anytime, day or night." I sighed and held the phone against my ear, not wanting to disconnect. Voice mail timed out and ended the call for me. What had I done?

I stood in the shower for a long time after rinsing the soap off my body. I let the water beat on my skin until it was no longer piping hot. My Chinese takeout, reminiscent of the day I'd been terminated, showed up shortly after I was dressed. Piping hot, sugar-covered doughnut holes pair nicely with scotch. I filled my tray with small white cartons, poured myself a second drink, and made my way into the living room. I couldn't get into the office until the next morning because accounts had to be recreated, which meant it was time to resume the self-pity movie-watching binge that had started this whole mess.

The guide screen popped up when I turned on the TV. The selection was still on the movie *Wild*. I'd watched it one last time the night before my flight to Amicalola Falls. I wasn't in the mood to watch it again. I flipped through the channels until I found something that wasn't a romantic comedy and didn't involve hiking. The Grammys were on a local network station. That would work. I welcomed the distraction and opened my container of kung pao chicken. *Welcome home.*

CHAPTER SEVENTEEN

I really thought I'd be more excited to get home, but nothing about being at home felt right. The house was too big and at the same time, too small. It was too quiet while also too noisy. Bottom line, it no longer felt like home. I wondered if it ever had.

Without Leslie's body up against me and her arms holding me close, sleep was fitful. I woke up restless and forced myself to get back into my old routine. The treadmill now seemed like a ridiculous invention, and even with the adjusting incline feature as part of my program, I felt like it wasted forty-five minutes of my life.

Nothing felt right, nothing felt normal. Even my strawberry and kale smoothie seemed off. It no longer hit the spot. I dumped it down the drain and broke into one of the yet-to-be mailed trail boxes, craving my AT breakfast of oatmeal with cream powder, raisins, and walnuts. I even used my camp stove since I still had the fuel canister that I'd had to leave behind when I flew to Georgia. The concoction smelled so good that my mouth watered.

I decided to eat outside on my rooftop patio. Titanium cup in hand, I sat at the picnic table that I hadn't previously realized was even out there and dug in. It would have been almost perfect except the city noises ruined the atmosphere, replacing birdsong and the sound leaves made when the wind rustled them gently. Not only that, but I longed for the morning chat with Leslie, something I'd come to associate with this sweet morning meal. One wasn't quite the same without the other. I missed the woman who'd pulled me out of my guarded existence. She'd helped me see who I was and who I wanted to be. I missed the woman who taught me to slow down and play. I missed Leslie.

I checked my phone for the hundredth time that morning. Two texts from Grayson and three from Sue but nothing back from Leslie. No texts. No calls. Not even a broken heart emoji. I reminded myself that I was the one who'd left, not her. But it was a short-term blip, wasn't it? A blip if they didn't offer me my old job back. But what if they did? Surely, she'd come around and give Hartford a try. Better question was, could I go back? Or was Leslie right, and I could only go forward? If I could go back, would I really want to? Being away from all of that stress had me feeling like a new woman.

I shook it away; none of it mattered. They'd picked Carl, and I wouldn't return if I wasn't the CEO.

I stared into space, feeling pulled in two different directions: one path my legacy and the expectations that went with it, and the other a path of openness and honesty and the unknown. The unknown had always been an unwelcome concept. After all, I was a planner. Somehow, with Leslie next to me, the unknown had morphed into something exciting and full of possibilities.

But what if they begged me to come back and met all my demands? Was I prepared with a list? I might consider going back if they begged. Jesus, I needed to stop this wishy-washy nonsense. I was putting the cart before the horse. Being back was definitely just a short-term blip. I'd go into the office and get the work done so I could get back to Leslie and the trail. We still had several months to figure out who we were to each other and how something between us could work.

I gave myself a good eye roll. I didn't need several more months to figure anything out. It'd been less than twenty-four hours away from her, and I already felt such a deep, inescapable heartache that had no cure. I thought back and couldn't recall this kind of profound sadness when Tiffany had moved out, or anyone else for that matter. What I had with Leslie was unlike anything I'd had with anyone else, of that I was certain.

Showered and dressed, I collected my things, slid behind the wheel of my car, and drove to the office. With the morning traffic, my drive took more than twenty-five minutes. It probably would have been faster if I'd walked. I shook my head and chuckled. I'd commuted to the same building for more than fifteen years, I'd been the CEO for seven, and not once had I ever considered walking to work. Jesus, had blaring horns always been so loud? I turned up the radio. Finally, I whipped into the parking garage and snaked up the levels. When I reached the blue level, I turned left and had to slam on the brakes in order to avoid hitting the Jaguar parked in the space my car had occupied those last many years. That was right. I was no longer the CEO. I backed up and made my way to guest parking.

An old familiar anxiety took ahold of my chest, blanketed in an altogether new uneasiness. I was about to walk into the building that had escorted me out. I wasn't returning as the chief executive; instead, I was a consultant, albeit a very well-paid consultant. No doubt, the smirk on my face looked like the Grinch plotting Christmas demise. I stepped into the elevator and through muscle memory, aimed for the floor that held my old corner suite.

I had to stop myself. The accounting department wasn't on the top floor. I pressed the button for two stories down, and the doors closed. *Here goes nothing.*

Sue was standing there when the elevator doors opened. She had two cups of coffee, one in each hand, and the cheesiest smile on her face. She was the only bright spot in my time away from the trail, my time away from Leslie.

"My, oh my, what a difference a day makes. Look at you, all cleaned up, smellin' pretty, and dressed for success. Thought maybe you'd like your usual. Grayson's been down here six times already, and you're not actually due in for another half hour." She handed me a cup.

"How long have you been standing here?"

"Seriously? Less than a minute. You always arrive promptly at six thirty. I could set my watch by it, which means I arrive at six twenty-five." She hooked her arm in mine. "Come on, we're set up over here."

"I pray Kelly's got it all done. Being here feels weird. It's like I'm in the Twilight Zone. I damn near parked on top of Carl's car."

"I'd have paid to see that happen." She laughed and led me into a wasteland of cubicles, apparently our temporary office. She guided me through the maze and into the conference room in the back, next to Kelly's old office.

Beth from IT walked in a few minutes later. "Excuse me, Ms. Shaw, I don't know if you remember me. I'm Beth. I'm here to get you back in the system." She set down two laptops, an armload of monitors, keyboards, and mice that were dangling from her extended pinky finger. She wiped her hand on her slacks and held it out to me. "Can I just say, we're all excited to have you back."

I shook her hand. "Of course I remember you, Beth. You were always there when I had issues. Thank you for the kind words, but I'm afraid my return is temporary."

"Your return has been the talk of the building. Everyone's hoping that the joker sitting in your office upstairs will be tossed out on his ear, and you'll be back permanently." She leaned a little closer. "It's been a colossal shit show since you left."

A throat cleared behind us. Beth looked over my shoulder, and her face flushed beet red. "I should probably get your stations set up. I'll be ready for you to test your credentials in just a bit."

"Thank you." I winked at her, and she smiled.

"I'm glad you're back. Punctual as always," Grayson said from the door. "Thank you, again, for agreeing to do this."

I turned slowly and channeled my mother's cold exterior. "I'm not back. I'm a consultant, merely passing through."

"If I had my way, you'd be back. You'd be upstairs where you belong." He was in his space now, his confident swagger on full display. I half expected him to flop in a chair at the conference table and start chatting as if nothing had ever happened.

"Let's not do this dance. I'm here to accomplish one task, and when that's done, I'm gone."

"We'll see. I've got a week or so to change your mind."

"You lost the leverage of loyalty when you walked me out the door, and as far as I know, the board hasn't called for Carl's termination, thus, there's no vacancy upstairs. Now, if you'll let me get to work, I'll be out of your hair in no time."

Was that sadness that flashed across his face? Like me, he'd never been one to show his emotions. The only emotion that ever broke through was the frustration that was hard for him to hide when his face reddened, and that vein popped out on his forehead.

"I'd like an update before end of day." He turned and disappeared.

"Ms. Shaw, I'm ready to test your access," Beth said from behind me. "You just went toe to toe with the chairman of the board. Damn, you're such a badass."

Sue chuckled. "You've been back all of five minutes, and I see that your momma has taken over your spirit. Cold as ice. Definitely got that hard-ass CEO hat on today."

"Correction, hard-ass consultant hat," I said.

The information I'd put together for the merger packet looked to have been hidden or deleted from the system, at least within the accounting department's files. Beth went to work on recovering my archived files, but in the meantime, Sue and I simply had to recompile the data and create the final quarterly report, along with the glossy, colorful annual report for the board and the SEC.

Putting the information together was more difficult than I remembered. Not because I'd forgotten what to do or where to get the data, but because my focus wasn't there. Here and there, day after day, I'd catch myself staring at the numbers, but my mind was out on the trail. I wondered how many miles Leslie, Bobber, and Cricket had covered. I'd been back for four days, which meant they could have traversed anywhere from sixty to more than eighty, depending on how hard they'd pushed. Knowing Leslie's pace when she was deep in thought, it could be closer to a hundred. My body was already sick of sitting in a chair all day, and my muscles twitched to be out there with them.

I'd also missed one of the photos from Leslie's mom's journal. I knew this because a text arrived the day before, shortly after lunch, with a photo attached. I saved it to my AT album and stared at it until my screen timed out and turned black. The text was from Cricket instead of Leslie, not that Cricket understood the significance of the picture or the pose, but I was happy she thought to share it with me.

Leslie held the *Rocky* pose that her mom was so fond of. Her smile was forced, and her eyes were filled with sadness. More than anything, her expression made me want to reach out and pull her into my arms. I hadn't heard from her yet. Deep down, I understood her silence. After all, the ball was in my court. I was the one who'd left and the longer I was home, the more I struggled with what to do. Was it really so easy for her to cut off all communication? Meanwhile, I sat there like a teenager, checking my phone every five minutes, hoping it would ring, and her name would pop up on the screen. I missed her with all my heart, and even those words didn't convey the depth of my feelings. Was this love? One thing for certain, I wanted the chance to find out.

"Sugar, you done got lost again, haven't you?" Sue's voice pulled me out of my thoughts.

"Yeah, sorry, I was just thinking."

"I know you was just thinking, cause the clickety clack on the keyboard slows, then stops altogether. You've been chewing on something on and off since you've been back, and it became much worse after yesterday's lunch. I'm about done waiting for you to talk to me." Sue rose from her chair at the far end of the table and sat in the chair next to me. "Tell me, was I wrong to come get you?"

"No, you weren't wrong. I needed to come back, and you know it. It is my name on the filing. Besides, I needed to know."

She folded her arms and leaned back in her chair. She remained quiet, and I knew she was waiting for more. It was something she'd done for as long as I'd known her. When we'd started working together so many years ago, it hadn't taken me long to realize that Sue had magical powers. It was like she was always playing a game of chess, and we were all just pieces on the board. She knew all the moves. Hell, she knew all the answers before a question was even asked. It was a gift that she'd chosen not to flaunt. Instead, she'd been content to be the master behind the curtain, or the coach standing on the sidelines, so to speak, and without a doubt, I was the player that had all the tools, and now it was a question of execution. Could I put everything together and come up with the answer she'd been privy to all along? Or would I flounder and need her guidance? Her expressions would tell me which scale I tipped. *I swear she knows me better than I've ever known myself.*

"Out there, I ignored it, just swept it all under the rug. I knew I had to deal with it, and I thought that maybe I had. Then, when I saw you and Grayson in the park, I realized that I still hadn't, and now that I'm back, I feel pulled in different directions." I turned my chair to face her, leaned back, and crossed one leg over the other.

She raised her eyebrows as if waiting for more.

"Being told I was too deep in the weeds and promoted beyond my skill set was a hard pill to swallow. Those words hurt. I was angry, and my ego was—"

"Kicked square in the balls?" Her pronunciation of balls was quite exaggerated, with a W somewhere midstream that made me laugh more than the figure of speech.

"Well, I was going to say bruised, but, yeah, all right, let's go with kicked in the balls."

"And how has being back turned you into the rope that's being tugged on at each end?"

"Because there's a part of me that wants the best of both worlds. The board might have felt like I was too deep in the weeds, but I was good at my job, and I've been missed. I think they can now see how my style worked, or at least enough people have said as much, and quite honestly, it feels good that they have regrets."

"Grayson's been down here several times a day asking what it will take to put you back upstairs. Does that mean you're considering one of his proposals?"

"Yeah, well, that's where I find myself getting angry all over again. You'd think they could at least match Carl's salary if they really wanted me back. I think they're just stalling until I finish the annual report, and then I'll be dismissed all over again." I sat there swimming in the melancholy of the moment. Grayson had been in the conference room several times each day, trying to negotiate between me and the board. So far, I'd declined each and every one of the offers. As much as he claimed that the board didn't like Carl, they still treated me like a "less than" candidate by not even matching his contract. Not that I was sure I'd accept the position, but it would have been nice to turn down a decent offer.

"Okay, let me ask you this, if Grayson came in here right now and offered you double Carl's salary to come back and lead this place, would ya do it?" She shot me a twitch of a smile. Yep, without a doubt, she already knew the answer.

"Double Carl's salary would definitely make the statement I've been yearning for, however, that offer hasn't come in, has it, my friend? Maybe this chapter of my life is over. All I know is that when this project is complete, I'm going back to finish my hike, and by my estimate, now that Beth has restored my old files for comparison, it should be complete and submitted by end of today. Leslie might just be right. I can't go back, only forward."

"That Leslie sounds like my kinda gal. So if you're outta the building, are you outta Hartford altogether?"

"I'm not entirely sure. Coming back has me thinking that Hartford isn't my home anymore. I'm not sure it's ever been home. It's been where I was expected to live because it's where successful people live, and I wanted to be successful, didn't I? Thank you for that, Mother." I drew in a breath and allowed myself a second to choose my words. "I don't regret my success or the choices I've made, but it hasn't come without a cost, and I see that now. I'm proud of my accomplishments, but I'll share a little secret: I achieved them to impress the wrong person and lost myself along the way. I'm done doing what's expected of me. I've earned the right, and I have enough money, to do what I want to do. It's time for me to focus on a different area of my life."

Sue grinned that "I told you so" grin. "Does your momma know that you just sent her a great big giant fuck you? By the way, I like that Cricket gal, too."

"No, I haven't talked with my parents yet, but I will. They still haven't returned my call telling them I was going hiking for six months. My decision doesn't impact them, so I don't expect them to care one way or the other."

"Good on ya for breaking the chains." She cocked her head. "Where do you go from here?"

"Nothing's firm yet, but I have a little something in the works. I'll let you know once it's finalized so you can come visit. Know of anyone who might want to buy a penthouse?" I asked.

"Geez, I'd love to, but I'm a little too poor to paint and too proud to whitewash, so I'll pass."

"Great, another saying I'll never get out of my head." I nudged the wheel of her chair with my foot.

"For the record, I like the version of you that I saw coming up that trail in Virginia. You were unapologetically you. Laughing with your friends like you didn't have a care in the world." She leaned forward and reached for my hand. "I know you say that you haven't put a label on it yet, but can I just say, love looks good on you, Amber. I'm happy for you. I think you found the gal who lights you up. Whatever you two do together, it'll be amazing."

Love. It was love, wasn't it? One thing was certain. I didn't like waking up without her next to me each morning. I'm sure I had that starry-eyed look I'd seen in countless rom-coms. Was I really one of those starry-eyed people now? Based on the look Sue was giving me, I'd say that was a safe bet.

"It feels good, and I miss her with every fiber of my being."

"Then let's get this report wrapped up and get you back to your gal."

Sue and I worked late to finish everything up and submitted the final numbers well before the deadline. Grayson didn't seem too surprised when I said good-bye. Instead, he thanked me, handed me an envelope, and wished me well. I wished him the same, and it felt good to mean it. I also gave him a list of professionals I trusted to take care of the company I'd dedicated fifteen years to. No matter which direction the board went, I knew it would all work out for the best. It was a great company, and they'd make it through the transition. I left that day with my head held high. Walking away felt better this time around because this time, it was my choice, my decision.

Home didn't feel so cavernous or claustrophobic once I'd decided it wasn't much more than a short-term storage unit. I coordinated my surprise return with Cricket and called the corporate hangar about my flight. It was my turn to be waiting on a park bench when they walked into town. Cricket swore to keep my secret. Luckily, she wasn't privy to all the details surrounding the surprise. I'd be back well before we reached McAfee Knob, and as far as I knew, I'd only missed one Mom photo.

I could only hope that Leslie welcomed me back with open arms.

CHAPTER EIGHTEEN

Sue must have had the patience of a saint. How she sat on that bench waiting for me in Damascus was beyond me. I hadn't been there long, and I was a fidgety mess. Part of me wanted to rush up the trail until I found her, but that wasn't the plan, so I forced myself to stay put. After what seemed like half a day, but was probably more like an hour, I finally spotted her. I'd never been so happy to see that tie-dye bandana in my life. She'd arrived in town early, just like Cricket expected she would. There was still plenty of time for everything to work. I only hoped my gesture wasn't too over-the-top. Remaining seated and waiting for her to get closer wasn't working. I couldn't handle waiting for one more minute. I leapt from the bench and ran toward her.

The moment our eyes met, Leslie's face lit up. She froze in place, just as I had done when I'd seen Sue, but her expression had nothing to do with being a little homesick. Her jaw dropped, then a huge smile formed, and those adorable dimples were on full display. A split second later, she bolted to cover the distance between us.

"You came back," she kept repeating as she ran toward me. "You really came back!" Her eyes sparkled, and the mixture of happiness and excitement showed up in her expression better than any words could've conveyed.

She scooped me up and held me close. In that moment, I knew that being wrapped up in her arms was the only home I needed.

"I'm not just back. With you is right where I belong." I cupped her face and kissed her. She returned the kiss with unbelievable passion, and every cell in my body responded. I wrapped my legs around her waist, and she cupped my ass to hold me in place. I was definitely right where I belonged.

"Get a room," someone walking by said.

I pulled back, breaking our kiss. Leslie and I laughed through our happy tears. Slowly, she lowered me until my feet were once again on the ground.

"I missed you so much. I'm so happy to see you. I thought you were going to call. I kept checking my phone, hoping you'd call to tell me you were on your way."

"What I need to say to you shouldn't be said over the phone." I leaned forward until our foreheads touched. "I needed to see your eyes when I tell you that I'm not broken after all. As it turns out, I just hadn't met the right woman. That is, until I met you. I love you. I'm in love with you, Leslie Brown. Starry-eyed, butterflies, head over heels in love with you. I've missed you so much."

She pulled her head back and stared at me long enough that I began to think she didn't feel the same way. "Really? Are you serious?" Her eyes crinkled in the corners, and a huge smile formed. "God, I hope you're serious. I feel the same way. There were so many times when I almost said something, but I didn't want you to feel cornered, so I waited. I love you, too. Totally in love with you. I fell for you back at Stover Creek, hell, probably on the airplane, and the feelings just keep getting stronger and stronger. I don't want to be apart ever again, even if it means we live in Hartford. I'll do it because I want to be with you."

A sacrifice like that had me falling for her even harder. "You're so sweet to say that, but you were right, Hartford isn't home. Which brings me to the other reason I'm here, right this moment, in this town. Something's come up. It's time sensitive, and we need to take a little trip."

Thunderous footfalls quickly approached from behind. I caught sight of Bobber and Cricket a moment before they engulfed the two of us in a huge hug.

"You're back. The dream team is together once again. We're so happy to have you back." Cricket rocked me side to side in her arms.

"Welcome back, First Class. It's good to see you, and look, Munch is no longer doom and gloom," Bobber said with an extra squeeze before releasing her hold on us. "You're not allowed to leave again. I don't think Munch would survive."

"It's so good to see you two again, too and I have no plans on leaving her again." I hugged Cricket, then Bobber. "I missed you both."

Leslie tugged on my hand. "Hey, you were just saying something about a trip?"

"I was." I turned and pointed at the Suburban parked in the parking lot. "I need the entire dream team to get into that vehicle, please?"

"Where are we off to?" Leslie asked with a quirked eyebrow. "Nothing's changed. I can't leave the trail."

"What if I say it's just for the afternoon? We'll be back here, in this town, before the end of the day, and I have already booked two hotel rooms for tonight, so there's no risk of not having a place to stay. Other than that, can it be a surprise for the moment?"

Three pair of eyes stared at me. Cricket was the first to break the silence. "What the hell, life's an adventure. I'm game."

Bobber and Leslie looked at one another. Bobber shrugged. "I'm in."

"We'll be back here, in this town, tonight?" Leslie asked. "You promise?"

"I promise."

"What are you up to? I've never seen that 'something up your sleeve' grin before," she asked.

I tried to neutralize my face, but instead, I'm certain my grin just broadened. I held out my hand, and she accepted it. The driver opened the tailgate of the SUV and added their three packs next to mine, and the four of us piled in. Cricket and Bobber ducked into the third row while Leslie and I snuggled into the middle seat.

"I'm glad you're back." Leslie draped her arm over my shoulders and leaned in so close that her lips brushed my ear. "You missed me. You love me. I'm so glad you didn't pick Hartford over me. I didn't want to think you would, at least, I hoped. It hasn't been the same without you."

I shivered from head to toe. Why hadn't I scheduled this part for tomorrow? I should be in a hotel room with Leslie instead of sitting in this truck. There were too many moving parts to change the plan now. I nuzzled into that sweet spot in her neck. "I'm glad to be back, and my, oh my, how I do love you. I'll show you how much, in great, extensive, exhaustive detail later this evening."

I could feel her smiling against the top of my head. It felt so wonderful to be cuddled in her arms, confirming once again that I was right where I belonged.

Fifteen minutes later, the driver parked the SUV next to a hangar at the small community airport. The pilot stood at the ready next to the corporate jet.

"Are you shittin' me? We're going for a ride in that sweet thing?" Bobber said behind me. "Sign me up."

Cricket squealed. "Is this what you asked for? Is this what you were paid? Did they give you a fucking jet for keeping them out of hot water with the SEC? Are you taking us to Paris for lunch?"

"Easy, Cricket, it's only a loan, and yes, we're going for a ride, but trust me, Paris is too far away to be back by tonight."

Leslie looked skeptical. She squinted and cocked her head slightly. "I thought you meant a road trip, not a private jet kind of trip."

"It's a good thing, trust me," I whispered in her ear.

"If you say so." Rather than wait for the driver, she opened her own door and exited the truck.

How I hoped I hadn't made a mistake.

Luckily, the contract hadn't yet been signed. We collected our packs and boarded the Cessna Citation X. Past business trips had taken me all over the country in this jet; it seemed fitting to take it to my final destination. Well, hopefully it worked out that way. Each of us settled into individual plush leather seats. Leslie and I sat side by side with about a foot of space between us. I already missed being snuggled up next to her. The copilot secured the hatch, and the plane whirled to life.

"Will lunch be served on this tin trap?" Leslie did not look enthused. "I'm starving."

"We can eat in thirty minutes when we land. Our car should be waiting."

Cricket, on the other hand, was all smiles. "Ah, big-time CEO life at its finest. Hey, shouldn't there be a bar somewhere on this bird, complete with crystal glasses and all that?"

I pointed behind her. When she turned back around, she had the best "wow" expression on her face. "We'll sit back there and have a drink on the way back, if that's okay?" I answered.

"Totally okay. This is so frickin' cool! Isn't it cool, Bobber?" Animated Cricket was so fun to watch.

"I can think of worse ways to get from one place to another." Bobber winked at me. "So, First Class, not that we're complaining, but why are we along for the ride? Seems like you and Munch would much prefer some alone time."

No doubt, I'd love some alone time with Leslie, but I wasn't kidding about the time sensitive nature to the trip. "Okay, for starters, just look at Cricket, isn't that reason enough? Seriously, it will all make sense very soon. I promise."

Leslie leaned over and draped her arm over my armrest. "Is this what your life in Hartford is like? Private jets and chauffeured cars?"

"Yes, at least, that's what it was like for the past seven years," I answered honestly. "Why? Are you changing your mind about city life?"

"No." She smiled. "I'm just wondering if your first-class seat on the plane to Atlanta wasn't sort of a downgrade for you if this is how you normally fly."

"I only use, excuse me, past tense, used this plane for business trips. If I planned a vacation, I sat right where you found me on the plane in Atlanta."

"Are you sure I'm someone who can fit in your world?" Leslie asked.

"The jet was too much, wasn't it? I wondered if it wasn't over-the-top." I left out the part that it was the only way to get there and back within the limited time we had. "Leslie, I could ask you the same question." I twisted so I could see her better and took the opportunity to hold her hand. "After today, my time in this jet will be over. This is a grand finale of sorts. Like I said, Hartford's not home. It will all make sense soon, okay?"

"Okay, I trust you." She winked and settled back. "The next time the suit flies in this plane, he's going to smell one sweaty hiker." She rubbed her arms all over the leather.

"Believe me, it won't be the first time. Do you remember how hot and humid it was that day when they picked me up? I sat in the seat Cricket's in right now. Grayson all but plugged his nose the entire flight back."

We all laughed.

Cricket ran her hands along the side of the chair and bumped a button. "Oh shit. Hey, the seats are powered. They recline, and there are flippers for your feet. First Class, you gotta keep the plane. Imagine the places we could visit."

Thirty minutes flew by in fun conversation, and before I knew it, we were already descending for the landing. The touchdown was every bit as smooth as I'd come to expect from my favorite pilot. We taxied up to the main hangar, where another SUV sized limo was waiting. The driver was standing at the bottom of the stairs when the copilot opened the cabin door and lowered the steps. He collected our packs, opened the car door, and waited for us to take our seats.

"Shall I follow the itinerary as planned?" The driver asked before I slid in next to Leslie.

"Yes, please, exactly as planned." I took my seat, and he closed the door gently.

"Where are we?" Leslie asked. "Better yet, how fast was that jet going?"

"Sneaky way to figure out how far we've traveled." I squeezed her thigh. "The wait is almost over."

We traveled for about ten minutes when Bobber and Cricket started pointing at different landmarks. "Hey, Creepy McCreeperson, why'd you fly us home?" Cricket pointed out the window. "Like, literally, that's our house."

We passed the city limit sign that read, "Port Clinton, Pennsylvania, Population, two hundred thirty-one."

Leslie's jaw dropped open. She whipped her head left and right. "Wait, Port Clinton, the hostel...the one that's for sale. The one I've been drooling over. This is the halfway point on the AT. Look, there's the trail. No fucking way! You two live here?"

"The hostel's for sale? How'd we not know about that? When did it go on the market? Are Kirk and Monica tossing in the towel?"

"I found it online a few weeks ago when we had the big rains and stayed at that fancy hotel for a couple of days. Hey, the Hungry Hiker. That was mentioned in the listing."

"Shut up! That's my restaurant." Bobber shoved Leslie's shoulder. "Wait, are you two buying the hostel? Are you moving here?" Bobber was so animated that I thought she was going to climb over the seat.

"No way. You own the Hungry Hiker? That's your place? Can we eat there? I'm starving," Leslie asked.

"Abso-fuckin-lutely." Bobber pounded on the back of our seat as if it was a set of drums.

The Hungry Hiker had been the primary stop all along. It was situated right next to the five-acre hostel, and I was pretty sure we could walk from the restaurant to the hostel entrance. The driver pulled into the parking lot, and the four of us spilled out of the car. I knew food was needed all around, and I knew there'd be a ton of questions. This was the perfect place to accomplish both needs. The bell jingled above the door when we walked inside.

The cook and the server came running out to the seating area. "Becca? Marie? What are you doing back? Did something happen?"

"Nothing's happened. We're good. We're only back for a couple of hours. Phoebe, Lucy, I'd like to introduce you to Munch, like, the Munch." Bobber picked up a menu and pointed at something. "And First Class. They are here to buy the hostel, then we're all going back to finish the trail."

"Wait...you're Munch, the hiker? You're the Munch that hiked all of the scenic eleven? You're that Munch?"

"I still have to finish the AT, but yes, I'm that Munch."

"We have a burger on the menu that's named after you. It's exactly how you described your favorite burger in the *Hiker Today* article. Green olives, medium cheddar cheese, grilled onion, down to the buttered bun slightly browned on the griddle. Can we get a photo with you?" Phoebe asked.

"Sure, if I can get a Munch Burger. I'm starving, and that sounds awesome."

"Munch burgers all around." I called out. It did sound fabulous.

Leslie posed with everyone while Bobber disappeared into the back.

Cricket wrapped her arm around my shoulder. "I'm so happy you're back. It really hasn't been the same without you. And this"— she held out her arms—"this is unbelievable. Thanks for bring us along. I've always dreamed of flying in a private jet." She hugged me.

"I missed you, too. It was a long week. I can't wait to tell you all about it."

"I can't wait to hear all about it."

Bobber returned with a tray filled with deep-fried appetizers and four frosty bottles of beer. We settled in at a large table. Phoebe joined us, which was odd, while Lucy disappeared into the back. I spotted her a moment later and heard meat sizzling on the grill. All a part of small-town living, I supposed.

"I can't believe you're considering the place next door. So tell me again, what happened that had you looking into Port Clinton?" Cricket asked.

"It was all Munch. She found the listing, and when I got back to Hartford, I looked it up again. The town's name sounded so familiar, and I remembered our conversation while we were kayaking on the lake. You told me that you two were from Port Clinton, and you mentioned that Bobber owned a restaurant. I did some digging in the public tax rolls, and what do you know, the hostel of Leslie's dreams is right next door to your restaurant. Now you know why the two of you had to join us on this trip. We couldn't come here to check out the property and not bring you along. Who better to tell us all about the area?"

Leslie wrapped an arm around my shoulder. "This is so cool. So, so cool. Way better than anything I expected. You did all of this so we can look at the hostel? A jet and cars with drivers. I know I made fun of it, but really, it's so cool."

I'd never seen her so excited. "The hostel is our next stop. Like I said back in Virginia, it's a little time sensitive. There's another interested party who has made a strong offer with a deadline of five o'clock today, so if it feels right, then we need to be prepared to outbid them and lock it in. I've been in contact with the owners and during one of our calls, I managed a little name drop. It made all the difference. They were so excited and impressed that they were willing to hold off on a response to the other offer until we could get here and make a decision. We have a two o'clock appointment to see if feels right."

"I didn't realize that your name had that much pull, even out here," Leslie said. "You're amazing. I can't believe you did all of this for me."

"Aw, you're sweet. My name isn't the one with pull, yours is. The moment they heard that Munch, who hiked the scenic eleven, and apparently has a local burger named after her, wanted to buy their place, they were ready to decline the other offer and sign papers then and there, but it didn't feel right to make that decision without you, hence, this marathon trip. Babe, your name made this happen, not mine."

"Are you shitting me? My name has pull? How cool is that? See, Bobber, I'm not a has been. The final credits aren't rolling. I'm in it baby." She clapped Bobber on the back. "We're going to be neighbors." Leslie turned with a concerned expression on her face. "Wait. How can we sign papers today? Did you look into my thing? Can I do this? Is there enough for me to do this?"

"Is it still your dream? Does it still feel right?" I asked, and Leslie started nodding before I even finished. "Your grandma was one smart cookie. I looked into what you asked me to, and yes, you could easily make this happen on your own, but not in the time that we have available. What if I said I took your suggested terms to heart? Rather than ask for the jet, as Cricket would've done, I asked for the money to do this. My fee for being pulled away from my adventure with you is the chance at building a future with you. We can call it a mutual reward for our shared sacrifice of being apart."

"Seriously? You really made the hostel your fee? You'd leave a life with chauffeured cars and private jets to run a hostel with me? Are we seriously doing this together? Wait, am I being punked? Is it my birthday or something? Because all of my wishes and dreams are coming true. And how cool is it that we already have friends here. This is unreal."

I nodded. "It feels right. More than I could ever put into words. What do you think of 'Munch's Place, the Halfway Hostel'? You're the draw, so your name needs to be on the sign. I'll be happy to ride your coattails into the future."

"Munch's Place...the Halfway Hostel, I like it." She leaned over and kissed me. "I can't believe you pulled all of this together, and here I was so hurt and pissed because you left me to help the suit."

"Being away from you was miserable, but it also helped me see how much I love you."

"I love you, too."

"It's going to be so awesome having you two here!" Cricket drummed the table. "The dream team lives on. Phoebe, I want a pic for the hiker wall of fame."

I hadn't noticed the wall until then. One wall was covered in photographs of hikers who had eaten in the restaurant.

"I think this one is getting framed and its own wall," Bobber said.

I couldn't agree more. This felt like home.

We devoured our burgers and walked down to the hostel. It looked even better than in the pictures, the perfect place to build a life with Leslie. The house was cozy yet spacious. The store had a rustic appearance, including tons of modern upgrades, and the property was set up every bit as well as the one we'd visited in Tennessee, if not better. The owners had another ten acres behind that included a very large pond.

Leslie lit up when she heard about the second lot, especially the pond, and the unlimited ability to go fishing. The ten-acre parcel had been listed separately, so we had the real estate agent modify the offer to include both.

We signed our names on the dotted line right there, and I wrote a check for the earnest money. We agreed to close when we made it there on foot in a month and a half, after a few contingencies had been met. The owners even offered to run it until we finished our hike in the fall, knowing how important it was to Leslie to accomplish the last of the scenic eleven.

I'd never had a negotiation go so well. I didn't even have to put on my badass corporate negotiation hat, so to speak. When it was meant to be, it became so easy. Everything with Leslie was easy.

We spent the entire afternoon and early evening there. We even stopped in at the Hungry Hiker again for dinner before heading back to the community airport. I don't think Leslie wanted to leave. I could have stayed longer, too, but we had a trail to finish. The last of the scenic eleven. We all boarded the jet just before dark and enjoyed that much anticipated drink, toasting to new adventures yet to be had.

❖

"I'm going to have to pinch myself every single day until we finish our hike. Hell, I'll probably have to pinch myself for the rest of my life. I can't believe we'll own that place in just a few weeks. What a whirlwind." Leslie scooped me up and carried me through the hotel door after our flight back to Virginia. "Thank you for being all in on this. I can't believe how much I love you. I can't believe we're going to do this together."

"Thank you for being all in on this, too. You've shown me a world that I never knew existed. I've never been so excited for the future, our future. We're already amazing together, I can't wait to see what our life will be like once we're there full time. I love you with all my heart. I have never felt this way about anyone, ever."

She lowered me onto the bed. "How did I get so lucky to have you in my life?"

I pulled her on top of me. "I was just thinking the same thing. Thank goodness for a full flight and diamond status membership." I stared into her eyes. "When I started this adventure, there was this void inside that no amount of money or success could fill. I've struggled with it for as long as I can remember. Little did I know, it wasn't a thing that was missing. It was a very specific person. You complete me."

"You complete me, too. I can't imagine any of this without you. Hey, because of you, I'll actually own something that's too big to fit in my pack, like, way too big. Do you realize this will be my first real home since I sold Grandma's place twenty-one years ago? I couldn't have done it without you."

"Actually, you could've, which makes it mean so much more that we're doing it together."

She kissed me "I don't want to think about doing this without you."

The week we'd been apart caught up with me in an instant. "Naked, now. I need to feel all of you." I tugged on her shirt, and she broke another kiss long enough to lift it, and her sports bra, over her head in one fluid motion. I sat up and removed my shirt and bra.

Leslie helped me out of my shorts and panties, then quickly shed hers before lowering her naked body on top of mine. Our passionate kiss made every cell come alive and sizzle with excitement. The weight of her was exactly what I needed. I raked my nails up the bare skin of her back. Her moan caused shocks to pulsate inside me. I'd only been gone for a week, and yet, I'd missed her so much. I missed how well we fit together, regardless of what we were doing but especially when we were doing this.

I slid my hand between our bodies, then between her legs. She was already so wet. I circled her clit with two fingers until she quivered, and her breath came in gulps next to my ear, then I slid those fingers inside her. She shifted slightly and touched me, too. We could take our time and savor each other all night long, but at that moment, I had an insatiable need that only she could satisfy.

I needed to come with her inside me. I needed to be inside her. I needed to feel that deeply pleasurable relief that only she could offer. I pushed into her hand with my hips, and she rewarded me by going as deep as she could go. The pressure felt incredible.

"I want to come with you," she whispered in my ear. "I love it when we come together."

Her words and her touch had me on the edge. I loved it, too. We rocked against each other with an urgent pace until I felt her tighten inside.

"Oh, yeah, baby…that's it. Come for me," I cried.

"I'm—" Her body finished her sentence for her, and her breath stuck in her chest. I was right there with her, frozen with pulsating aftershocks that jerked my hips against her hand.

I rolled over, holding her fingers inside me and circled my hips against the heavenly pressure.

"I love you," she whispered in my ear.

"Hmm, I'll never grow tired of hearing that. I love you, too."

We spent the next several hours making love. I couldn't get enough of her, which now seemed to be a theme for me. I'd spend the rest of my life savoring each moment we shared.

EPILOGUE

Closing on the hostel in Port Clinton occurred six weeks later, coinciding with the conclusion of Leslie's mom's trail photos, along with Bobber and Cricket's hike. While I'd enjoyed hiking with them tremendously, I was excited about the notion of having Leslie all to myself for the last three months of our trek. I couldn't get enough time with her. Seriously, a lifetime seemed lacking, and I wanted more. *If this is love, let me bathe in it, head to toe, for all eternity.*

We stayed in town for the night to celebrate our purchase, and then we were off. One foot in front of the other, we worked our way up the east coast from Pennsylvania to Maine. The views along the way exceeded any photograph I'd ever viewed online. There was something surreal about experiencing the spectacle in person. The way the wind felt in my hair heightened the lovely scents carried within the breeze. The way the earth smelled after a warm summer rain or when the next set of wildflowers bloomed. Leslie was right, each day, down to each step, offered something new and incredible. I'd never worked so hard or climbed so high to experience something so beautiful in all my life.

While I knew the Appalachian Trail extended some two thousand, one hundred and ninety-ish miles, that didn't take into account the elevation changes. The path stretched all along the Appalachian Mountain range, and very few steps landed on level ground. If we weren't climbing up a steep grade, we were traversing sharp, indescribable descents, and one didn't occur without the other, sometimes immediately following. I didn't understand how difficult the miles would be when I set off, and I was grateful for my ignorance. I swear, if someone had stretched the trail out and removed the ups and downs, it would have been twice as long of a hike. Had I known, I might have looked elsewhere for my answers, and it would have been the greatest, most profound mistake of my life.

I found so much more than the love of my life out on that trail. I found a drive and a fortitude that I hadn't known I'd had. I found out who I was and embraced my newly discovered badass abilities. I found friendships that knew no bounds, and while I certainly had grit and determination in my professional career, I summoned a maximum level in my hiking life.

I waded chest-deep through rivers of ice-cold water, holding my pack above my head to keep it dry. I survived the adorable handstand of the spotted skunk, one of the many touching, scary, and brilliant wildlife encounters over the almost six months of our trek. I kept going whether it was freezing cold or sweltering hot, and I thought my skin would melt, and just when I couldn't take one more step, we'd find solace in the cool waters beneath a gentle waterfall.

I ate wild blueberries in my oatmeal. I caught my first fish, cleaned it, and ate it for dinner. It tasted amazing. I think Leslie had fun watching me discover it all.

The best part was the knowledge that our adventure in life was just beginning.

Finally, we navigated the most remote section of trail in Maine, the hundred mile wilderness, a trek so difficult and remote that it earned its own patch. Then, we climbed, at times completely vertical, to the peak of Mount Katahdin. I'd never felt more in shape and more alive than when I stood on the highest peak in Maine, celebrating Leslie's dream, twenty-one years in the making.

I couldn't have been prouder of her, although our journey was not quite complete. She wouldn't let me off that easy. We flew back to Damascus, Virginia and hiked my missing seventy-five miles before honoring all criteria and claiming victory as official AT thru-hikers.

At least she didn't insist that I hiked that last missing section alone. For that, I was extremely grateful, although, without a doubt, I could have done it if I'd had to.

Kirk and Monica, the Halfway Hostel's previous owners, spent a week with us in early September, showing us the ins and outs of the hostel before they retired to a life of leisure in Florida. Shortly after, my home in Hartford sold, and the movers showed up a couple of weeks later with way too much furniture for our new house, along with boxes and boxes of smaller items.

Who knew I had so much shit? I honestly didn't recognize half of it. We kept what we wanted and donated the rest. At least it enabled us to set up our new bedroom with more than our full-sized sleeping pad and bag, although snuggling up as we had on the trail wasn't the worst thing.

We spent the next couple of months getting settled, cleaning and painting, celebrating the holidays with friends—a first in a long time for both of us—celebrating Leslie's fortieth birthday, and figuring out our new routine. Before we knew it, winter turned to spring, and it was time for the grand opening of Munch's Place, the Halfway Hostel. The entire town was invited, and Sue even made the trip down from Hartford. I was giddy with excitement for our first hiking season.

I stood just outside the store. I'd been setting up the last shipment of merchandise before we showed the place off. Sue strolled over amplifying her hip-swaying swagger that made her a force to be reckoned with. I was so thankful she'd made the journey.

"Hey there, sugar, ain't you just grinning like a possum eating a sweet tater."

I pulled her close. "I don't even know what that means."

"I guess you haven't shed all your city skin yet." She laughed. "The sayings will make more sense once you enjoy life out here in the country for a spell. Most possums eat bugs, and it's a good day when one gets ahold of a tasty sweet tater. You done found your sweet tater. This place is amazing, and your gal is the cat's meow.

She's nothing like any of the other gals you've been with, and when I see the two of you together, I just know all the others didn't work because they weren't her. She's your destiny."

I gave Sue an extra squeeze. "I'm so glad you see that, too. She's pretty spectacular, isn't she? I've never felt like this before. Until I met her, no one's known me like you know me, and as much as I've let her in, she's let me in, too. She's my person."

"Oh, honey, I can see it and rejoice with happiness for you. And wouldn't you know, now I have another great place to find peace from the madness at my house, just a hop, skip, and a jump away. I've been wondering how to use all them airline points from my credit card. All you need is a Jacuzzi, and I'll be as happy as a clam."

"I'll add anything if it means you'll visit more often. Over the last year, I didn't realize how much I've missed you until you're standing right in front of me, and I don't want you to go. You're the only friend I've had for longer than either of us care to admit. I've missed you."

"Aw, sugar, you couldn't be sweeter if you was my own blood. I've missed seeing you every day, too, but seeing you happy, happier than I've ever seen you before, well…it makes my heart swell somethin' fierce. But like I said, now I've got a new place to visit." She pulled me into another hug and rocked me in her arms. "I love you, sugar. You've found your happy place, and I'm so thrilled for you."

I relaxed into her. Having her confirm what I already felt made everything feel just right. Especially since my parents hadn't returned my calls. Having Sue in my life made their lack of involvement a little more tolerable. "I love you, too, Sue."

"I'm gonna go get cleaned up before the festivities get started. I just wanted you to know, I see you."

Sue gave me another squeeze and made her way back to her private cabin. I finished a few final touches and went in search of Leslie. There was something I wanted her to see before our guests arrived. I spotted her out by the picnic area close to the pavilion.

I tugged on her hand. "Hey, babe, before everyone gets here, I'd like to show you something."

"Just a minute. I have a few more chairs to set up."

"I'll help with that after. Come with me, please?" I gave her an extra tug. She followed me into the outfitters. I positioned her in front of the checkout counter. "What do you think?"

She looked at the countertop and finally raised her gaze to the wall behind the cash register. I knew the moment she saw it because she drew in a sharp breath.

Mounted on the wall was wooden sign with burned lettering that read, "Munch's Place, have a question, ask. I've hiked all eleven of the National Scenic Trails." Below the sign was a glass case displaying the three-by-three, shield-shaped patches for each of the eleven trails. A patch in the center read, "Hiker Trash—National Trail Addict," which seemed fitting for my sweet and sexy trail addict.

She stepped around the counter to get a closer look. "Oh, Amber, this is incredible. Where'd you get the patches? I stopped collecting them because they were useless weight in my pack." She turned with happy tears teasing the corner of her eyes.

"I contacted the organization for each of the trails, and once I'd verified your information and proved you were the one who'd hiked all eleven but hadn't collected the patches, they mailed them to me and asked for a picture to put in their newsletter. I'm so proud of you. I love you."

"This is unbelievable. Thank you. I love you, too. These patches are unreal. The sign, the case, wow." She ran her hand across the wood. "This is beautiful."

While she was occupied, I retrieved the second part of the surprise and tucked it into her hand. I'd had a replica of her bandana manufactured with, "Munch's Place—the Halfway Hostel," embroidered in black on each side when it was tied as a head covering, just as she had worn hers all along the trail.

She put it on and tied the knot in the back. "Holy wow! This is awesome. I love it. You had this made?"

"There's all sorts of swag back there with our name and logo, but nothing would be complete without the Munch bandana. It's your signature item. There's a box of stuff to hand out today if you'd like."

"This is such a great idea." She pulled a T-shirt on over her long-sleeve shirt. "I can't believe this is really happening! It's all so overwhelming. I love our life."

"Hmm, me, too, totally."

"Aw, Bobber, aren't they cute?" Cricket said from the doorway.

"As a button." Bobber stood behind her. "Hey, lovebirds, people are starting to arrive, and the band is here. If you want them in the pavilion, I can show them where to set up."

Leslie gave my hand a little squeeze, and we jumped into action. We had a grand opening to host, and before it was over, we had our first set of hikers check in to the bunk house. They'd been section hiking the trail for the last four years, and this year, our little hostel was their kickoff point. Of course, each wanted a picture with the famous Munch.

It couldn't have been a more perfect start to the season, not to mention, the rest of our lives.

About the Author

Nance Sparks lives in Wisconsin with her spouse. Her passion for photography, homesteading, hiking, gardening, and most anything outdoors comes through in her stories. When the sun is out and the sky is blue, especially during the golden hour, Nance can be found on the Wisconsin River with a camera in hand capturing shots of large birds in flight.

Books Available from Bold Strokes Books

All Things Beautiful by Alaina Erdell. Casey Norford only planned to learn to paint like her mentor, Leighton Vaughn, not sleep with her. (978-1-63679-479-2)

Appalachian Awakening by Nance Sparks. The more Amber's and Leslie's paths cross, the more this hike of a lifetime begins to look like a love of a lifetime. (978-1-63679-527-0)

Dreamer by Kris Bryant. When life seems to be too good to be true and love is within reach, Sawyer and Macey discover the truth about the town of Ladybug Junction, and the cold light of reality tests the hearts of these dreamers. (978-1-63679-378-8)

Eyes on Her by Eden Darry. When increasingly violent acts of sabotage threaten to derail the opening of her glamping business, Callie Pope is sure her ex, Jules, has something to do with it. But Jules is dead…isn't she? (978-1-63679-214-9)

Head Over Heelflip by Sander Santiago. To secure the biggest prizes at the Colorado Amateur Street Sports Tour, Thomas Jefferson will do almost anything, even marrying his best friend and crush—Arturo "Uno" Ortiz. (978-1-63679-489-1)

Letters from Sarah by Joy Argento. A simple mistake brought them together, but Sarah must release past love to create a future with Lindsey she never dreamed possible. (978-1-63679-509-6)

Lost in the Wild by Kadyan. When their plane crash-lands, Allison and Mike face hunger, cold, a terrifying encounter with a bear, and feelings for each other neither expects. (978-1-63679-545-4)

Not Just Friends by Jordan Meadows. A tragedy leaves Jen struggling to figure out who she is and what is important to her. (978-1-63679-517-1)

Of Auras and Shadows by Jennifer Karter. Eryn and Rina's unexpected love may be exactly what the Community needs to heal the rot that comes not from the fetid Dark Lands that surround the Community but from within. (978-1-63679-541-6)

The Secret Duchess by Jane Walsh. A determined widow defies a duke and falls in love with a fashionable spinster in a fight for her rightful home. (978-1-63679-519-5)

Winter's Spell by Ursula Klein. When former college roommates reunite at a wedding in Provincetown, sparks fly, but can they find true love when evil sirens and trickster mermaids get in the way? (978-1-63679-503-4)

Coasting and Crashing by Ana Hartnett Reichardt. Life comes easy to Emma Wilson until Lake Palmer shows up at Alder University and derails her every plan. (978-1-63679-511-9)

Every Beat of Her Heart by KC Richardson. Piper and Gillian have their own fears about falling in love, but will they be able to overcome those feelings once they learn each other's secrets? (978-1-63679-515-7)

Grave Consequences by Sandra Barret. A decade after necromancy became licensed and legalized, can Tamar and Maddy overcome the lingering prejudice against their kind and their growing attraction to each other to uncover a plot that threatens both their lives? (978-1-63679-467-9)

Haunted by Myth by Barbara Ann Wright. When ghost-hunter Chloe seeks an answer to the current spectral epidemic, all clues point to one very famous face: Helen of Troy, whose motives are more complicated than history suggests and whose charms few can resist. (978-1-63679-461-7)

Invisible by Anna Larner. When medical school dropout Phoebe Frink falls for the shy costume shop assistant Violet Unwin, everything about their love feels certain, but can the same be said about their future? (978-1-63679-469-3)

Like They Do in the Movies by Nan Campbell. Celebrity gossip writer Fran Underhill becomes Chelsea Cartwright's personal assistant with the aim of taking the popular actress down, but neither of them anticipates the clash of their attraction. (978-1-63679-525-6)

Limelight by Gun Brooke. Liberty Bell and Palmer Elliston loathe each other. They clash every week on the hottest new TV show, until Liberty starts to sing and the impossible happens. (978-1-63679-192-0)

Playing with Matches by Georgia Beers. To help save Cori's store and help Liz survive her ex's wedding they strike a deal: a fake relationship, but just for one week. There's no way this will turn into the real deal. (978-1-63679-507-2)

The Memories of Marlie Rose by Morgan Lee Miller. Broadway legend Marlie Rose undergoes a procedure to erase all of her unwanted memories, but as she starts regretting her decision, she discovers that the only person who could help is the love she's trying to forget. (978-1-63679-347-4)

The Murders at Sugar Mill Farm by Ronica Black. A serial killer is on the loose in southern Louisiana and it's up to three women to solve the case while carefully dancing around feelings for each other. (978-1-63679-455-6)

Fire in the Sky by Radclyffe and Julie Cannon. Two women from different worlds have nothing in common and every reason to wish they'd never met—except for the attraction neither can deny. (978-1-63679-573-7)

A Talent Ignited by Suzanne Lenoir. When Evelyne is abducted and Annika believes she has been abandoned, they must risk everything to find each other again. (978-1-63679-483-9)

An Atlas to Forever by Krystina Rivers. Can Atlas, a difficult dog Ellie inherits after the death of her best friend, help the busy hopeless romantic find forever love with commitment-phobic animal behaviorist Hayden Brandt? (978-1-63679-451-8)

Bait and Witch by Clifford Mae Henderson. When Zeddi gets an unexpected inheritance from her client Mags, she discovers that Mags served as high priestess to a dwindling coven of old witches—who are positive that Mags was murdered. Zeddi owes it to her to uncover the truth. (978-1-63679-535-5)

Buried Secrets by Sheri Lewis Wohl. Tuesday and Addie, along with Tuesday's dog, Tripper, struggle to solve a twenty-five-year-old mystery while searching for love and redemption along the way. (978-1-63679-396-2)

Come Find Me in the Midnight Sun by Bailey Bridgewater. In Alaska, disappearing is the easy part. When two men go missing, state trooper Louisa Linebach must solve the case, and when she thinks she's coming close, she's wrong. (978-1-63679-566-9)

Death on the Water by CJ Birch. The Ocean Summit's authorities have ruled a death on board its inaugural cruise as a suicide, but Claire suspects murder and with the help of Assistant Cruise Director Moira, Claire conducts her own investigation. (978-1-63679-497-6)

Living For You by Jenny Frame. Can Sera Debrek face real and personal demons to help save the world from darkness and open her heart to love? (978-1-63679-491-4)

Mississippi River Mischief by Greg Herren. When a politician turns up dead and Scotty's client is the most obvious suspect, Scotty and his friends set out to prove his client's innocence. (978-1-63679-353-5)

Ride with Me by Jenna Jarvis. When Lucy's vacation to find herself becomes Emma's chance to remember herself, they realize that everything they're looking for might already be sitting right next to them—if they're willing to reach for it. (978-1-63679-499-0)

Whiskey and Wine by Kelly and Tana Fireside. Winemaker Tessa Williams and sex toy shop owner Lace Reynolds are both used to taking risks, but will they be willing to put their friendship on the line if it gives them a shot at finding forever love? (978-1-63679-531-7)

Hands of the Morri by Heather K O'Malley. Discovering she is a Lost Sister and growing acquainted with her new body, Asche learns how to be a warrior and commune with the Goddess the Hands serve, the Morri. (978-1-63679-465-5)

I Know About You by Erin Kaste. With her stalker inching closer to the truth, Cary Smith is forced to face the past she's tried desperately to forget. (978-1-63679-513-3)

Mate of Her Own by Elena Abbott. When Heather McKenna finally confronts the family who cursed her, her werewolf is shocked to discover her one true mate, and that's only the beginning. (978-1-63679-481-5)

Pumpkin Spice by Tagan Shepard. For Nicki, new love is making this pumpkin spice season sweeter than expected. (978-1-63679-388-7)

Rivals for Love by Ali Vali. Brooks Boseman's brother Curtis is getting married, and Brooks needs to be at the engagement party. Only she can't possibly go, not with Curtis set to marry the secret love of her youth, Fallon Goodwin. (978-1-63679-384-9)

Sweat Equity by Aurora Rey. When cheesemaker Sy Travino takes a job in rural Vermont and hires contractor Maddie Barrow to rehab a house she buys sight unseen, they both wind up with a lot more than they bargained for. (978-1-63679-487-7)

Taking the Plunge by Amanda Radley. When Regina Avery meets model Grace Holland—the most beautiful woman she's ever seen— she doesn't have a clue how to flirt, date, or hold on to a relationship. But Regina must take the plunge with Grace and hope she manages to swim. (978-1-63679-400-6)

We Met in a Bar by Claire Forsythe. Wealthy nightclub owner Erica turns undercover bartender on a mission to catch a thief where she meets no-strings, no-commitments Charlie, who couldn't be further from Erica's type. Right? (978-1-63679-521-8)

Western Blue by Suzie Clarke. Step back in time to this historic western filled with heroism, loyalty, friendship, and love. The odds are against this unlikely group—but never underestimate women who have nothing to lose. (978-1-63679-095-4)

Windswept by Patricia Evans. The windswept shores of the Scottish Highlands weave magic for two people convinced they'd never fall in love again. (978-1-63679-382-5)